COUNTING THYME

COUNTING THYME

Melanie Conklin

G. P. PUTNAM'S SONS

G. P. Putnam's Sons
an imprint of Penguin Random House LLC
375 Hudson Street
New York, NY 10014

Library of Congress Cataloging-in-Publication Data is available upon request.

Printed in the United States of America.
ISBN 978-0-399-17330-1
1 3 5 7 9 10 8 6 4 2

Design by Marikka Tamura.
Text set in Bembo Book MT Std.

For my mother, the truth-teller

1

NEW YORK CITY

WHEN SOMEONE TELLS YOU YOUR LITTLE BROTHER MIGHT DIE, you're quick to agree to anything. You give up after-school activities because no one can take you to practice. You start eating kale chips instead of regular sour cream 'n' onion because your mom says kale is rich in antioxidants, which means healthy. You even agree to move across the country, if that's what it takes.

That's how I ended up in New York City.

We came for my brother, Val, and the drug trial that might save his life. I didn't know if the treatment would work or when we would go home again. All I knew was that Val needed to be in New York and we had to go with him. So I came.

It was November. Thanksgiving Day, nine months since we'd found out that Val was sick. Dad met us at the airport. He'd flown ahead to meet the movers while we spent our last week in San Diego with Grandma Kay. When I spotted him at the baggage claim, he looked older—his beard grayer, his face thinner than just a week before. But he was still tall as a tree and he smiled like he was glad to see me.

1

Which was nice, considering Mom had hardly looked at me all day. She'd been too busy taking care of Val, making sure he washed his hands to avoid germs and ate granola to keep his energy up. When our bags arrived, she didn't notice that I took Val's suitcase, too, or that I almost got lost in the crowd on the way to the taxi stand. I guess I should've been used to it by then, but something about being in a strange airport in a strange city made me wish the old Mom would come back just long enough to give me a squeeze, like she used to before Val got sick.

Instead, when our turn came, she just said, "Hurry up, Thyme," like I was the one slowing us down, when in fact I was being way more helpful than my big sister Cori, who was so busy reading her city guide that she almost got left on the sidewalk.

Sitting in the back of the taxi, I tried to remember the order of the flowers Grandma Kay and I had planted before we left. Sugar-bush, hummingbird sage, and thyme, of course, tucked right up against the fence where Mom would see them from the kitchen. It was supposed to be a surprise for the spring. Something to look forward to. Only now, the thought of leaving all of those plants behind just made my stomach twist, so I put them out of my mind.

Val was curled up against my side. He had to be tired of sitting, but he'd barely complained all day. He was actually pretty tough for a five-year-old.

I tapped his shoulder and he looked at me, his little blue eyes curious. "Back rub?"

He nodded eagerly, laying his skinny body across my legs so I could run my fingers over the back of his Batman costume. His hair was finally starting to grow back again. Brown and fuzzy, like baby's hair. And over each ear, a plastic loop connected to a pale blue battery pack—the hearing aids he'd started wearing a few weeks earlier. He still wasn't used to them. Mom was always checking his volume to make sure he didn't crank them up too high or turn them off completely.

Next to us, Mom had her checklists out again. She frowned and marked something off, her eyes never leaving the page even when Cori shouted, "Look! It's the Empire State Building!"

Dad was up front with the taxi driver. They were talking about construction on East River Drive, wherever that was. It was hard to believe we were actually in New York. It had only been a few weeks since Val got into the drug trial and Mom and Dad told us we were moving. The plane had crossed the country with no problem, but my mind was having trouble catching up.

"Tell me about the trains again," I said, and Val's eyes brightened.

"There are twenty-four subway lines," he recited from memory. "Each line has a different letter or number, and there are ten different colors."

"Which one is your favorite?"

He thought for a moment. "The A train."

"Why?"

"Because it's the longest ride."

I made a face, and Val giggled. He knew I wasn't super excited about riding the subway.

"I want to ride them all," he said, the way other kids said they wanted to fly.

I rubbed his back some more, and he relaxed against me. After a minute, he said, "The hospital's on the green line. It's two stops from 86th Street. I counted."

"I guess that doesn't sound too bad, then."

He shut his eyes, and I looked out the window. Streetlights glinted off cars and buildings. Signs flashed and people hurried by in heavy coats. The city was alive.

As the taxi bumped down the street, I tried not to think about what I was missing at home. Grandma Kay had made us an early turkey dinner, but it still didn't seem right to leave her alone on Thanksgiving Day. My best friend, Shani, had a soccer game on Saturday. Plus, we were right in the middle of our big social studies project. Shani said she was fine finishing it on her own, but I wasn't fine. Not at all. I felt like I'd left my own skin behind.

According to Mom, they didn't know how long we had to stay in New York. Which meant either she really didn't know, or she wasn't telling me the truth.

Val's new treatment would last a week out of every month—but for how many months? What about Christmas? Would we get to see Grandma Kay? Would Shani and I celebrate our birthdays together, like we always did? Or would I still be gone?

That's when Mom said she didn't have all the answers and

could I please stop giving her the third degree. I'd wanted to know why she wouldn't talk to me, but I was pretty sure that if I asked one more question, she'd explode.

"I think the doctor said three months," Dad had said, before Mom gave him a look. "But it's a drug trial, so we don't know for sure," he added quickly.

Three months meant December, January, and February in New York.

"So we'll be back by March?" Shani's birthday was March sixth. Mine was March twelfth.

Dad had rubbed at his beard, thinking. "Well . . . the thing is—"

"You don't need to worry about that," Mom said. "What matters is that your brother has this opportunity. Just because he's stable now doesn't mean we're done. The cancer could come back."

We all got quiet then. That word is so loud, it's hard to talk over it.

After a minute, Dad took my hand. His fingers were long and thin, but strong, like the rest of him.

"Our family is like a printing press," he said. "You remember how complicated they are?"

I nodded. Dad was in advertising. He worked at a company that made special handmade posters on big machines that gave the colors just the right look.

"There are lots of parts that make a press work," he said. "Rollers, wheels, clamps. If one of the wheels is broken, the whole operation stops. You've got to fix the broken part

5

before you get the print you want." He looked at me like he'd made all the sense in the world, instead of talking about the machines at his office like they were people.

But the truth was, I knew what he meant.

Val was the broken wheel.

He was the one who counted.

2

THIS IS IT

DAD SAID OUR APARTMENT BUILDING WAS PREWAR AND IN A good part of town, but I was skeptical. After eight months of Val being sick and getting better, then worse, then better, then worse again, I knew how to be skeptical.

In this case, I wondered exactly what *prewar* meant. Was the building so old that everything was peeling and crumbling and falling apart? Or was it super old-fashioned, with a pull string overhead for the toilet? Mrs. Bellweather had shown us pictures of bathrooms like that in social studies, to illustrate how far civilization had come so we would be grateful for our high-efficiency toilets with their push buttons and clean porcelain bowls.

We turned onto 87th Street, where the buildings were sandwiched together like books on a shelf. The trees were bare, the sidewalks slushy and gray. There wasn't a scrap of green in sight.

Our taxi stopped in front of a four-story brick building with a windowless black door and a row of trash cans out front, behind a wrought-iron fence. Up above, a rusty metal fire escape clung to the red-and-brown bricks, leading nowhere.

This can't be it, I thought just as Dad clapped his hands and announced, "This is it!"

Dad was our Official Family Cheerleader. He was the opposite of skeptical. He even had a sign over his desk that said "Open for Possibilities." Before he left San Diego, he'd been selling me hard on New York with slogans on sticky notes in my lunch:

Take a Bite Out of the Big Apple!

The City So Nice They Named It Twice!

Standing on the sidewalk, I was still skeptical. The air was so cold we could see our breath, and the light was fading fast. Thanks to the time zone difference, it was already six o'clock. Which meant it was three o'clock back at home, the exact time we would have started Thanksgiving dinner at Grandma's. It had always been my job to snap the green beans.

Mom watched the cabbie unload our bags, counting to make sure nothing got left behind. She made him check the trunk twice just to be sure, even though the rest of us were chattering with cold. Grandma Kay had warned me that New York would be chilly, but she didn't say it would be *freezing*.

"Let's get you inside," Dad said, swooping Val into his arms. He rubbed his beard against Val's cheeks, making him laugh. I wished he would hug me, too, but I was eleven and I was supposed to be tougher than that, so I grabbed my suitcase and followed them through the front door.

Cori and Val and I waited in the foyer while Dad went

back out to help Mom with the rest of the luggage. Next to me, Val eyed the shadowy staircase. "It looks spooky," he said.

"That's no big deal for Batman, right?" Cori flapped Val's cape, and he smiled a little.

When Mom and Dad came back, we grabbed our bags and Mom and Cori took the lead. Dad asked Val if he needed a lift, but Val shook his head. "I'm not tired. I can do it myself." He stood up straighter, like a soldier reporting for duty. He did the same thing every time we pulled up to the hospital.

"Let's count the steps together," I said, and he smiled and slipped his hand into mine.

We followed Mom and Cori while Dad brought up the rear, dragging the rest of the bags like a cart horse trailing a royal procession.

"One, two, three," Val counted as I bumped my roller case up the steps.

Step, *thump*. Step, *thump*.

The sound was like a heartbeat, with Val counting out the time as we climbed. There were two apartments on each floor. Ours was all the way at the top. Apartment 4B. "The penthouse," Dad joked. I nodded, but it wouldn't have mattered if we were in a fancy New York building like the ones I'd seen in the movies. The only house I wanted to sleep in was three thousand miles away.

"Four B," Val said. "That's like the green train and the orange train put together. That would make it . . ." His brow furrowed.

"The *brown* train," Dad said, and Val cracked up. I didn't know how they could be making jokes about the subway. We were about to see the place we had to live in for the very first time, the place we were supposed to call home. An impossible idea.

On the third-floor landing, I heard a creak and looked around. A pair of hard gray eyes stared back at me from the door to apartment 3B.

I jerked Val to a stop, and Dad ran into us from behind. "What is it?" he said.

"There's a man." I pointed at the crack in the door, at the guy watching us. What kind of a person spied on other people like that? He had to be a weirdo of the highest order.

Dad looked, and the door clicked shut.

"Was that the boogieman?" Val asked.

"No, buddy. That's just Mr. Lipinsky. He's a little particular, but he's completely harmless. Promise."

"What's wrong with him?" I asked.

"He looks sad," Val said.

Dad smiled. "Let's just say he's set in his ways. He leaves the occasional note. Sometimes he thumps on his ceiling. But it's fine, really. He just might take some time to get used to us."

I wasn't convinced. "But what about—"

"Thyme," Dad said. "It's going to be all right. Let's just focus on getting settled in, okay? How about I show you your new room when we get inside?"

The last thing I wanted was to settle in, but I said okay.

Dad liked to believe that things would get better. He'd said the same thing about our middle school bus driver back home. Charles was as old as the bus, and extra cranky in the mornings. If you didn't sit down within 2.5 seconds, he'd shout, "I haven't got all day here!" I know because Shani and I timed him with her new watch, which had a very reliable second hand. The funny thing was, it's not like there was anywhere else Charles had to be. He was the *bus driver*. Dad thought things would get better with him, too, but Charles never got any nicer.

Mr. Lipinsky wasn't happy about us moving in? Fine. That made two of us.

◎◎

The apartment was even smaller than I'd expected. There was no living room or dining room, just a single narrow space with windows at one end that overlooked the street. Our old brown couch and Val's Lego table were in front of the windows, opposite the TV. The rest of the room was full of moving boxes, with our dining table buried in the middle of the pile. Past that, a big square cutout looked into the kitchen and a dimly lit hall led back to the bedrooms. I squeezed the handle of my roller case, wondering how many people had lived in this place before us.

Cori went straight to the windows to look for more landmarks from her tourist guide. Mom set her bags down and got out her list and her phone. Dad started helping Val take his boots off, a process that involved goofy voices and could take well over ten minutes.

"Help! I'm under attack," Dad exclaimed as Val giggled.

"We don't have time for this," Mom said, looking at her list. "We need to order dinner."

"There's always time for . . . Captain Stinky Toes!" Dad said, dancing Val's feet through the air. Dad was already caught up playing with Val. Clearly, he'd forgotten about showing me my room. Mom said his brain liked to go on vacation, but I think he just liked to take a break from all the lists sometimes.

I rolled my suitcase down the hall, trying not to think about how much I loved my room at home. How the walls were the perfect shade of blue, with pictures of sea horses and waves and me and Shani . . . Anyway, those pictures weren't there anymore. They were in storage with the rest of our stuff. Dad had said they needed to rent our house while we were gone, to help pay for things, but Mom had cut him off before he could explain what things. She didn't want me to worry about it. But worries have a way of finding you, no matter how much you try to avoid them.

I passed a tiny kitchen, which looked like something you would have on a boat rather than a house. Next came a bathroom with black and white tiles on the floor. Then a room that wasn't much bigger than a closet, with Val's Lightning McQueen bed taking up most of the space. That left two more doors. The one at the end of the hall was open, and I could see the corner of Mom and Dad's rainbow-colored rag rug on the floor. Which left one door for me and Cori. A knot of worry tugged at my chest.

I pushed the last door open. There were two twin beds inside.

Cori walked up behind me, took one look at the room, and said, "Oh, no. This is *so* not happening." She shouted for Mom and stood there glaring at me, as though I'd had something to do with the way the rooms were set up. Ever since Cori started high school, she'd done her best to avoid me at all times, like being in middle school was contagious or something. This new Cori didn't talk to me. She hung out after school at one of her million clubs and wore eyeliner that made her look like an owl—though, thanks to Dad's genes, a very tall, long-limbed owl.

"I didn't know, I swear," I said, but she just rolled her owl eyes like she didn't believe me. But she should have known better. Of course Mom hadn't told me.

Mom walked up. "What's the problem?"

"Duh." Cori waved at the beds.

"If that's supposed to be a question regarding sleeping arrangements, yes, you two are sharing a room. Thyme, you're on the right. Make sure you only use the dresser. Cori's on the left. She gets the closet, okay?"

I nodded. Cori's mouth fell open. "You have *got* to be kidding me."

"No, I'm not kidding," Mom said. "In fact, you girls should be glad we managed to find a three-bedroom on such short notice. We're very lucky."

"Lucky? This is the unluckiest day of my life," Cori said.

"Think before you say that," Mom warned, and Cori

froze. Mom was small enough to walk right under Dad's arm without ducking, but when she and Cori argued, Mom always seemed like the tallest person in the room. That was one of her superpowers, along with list-making.

"Sorry," Cori said, though she didn't sound very sorry at all.

"You girls should get unpacked," Mom said. "Dinner will be here soon."

"Did you get a turkey for Thanksgiving?" I asked.

Mom sighed and ran her hand through her hair. She'd cut it short over the summer, but it looked good—dark and wavy, unlike my dead straight, boring brown flyaways. "We're ordering in from a pizzeria," she said. "They have whole grain pasta for Val."

Then she left, and Cori fixed her owl eyes on me. "Don't think that just because we have to share, you can put your little-kid junk all over the place." That was the other thing about the new Cori. Avoiding me wasn't enough; when she did talk to me, she had to be mean, too.

While Cori went to get her bags, I unzipped my suitcase and pulled out a calendar. It was a gift from Shani. She called it the Calendar of Us. Inside were pictures: us on her trampoline, us at the pool, us on the first day of middle school with our matching red shoes. We hadn't planned it, but that kind of thing happens when you've known someone your whole life.

I pulled a roll of tape from my suitcase and stuck the Calendar of Us to the wall above my bed. On the page for March,

Shani had circled our birthdays in bright red marker, just six days apart. We'd always celebrated them together. Our moms had started the tradition because we lived right next door to each other and went to the same preschool. It made perfect sense.

That night, I lay in my bed, in a room that was dull tan instead of robin's egg blue, staring at the calendar while Cori snored and the radiator hissed like it was possessed. Three months of treatment for Val: December, January, February. I counted the days until March first. Ninety-nine days, including today. Just shy of one hundred. The number was big enough to scare me.

Before I left, Shani had told me she was worried I might not make it back in time for our birthdays. I think she was also worried about what might happen if I was gone too long, about whether we would still be best friends by the time I got back.

I was worried, too. I'd never felt so alone in my life. But I also had a plan, and I hoped that if I worked hard enough, I would be back in San Diego sooner rather than later.

3

THE THYME JAR

THE NEXT MORNING, I SEARCHED FOR A BOX WITH THE word FRAGILE written on the sides in my own handwriting. But there were so many boxes, too many to find anything quickly.

"What if they lost it?" I asked Dad.

"They didn't lose it," he promised.

Soon, Dad found it, buried behind smaller boxes under the dining table. I dragged the box to my room and peeled off the tape, praying that the jar inside was in one piece. Thankfully, Cori was in the bathroom, claiming most of the medicine cabinet for herself. She thought the Thyme Jar was lame. Another stupid kid thing.

But the Thyme Jar wasn't lame. It was my ticket back to San Diego.

At first, the Thyme Jar was just a paper cup that sat on the dresser next to my bed. I used one of Dad's Sharpies to draw stars all over the outside and write my name around the middle. The cup sat there for months, and every time I finished a chore, or got a good grade, or helped Mom by being extra super patient, she gave me a little slip of paper to put in the cup.

The slips were like free passes to do whatever I wanted for a certain amount of time. Sometimes the slips were worth an hour. Sometimes thirty minutes. It depended on what I did to earn the time, and how good of a mood Mom was in. This was bonus time. Time to do special things. *Me time.*

Me time started after my eleventh birthday, also known as the week we found out that Val was sick. The kind of sick that makes you miss your own birthday party, the one you've shared with your best friend every year of your life. Mom felt bad, so she gave me an IOU on a slip of paper and promised to make it up to me, even though I could have cared less about my birthday with Val so sick. That's when the Thyme Jar was born. Earning time didn't make up for everything I missed, but it was something.

Whenever I could, I cashed in my time and spent thirty minutes or an hour doing something special with Shani, or keeping the iPad all to myself . . . as long as Val didn't have a doctor's appointment, or we didn't have to pick Cori up from one of her clubs after school, or there wasn't something else that absolutely had to be done no matter what. Even though those things happened a lot, I always managed to spend my time. My cup never filled up. But that was before I found out we had to move to New York so Val could go to a special hospital.

Since then, the Thyme Jar has been a for-real jar, a thick

glass one like the kind stuffed with eggs or peppers in restaurants. Dad brought it home from work. He was making posters for a candy company, and they had taken pictures of these big jars full of candy in the ads, but the company didn't want them back. Which was fine by me. The jar was perfect. The glass had a hint of green to it, and a thick cork plug.

I'd wanted to carry the jar with me on the plane, but Dad had said it wasn't safe. "Trust me, T. They won't let you bring a big glass jar on the plane." At the time, he was sorting through his endless record collection, deciding which to pack and which to store.

"But what if I say it's really important? Like, that I need it for a medical reason?"

He'd paused with a battered Moody Blues album in his hand. "Is that something you'd say? Even if it's not the truth?"

"I guess not." Although, to be honest, I hadn't thought it was that bad of a lie. Not in those circumstances. Desperate times and all.

In the end, I'd wrapped the Thyme Jar in a ton of blankets, stuffed it in a box, sealed the box with ten loops of tape, and written FRAGILE in big black letters all over the sides.

But then the movers had dropped Mom's antique rocking chair on the driveway and scratched the wood. They claimed to have slipped on a toy. Of course Mom sent me and Cori to clean up after Val, who'd left one tiny toy truck in the yard. But I was watching through the window, and saw the whole thing. The movers weren't anywhere near the truck when they dropped Mom's chair. Which meant there was no guarantee the Thyme Jar would make it safely across the country, either.

Just in case, I'd begged Dad to cut the big brown box open again so I could shake the paper slips out of the Thyme Jar and pack them in my suitcase instead. Then I'd crossed my fingers and my toes that the jar would make it to New York in one piece.

Now, when I finally opened the box in New York, I held my breath and looked inside.

The glass was fine!

I pulled the cork free and dropped the paper time slips inside, counting the time as I went. When I pressed the cork back into place, I felt better. Like my feet were finally on the ground, even if the apartment's creaky wooden floors were a sad substitute for our cool, even tiles back home.

All weekend, I added more time to the jar—for unpacking boxes, for lugging laundry to the Super Sudz Laundromat, for loading the tiny, apartment-sized dishwasher after meals. In that first weekend in New York, I saved up six hours of me time, which brought my total to twenty-seven hours.

And I didn't spend a minute of it.

Not one.

I hadn't cashed in for a single reward since Mom and Dad had told us we were moving (and that I had to say good-bye to Shani, and start sixth grade over in the middle of the year at a brand-new school, and leave Grandma Kay to tend our garden by herself, and share a bedroom with my sister who hated me, and risk going back to having no best friend at all) because I had a plan. Mom and Dad always told me to spend my time on what I wanted most, and I hoped that if I saved up enough, there was a chance I could convince them to let me go home early. I could stay with Grandma Kay, or maybe even Shani, just until Val was done with the trial. I knew it was a long shot and they would probably say no. But I had to try.

That meant I wasn't spending any more me time. Not until I'd saved up a week, minimum (although a month would have been better). The hours had to count, not just to me, but to them. If I cashed in enough slips, they would have to give me the thing I wanted most—and even though I wanted my brother to get better, the only thing I wanted to spend my time on anymore was going back home.

4

NEW

ON MONDAY MORNING, I WENT TO SCHOOL, ONLY MY NEW school didn't even look like a school. Other than the name over the red double doors—MS 221—and the American flag hanging outside, it could have been any other gray stone building in a block full of gray stone buildings.

Mom said I should have been happy they had an opening for me at the school closest to our apartment, but I thought that asking to get into school was ridiculous. I mean, in San Diego, I just showed up at the school in my neighborhood. And that was my school. A nice, normal-looking stucco building with big green fields all around.

"Do you want us to walk you in?" Mom asked as she parked Val's stroller in front of MS 221. He was feeling too tired that morning to walk all the way on his own, but he'd wanted to come with us, so Mom had him bundled up from head to toe so that only his little blue eyes peeked out.

Part of me really wanted her to walk inside for a minute. But there were four big stone steps leading up to the double doors, and if she had to drag Val's stroller with her, they would make a scene. And some kid would notice. And then I'd have to explain why my five-year-old brother was still riding in a stroller like a baby.

The questions were always the same:

What's wrong with your brother?

Where are his eyebrows?

What are those things on his ears?

"It's okay," I said. "I can go in on my own."

Mom squeezed my arm through my brand-new, puffy winter coat. I'd never owned such a thick jacket before. "Do you know where to go?"

"Principal Williams's office, room 107."

"That's my girl. Remind me that I owe you a time slip for cleaning up the dishes this morning. We'll see you at three fifteen, okay?" She was already unlocking Val's stroller. He reached his arms out for a quick hug. I leaned in. "We're taking the green line to the hospital," he said. "The 6 train."

I'd seen Mom's list that morning, so I knew he was going to meet his new doctors.

"You got this, V," I said. That was a thing we did. Me, Val, and Cori: *T*, *V*, and *C*. When things were good between us, we called each other by our initials, because they rhymed and because it felt special. At least when Cori wasn't acting like a total jerk.

My eyes were feeling watery, so I gave Val one last squeeze and ran inside.

With the holiday weekend, there hadn't been time for a

tour. Cori and Dad had taken a practice run to the high school because they had to take the subway to get there. After just one trip, Cori wanted to take the train by herself, but Mom said fourteen wasn't old enough to ride the subway alone. Which made me secretly happy (and not just because it was insane to ride the subway alone). So far, Cori and New York were getting along far too well. It was like she didn't miss San Diego at all. But at least at home, she'd been able to ride the bus to school on her own, a fact I'd been sure to remind her of.

Luckily, Principal Williams's office was pretty easy to find. It was on the first floor, just past the main office. Her door was shut when I got there. I knocked and waited as a stream of students wove by. They all looked about a foot taller than me, which was scary, but at least the building smelled nice. Like wood and books. Old, but in a good way. The other kids were all smiling, or laughing, or goofing off. Like it was just a normal day. Which it was—for them. But for me, it was the first day of school. Which meant I felt like barfing.

"Are you lost?"

I turned to find a tall girl with super shiny black hair standing right next me. She was wearing a fuzzy white hat that practically glowed against her olive skin.

"No," I said. Then a bell rang, and for a split second, panic rippled through my chest. I was in the right place, wasn't I? "I mean, this is Principal Williams's office, right?"

The tall girl nodded her white fluff at me. "Are you new?"

"Yeah." I was starting to sweat. I wished I'd taken off

my jacket. I pulled the zipper down to let in a little fresh air, and the girl's eyes trailed over my hand-knitted sweater from Grandma Kay with a look that said, *Really?* I guess she thought my fashion sense left a lot to be desired.

"I'm Emily," she said. "What's your name?"

"Thyme."

She cocked her head to the side. "Time? Like a clock?"

"No. Thyme, like the plant. With an H-Y."

The smile flashed again. "Oh. That's different!"

Emily didn't say whether she considered different to be a good thing or not. My parents had, obviously. Grandma Kay had started the tradition when she named my mom Rosemary. Mom had continued the herbal theme with Coriander, Thyme, and Valerian. Not exactly top-ten names. More like weird ones. The kind that get you the wrong kind of attention. That's what happened when I face-planted on my first day of middle school back home. This boy I didn't even know kept saying, "Better luck next *time*," until Shani pointed out that his nose was shaped like a pig's. That shut him up quick.

Just then, the principal's door popped open. A sharp-looking woman in a navy dress suit appeared. She had her hair pulled back so tightly it shone. "I thought I heard a knock. Hello, Emily. And you must be Thyme." She smiled briefly. "I'm Principal Williams. Pleased to meet you. I hope you don't mind, but I asked Emily to join us for a quick tour. Then she can take you to Mr. Ellison's homeroom."

I glanced back at Emily. So, she had already known I was new when she'd asked me.

Principal Williams gave me a schedule, locker assignment, and school manual. Then we left for a tour. The principal talked as she walked, moving at the same brisk pace as the people on the sidewalk. On our street, there were trash bags mixed in with the half-melted snow. Everyone just squeezed by the bags like it was perfectly okay to rub up against a pile of trash on the way to work or school or wherever. Little rivers of yuck ran out of the bags during the day. Then, when the light faded, the yuck froze into slippery brown trails. I tried to avoid anything brown when we were out, but it's impossible to dodge everything when you're practically sprinting everywhere.

"Here we have the computer lab." Principal Williams waved a hand at an open door and kept right on walking. I caught a glimpse of the room as we hurried by, all gray and quiet and full of sleek flat screens on wide black tables.

"The lab's fun," Emily said. "But Mr. Sanders will *kill* you if you chew gum in there. You should've seen the old carpet. Barf-o-rama." She stuck her tongue out, and I smiled, though I wondered if she was really being nice or just acting that way because the principal was there.

As we walked through the halls, Emily said hi to just about everybody, even the older kids. She seemed to love parading around, but I wished I could be anywhere else. Middle school was the worst. Girls went boy-crazy overnight. Friends argued over who sat next to who at the lunch table. I wasn't looking forward to dealing with all of that stuff again, without Shani this time. Then I thought of Val. He would've loved being in kindergarten for real. He missed his friends at his old preschool. He was always asking Mom when he could go back, but he never complained. I had to be tough, too.

Principal Williams pointed out the art room and the music room. Then the math and science classrooms. Upstairs, she circled through the social studies, English, and language arts halls. I checked my schedule and found Spanish.

Emily saw and made a sad face. "You didn't get Chinese? Too bad. It's fun."

"I like Spanish," I said. I'd studied it at home for two years.

"Spanish is totally fine. It's supposed to be really *useful*."

The way Emily emphasized the word *useful* made me think she was making fun of me. I almost told her that my best friend took Mandarin, and that she was good enough to study at the high school. But then I reminded myself that it didn't matter what this girl thought of me. I was going back to my real school and my real best friend as soon as possible.

On our way back downstairs, a blond girl with thick purple glasses rushed past us, taking the stairs two at a time. "Hey, Emily!" she said, waving at us. Her hair was in pigtails, which was the exact kind of thing Cori would make fun of— not to mention the pins and ribbons decorating her book bag.

Emily flashed the smile. "Hey, Lizzie."

"They're calling for a polar vortex!" Lizzie called as she disappeared up the stairs.

"What's that?" I asked.

"Oh, just nerd-speak for cold weather," Emily said,

frowning a little. Maybe she wasn't a big fan of the weather. Val had been seriously obsessed with clouds before his current fascination with trains kicked in. Dad had papered Val's ceiling with different cloud formations: cirrus, stratus, and Val's favorite, cumulonimbus. I missed those clouds.

We breezed past the gymnasium, the cafeteria, and the library. When we finished with that floor, another bell rang. "That's the late bell," Principal Williams said. "You'd better get to Mr. Ellison's room. Emily, I trust you'll introduce Thyme to your friends. After all, being new can be challenging."

The principal patted my shoulder like I was completely hopeless, right in front of Emily, who just smiled that big fake smile of hers. I wished I could disappear, or that I'd at least been smart enough to take off my jacket when I'd thought of it earlier. There had to be a gallon of sweat in my armpits from racing through the building so fast.

"If you need anything, come see me," Principal Williams said as she walked away.

"Thanks," I said, with zero intentions of ever doing that. She didn't seem like the kind of person who had time for anybody else. With the way she busted through the tour at light speed, she reminded me a lot of Mom these days. Focused on her goals, no matter what.

"So, are you ready?" Emily asked.

Was I ready? To start middle school all over again? To meet a roomful of new kids, who'd probably stare at me like I was some kind of creature from another planet? To explain a bazillion times over that my name was Thyme with an H-Y? To explain what brought me here in the first place? Not really. But this move was only temporary. Just like this school. Just like New York.

5

WHAT BROUGHT ME HERE

MR. ELLISON HAD A PRETTY DIFFERENT WAY OF CALLING class to order, which I noticed the second I followed Emily into homeroom. James Brown's raspy voice was bouncing off the walls, and every single kid was jumping in time to the music next to their desks. And Mr. Ellison, who had to be the tallest human being I'd ever seen, was spinning in place at the head of the room with his eyes squeezed shut.

"Excuse me, Mr. Ellison!" Emily shouted, and the teacher fell out of his spin and nearly flattened me before he caught the edge of his desk.

"Whoa!" His stubbly chin stopped just inches from my face. He grinned, and a bead of sweat tracked down his dark brown cheek. "That was a close call, little lady." He straightened up, towering over us. He had broad shoulders and huge hands, but his eyes were kind. He reminded me of one of the nurses at the hospital in San Diego, a guy who used to come to work in different costumes every single day, just to make the kids laugh. I liked that. So did Val.

"One second," he said. Then he cut the music off, and all the kids stopped dancing and looked to see what was up. As

Mr. Ellison pointed out my desk, I could feel every single eye in the classroom boring into my skin, straight through my stupid winter coat.

I walked to my row with my eyes on the floor, but halfway to my desk, a boy's leg blocked the aisle. "Excuse me," I said, but he didn't move his leg out of the way.

"We had to switch seats so you could sit in alphabetical order." I looked up. The boy was small for a sixth grader. He had spindly arms and a snub nose, along with a nasty smile. "You bumped Jimmy out of our row. Now he's stuck at the front."

"Sorry." I wished I could disappear. Again.

I stepped over his leg, dumped my bag by my desk, and shrugged off my coat as quickly as possible. Which wasn't quickly at all. My sweater seemed to have bonded to the jacket's fleecy lining. After an embarrassing amount of shaking and wiggling, I finally gripped the end of one sleeve with my teeth, ripped the coat off, and flopped miserably into my seat.

"Don't hurt yourself," the boy with the snub nose said, loud enough to cue a ripple of laughter from his buddies. I wondered if he liked to pick on everyone or if I was just super lucky.

Mr. Ellison clapped his hands. "Everyone, let's welcome Thyme Owens to our homeroom," he said, and the other kids clapped along with him, which only made me wish I could disappear even more.

"Now let's all introduce ourselves. Share your name and something about yourself."

One by one, the other kids stood up and said their names and something short, like what their favorite subject was. When it was Emily's turn, she shot to her feet and said she was a singer *and* a dancer, and that she couldn't wait for the Spring Fling, whatever that was. There were more than a few claps, and I realized that Emily wasn't just nice. She was popular. The kind of girl you ask to show the new kid around. Not the kind of girl who made friends with me.

Which was fine, I told myself. I wasn't looking for new friends, anyway.

Emily went on about how she hoped to win the lead in the Spring Fling, and how excited she was that they'd chosen *The Wizard of Oz*. I got the feeling she would've gone on forever if Mr. Ellison hadn't stopped her. "That's quite enough, Emily. Let's move on. We've got ten minutes until the bell."

Emily beamed at the class one last time and slid gracefully into her seat. Then the boy behind her stood up and mumbled a name that sounded like Dusty Hairnet. Followed by a Sheila Turnip—or was it Hurtlip? I didn't know if it was the blood rushing in my ears or the echo in the room, but I didn't really learn anyone's name until the row next to me, when two identical girls in matching dresses stood up and spoke loudly enough to make me jump.

"I'm Delia," one said.

"And I'm Celia," said her twin.

"We like fashion and making videos," Delia said.

"And you should totally sit with us at lunch!" finished Celia. They bowed and dropped back into their seats while the other kids laughed and groaned.

The introductions continued down our row. When we got to the boy in front of me, the one who hadn't moved his leg, he announced his name was Darien without even looking back. Obviously, he hated my guts. *It doesn't matter,* I told myself. I really wanted to believe that.

Then someone tapped my shoulder. I twisted around. The boy behind me waved. He had brown skin and hair that stuck out like springs all around his head, dark at the root and sandy brown at the end, as though he'd spent a lot of time in the sun.

"Hey. I'm Jake Reese." A pair of white earbuds hung from his shirt collar. He stuck out his hand, and I shook it. Then he smiled. I smiled back, and a floaty feeling sloshed through my insides. Not a bad feeling, but not an entirely good feeling, either.

"Thyme, huh? Just like Simon and Garfunkel," he said.

My smile slipped. Was he making fun of me, too?

"Um, can I have my hand back?" His fingers tugged against mine.

"Sorry." I dropped his hand like a rock and spun around. As the last few kids introduced themselves, I silently begged the bell to ring so that I could escape without having to introduce myself.

"Thyme, would you like to tell us a little bit about your-self now?" Mr. Ellison said. "Where you moved from, and what brought you here? Maybe your favorite subject?" He nodded three times, as if his enthusiasm would make me eager to answer, too.

I stood up. Emily was busy whispering with the girl next to her. I sucked in a breath and fixed my eyes on the clock over the door. "I'm Thyme," I said, still looking at the clock.

The second hand clicked. 8:59.

"I moved here from California."

There was a rumble of interest.

"My favorite subjects are social studies and math."

The clock was frozen at one minute to nine. Mr. Ellison nodded again.

"And we came here . . ."

I glanced at Emily. She stared back at me.

"We came here because of my dad's job."

The bell finally rang, and I plopped back into my chair without mentioning what had *really* brought me to New York. Because at some point, they'd all find out what had brought me here anyway.

One day, someone would notice Val, with his bald head, and his hearing aids, and his scars that showed if his shirt hung too low. Then, no matter what anyone thought of me, I'd become the poor girl whose brother has cancer. Neuro-blastoma, to be specific. That's nerve cancer. The worst kind. And then that's all they would care about, because cancer is the most fascinating thing in the world when it isn't happening to you. It's like a train wreck in slow motion. Everybody stares. They can't help it.

And they can't help assuming things, either. Like, that cancer boy's sister wouldn't want to participate in the end-of-year talent show, because, obviously, she's too busy with cancer-y things to do a skit (not that I was particularly talented—but, really, how much talent did it take to put on a grass skirt and lip-sync to music?).

Once people knew about the cancer, I wouldn't be able to stop them from talking about Val every time they saw me. And then I would stop being me, because me time was something I could only buy at home.

6

IT COMES FROM MICE

BY THE TIME THE FINAL BELL RANG, I WAS SO BEAT, I HATED the idea of walking home, even though the apartment was only a few blocks away. But when I spotted Mom and Val waiting at the bottom of the steps, I forced my face into something like a smile.

"T!" Val shouted when he saw me.

Mom was tapping at her phone. "Everything go okay?" she asked, without looking at me.

"Fine." I squatted down to see Val, who was tucked into the stroller wearing his Batman mask. He reached his arms out, and I let him pull me into his warm, stinky nest of blankets.

"I missed you, T."

I kissed his cheek. "I missed you, too, V. How was the train?"

His face lit up. "There was a turny thing, and we had to buy a card but Mom didn't know which one, and Dad said it didn't matter but I got to keep it." He held up a shiny yellow and blue card with MTA written across the front.

"We should get going," Mom said. "Val needs to rest, and I need to get these groceries put away." There were grocery bags hanging from the stroller handles. She put her phone away and glanced at me. "You look tired. Let's hang your bag on the stroller." She reached for my shoulder strap.

"It's okay," I said. "I've got it." I straightened my spine, even though my shoulders ached from carrying a full bag all day. I hadn't exactly gotten the hang of my locker. Mr. Ellison said I needed to check the combination with Principal Williams, but I hadn't had a chance to.

Mom smiled. "You're such a trouper, Thyme." She looked like she meant it, too.

I spotted Emily hopping into a sleek black car at the curb.

"Let's go," I said, pushing Val's stroller away before she saw us.

After that, I kept quiet and concentrated on dodging sidewalk muck. Mom surprised me by telling me about Val's checkup, although I think she was talking to herself more than anything because she kept stopping to make notes on her phone.

Val had gotten a set of scans, which were like pictures of the inside of his body. The doctors needed to look at them before he could start his new medicine. This new medicine—called 3F8—was a special kind of antibody, as well as the reason we'd moved all the way to New York. Thanks to months of chemotherapy, Val's cancer was mostly gone. But cancer has a way of coming back, especially neuroblastoma. That's why Val needed the 3F8. The antibodies would kill off any cancer cells that Val's chemo had missed and, hopefully, keep it from coming back.

"The medicine comes from mice!" Val shouted from the stroller.

"That's cool, V." I was happy for him, but I was also wishing we were already back at the apartment, and that San Diego was in the same time zone as New York so I could talk with Shani. We'd only managed a quick phone call over the weekend. Between the time difference and her soccer schedule, it was going to be difficult to stay in touch. I tried to ignore what that might mean for us and focused on the twenty-seven hours of time sitting in the Thyme Jar next to my bed.

When we got to our building, Mom folded the stroller and slung it over her shoulder. We started up the stairs to our apartment, with Val counting the steps as we went. Mom hovered behind him in case he crashed. The hospital always wore him out, even if he was just getting scans. I saw how it worked once, when Dad took me to visit. Val had to lie in the doughnut hole of a big white machine and stay perfectly still. For a whole hour. I wondered if I could ever be that patient about anything in my whole life.

When we got to the third-floor landing, I spotted Mr. Lipinsky watching us again, but he shut his door before I could get Mom's attention. Her focus was on Val, anyway. He was looking pale.

"Take this," she said, passing me the stroller. She scooped Val into her arms, which wasn't easy at her small size. He collapsed against her like a rag doll, too tired to hold his head up. His body was still weak from months of surgeries and chemotherapy. He could go from okay to exhausted in minutes. What was I doing, worrying about Shani and Mr. Lipinsky when I should have been thinking about Val?

One time, right before Val was diagnosed, I'd come home to find him crying on the couch and saying strange things, like he didn't know where he was or who we were. He'd had a fever on and off for two weeks, and Mom and Dad had taken him to three different doctors. The last doctor said it was the flu, but my parents knew it was something else. Something worse.

That night, they left me and Cori at Shani's while they took Val to the emergency room. Shani had these glow-in-the-dark stars on her ceiling. Her mother said the adhesive would ruin the paint, but Shani said sleeping under the stars was worth getting grounded. I remember staying up late into the night, counting stars and making promises long after Shani and Cori fell asleep, offering to trade every good grade and every nice thing I had—anything for Val to be okay.

That was the most terrible day ever. Every other day seemed easy by comparison. That night, I hadn't known if I would still have a brother when I woke up in the morning. And once you've had that feeling, it never really goes away.

Inside the apartment, Mom settled Val on the couch for a rest. Dad had gone to get Cori, so it was just the three of us. I went into the kitchen and put the groceries away: kale chips, pomegranate juice drinks, and enriched milk shakes for when Val was feeling low on energy. But no turkey and no Swiss for me. I would have to take Chinese leftovers for lunch again.

When I went back into the living room, Mom was reading a story with Val.

I told her that I put the groceries away, and she said, "That's right. I owe you time." I got the notepad from next to the phone, and she wrote me a slip. "There's an extra hour for you," she said. "I'm really proud of you for how well you did today." Which was strange, because I hadn't really told her much about my day. Not about getting lost trying to find my classes or listening to the twins finish each other's sentences at lunch. Or how it was impossible not to notice Jake. I blamed this on his springy brown hair, which stood out above the crowd.

Mom went back to the book she was reading with Val, so I went to my room and dropped the new time slip into my jar. I thought about Mom giving me extra time for trying so hard at my new school, and I felt a pang of guilt. If only she knew what I was saving for.

When Dad got home, I asked him if he'd ever heard of a "Simon and Garfunkel."

"Sure," he said. "Simon and Garfunkel is a classic band.

They even have a song about you. 'Parsley, sage, rosemary, and thyme.' Why do you ask?"

"No reason," I said, but I was surprised at how nice it felt that Jake hadn't been making fun of me after all. He'd even gotten my name right.

7

DRAMA

AFTER I FOUND OUT ABOUT THE SONG, IT WAS HARD NOT TO blush every time Jake Reese glanced in my direction. Dad had played the record for me. There were all these lyrics about a "true love of mine." Was Jake thinking about that when he'd mentioned it? Or had the song just popped into his head when he'd heard my name? He listened to his ear-buds all the time, at least until Mr. Ellison flagged him down for it. He probably just liked music a lot, but I still felt weird every time I looked at him.

Instead, I kept my head down and focused on my classes.

I had to admit I liked Mrs. Harris, my fourth-period math teacher. She wore the strangest clothes—vests with embroidered cats, and bright plaid pants. Dad would have called her outfits unique. Cori would have called them hideous. But Mrs. Harris called people up to the board like a game-show host, and that made me smile in spite of myself.

As expected, Emily didn't glance in my direction, much less say a word to me after that first day. But neither did Jake, to be fair. He and Lizzie with the pigtails were both in Mrs. Harris's math class with me. We all went to lunch together. Lizzie sat with Emily, while I ate with the twins, who were annoying, but mostly argued with each other and left me alone. I was fine with that, though I felt lonely without Shani at my side, cracking jokes about the seaweed snacks in my lunch. Mom had finally bought me some turkey, but I had to make my own sandwiches. She and Val had joined a support group at the hospital that met first thing in the morning.

Unlike me, Cori was having no trouble getting right into the swing of things. On Thursday afternoon, she walked into the apartment and announced she was joining the drama club at her school. I was doing my homework at the dining table while Mom and Val read in his room. She was determined to keep him caught up with kindergarten, and for that, he had to concentrate. I guess I was too much of a distraction to share a table with them.

"You've always had a flair for drama," Dad told Cori as he hung his coat by the door.

She put her hands on her hips. "I have *no* idea what you're talking about."

Dad laughed and went straight to his laptop. He was working on a freelance project for a big advertising agency. It had to do with selling dog food, which sounded really different from the ads he'd made at home, but he'd said it was time to try something new. He spent every spare minute on it.

"Seriously, Dad," Cori said. "My friends say drama is the best club at school."

"Since when do you have friends?" I asked. "We just got here last week."

She flipped her long, dark hair over her shoulder. "Since always, loser bait."

"*Cori*," Dad warned.

"What? All she does is mope around the apartment."

"I do not!"

Cori stuck her tongue out at me, and Dad held up his hands for us to stop. "All right, calm down, you guys," he said. "I've got work to do. Was there a point to all of this?"

Cori stopped giving me the death stare and looked at Dad. "The *point* is, we're working on proposals for spring projects until our adviser gets the new budget, so I need to stay after school. And I want to get a student pass to take the train home with everyone else."

"There's a pass?" Dad said right as I said, "Mom says you can't go by yourself."

Cori ignored me. "It works like a regular train or bus pass, but it's for students."

Dad glanced at the ceiling. That's what he did when he was thinking. When I was little, I used to think the answers were written up there somewhere, like some kind of magical answer map that only he could see. I was sure the only answer he would find for Cori was *no*.

"We'll think about it," Dad finally said, and Cori smirked.

"Well, maybe I already signed up."

The smile vanished from Dad's face. "Cori. We talked about this. You can't just do things without asking us first."

"When should I ask you, exactly? You're always working or taking Val somewhere."

"That's not fair," Dad said.

"Fair," Cori huffed. "You have no idea."

They stood there, neither of them giving way, until Dad shook his head and said, "I'll talk to your mother. But I can't promise anything. And you know that if there's any trouble, any at all, it's over." Then he put his headphones on, which meant he was working and we should leave him alone.

Cori gave me a smug look and strutted off to our room.

I went back to my homework, though I found it hard to concentrate after what she'd said. I wasn't loser bait. I just wasn't like her. I didn't want new friends. I wanted to ride the bus with Shani and have sleepovers on the weekends. I wanted to fall asleep in my own room at night, and wake up in my own house and eat pancakes on the back porch. Just because New York was new didn't make it better.

⟡

On Friday, when Mrs. Harris excused us for lunch, I reached into the front pocket of my book bag and found it empty. Either I'd forgotten to grab my lunch bag off the counter or I'd forgotten to make one in the first place. So, instead of heading into the cafeteria to meet the twins at their table, I joined the lunch line. Mom said school lunch was full of chemicals, but she still made me hide a twenty-dollar bill in my book bag in case of emergencies. Because emergencies were a thing that tended to happen to us—people got left at school, or at swim practice, or even at the grocery store, because when you're trying to keep one family member alive, losing someone else for a little while doesn't seem like that big of a deal.

It was chicken nugget day at MS 221. I followed in line, adding food to my tray, getting closer to the lunch lady and her tapping red nails. Her name tag read *S. Carlson*, and she didn't smile once, not even a crack. "Next!" she called, waving at me like she was directing traffic.

I stepped up to the register and held out my twenty-dollar bill.

She looked at me like I had two heads. "No cash," she said, pointing to a sign in front of the register that read: EASY PAY LUNCH ACCOUNTS ONLY!

"What's your account number?" Her nails hovered over the keyboard, waiting.

"I don't know my number," I said. My face grew hot. "I'm new."

"Fine. Name?"

I spelled my name for her. The nails tapped. All I could think was that it sucked so much being new.

"I'm not showing any money in your account. If you can't pay, you have to take a free and reduced lunch." She pointed at a tray of sandwiches near the end of the lunch line. "Next!" she called loudly.

I felt like the biggest loser ever. Cori was right. I would

have to put all my food back in front of everyone in line. There were sure to be stares.

I gripped the edges of my plastic tray. Turned around . . . and ran right into Emily.

She was wearing a sparkly gray sweater over black leggings. With her perfect high ponytail, she looked like she'd stepped right out of a commercial.

Emily looked past me, to the lunch lady. "I'll pay for her, Mrs. Carlson."

The lunch lady sighed, entered Emily's lunch number, and shouted, "Next!"

"Come on," Emily whispered. "Get moving before people think I'm taking on charity cases."

I followed her out of the lunch line and into the cafeteria, which was in the basement and super loud thanks to the voices bouncing off the cinder-block walls. Emily kind of paused and looked at me. I felt like the word LOSER was printed in big block letters across my forehead. I was sure she was about to say something snappy.

Instead, she just said, "See you around," and walked off to her usual table, where her friends were waiting. It was only after she left that I realized maybe she'd been waiting for me to say thank you. She had just paid for my lunch, after all. I felt like a total flake, but more than that, I was surprised. Maybe there was more to Emily than I'd thought.

@@

That weekend, I finally got to call Shani again. We used our tablets so we could see each other while we talked. I hadn't realized how much I'd missed seeing her face until she showed up on the screen. She had an easy smile that made me want to smile, too. She also had high cheekbones that came from her mother's side of the family and made her look older than she really was. Shani said people could think what they wanted. That if it were up to her, she'd rather be the best soccer player in the world than the prettiest girl at school.

I carried the tablet around the apartment so she could see how tiny the rooms were, and I made sure to tell her all the worst parts about being in New York so that she wouldn't think I was having any fun without her—how it was so cold some days I couldn't feel my fingers inside my gloves, how we had to drag our laundry to the Super Sudz and wash our clothes next to a bunch of strangers, how Cori left her stuff all over our room *all the time*.

Then Shani said she had news. I thought she'd come up with some brilliant new ideas to help me earn more time so I could get back home even faster. Instead, she started talking about our big social studies project, the one I'd left her to finish by herself.

"Mrs. Bellweather says I have to work with Jenny Hargrove on the pyramid model now."

"Jenny, chews-her-hair Jenny?"

"The one and only."

Jenny Hargrove lived two blocks away from us. She had long strawberry-blond hair that she chewed on all the time. When she switched sections, you could hear the dried spit crunch between her teeth, which gave me the shivers.

"Gross. I wish I could be there."

"I know," Shani said. "Why can't you just come back *now*?"

"I'm working on it."

Shani smiled, but I could tell she was sad. "I have to go," she said. "I have a game at ten."

We promised to talk again soon, crossed our hearts, and said good-bye. After she hung up, I sat on my bed and counted the paper slips in the Thyme Jar. Thirty hours. Not even two days' worth of time. It wasn't enough to make an impression on Mom and Dad. Plus, we'd only been in New York for a little over a week, and Val was about to start his first round of treatment. There was no way they'd let me go back home. Not yet.

8

RAVIOLI

ON MONDAY MORNING, IT WAS TIME FOR VAL TO GO TO THE hospital, which meant we were back on his schedule again. That included getting up extra early, staying out of Mom's way, and trying not to do anything that would make them late for their appointment. For Mom, being late was the worst sin a person could ever commit. Ever.

"Thyme, are you in there?" Dad called from outside the bathroom door.

I spit into the sink and garbled, "Uh-huh!"

"Okay, well, wrap it up. We have to leave for the hospital in a few minutes."

"Okay!"

I swished and spit again before dropping my toothbrush into my cup.

As I walked down the hall to the kitchen, I pulled my hair back and tied it with one of Cori's new hair bands, a tiny green one with white stripes—a gift from one of her new drama club friends. She'd braided her long, wavy hair into a million skinny braids before she went to bed. Her hair looked cool. But not like Cori.

"There you are," Mom said when I poked my head into the kitchen, like she'd been waiting on me for at least a century. Which was totally unfair. Especially after I'd spent all weekend unpacking her moving boxes to earn time. But I didn't say anything because Mom wasn't alone. There was an old lady standing next to her.

"I'd like you to meet Mrs. Ravelli," Mom said. "She's going to help us out with school and dinner for a while." She didn't say *because of Val* because by that point everything we did was because of Val. We'd had lots of helpers since he got sick. I just hadn't known we were getting a new one.

I offered my hand to Mrs. Ravelli like I was supposed to. "Pleased to meet you."

"Hello, Thyme." She wrapped her warm, squishy fingers around mine. She had a white shawl draped over her shoulders and a huge quilted bag on her arm. "I'm so happy to meet with you." The way she said things was a little odd. Every vowel stood out.

She must really be Italian, I thought.

That's when Val barreled into the room and wrapped his arms around Mrs. Ravelli's legs.

"*Ay!*" she exclaimed, although she didn't look upset at all, just amused.

"I'm so sorry," Mom said, peeling him off her. "He does that sometimes." Then to Val. "Remember what we talked about, honey. No hug attacks. Now go get your costume on. We don't want to be late."

Val giggled, and Mom called Dad to collect him. Then she gave Mrs. Ravelli some quick instructions on dinner and apologized for the state of our refrigerator. Mrs. Ravelli took one look at the embarrassing number of take-out containers on the shelves and asked if we liked fresh bread.

"I bake for you," she said, and then she winked, like this was no big deal.

"Great," Mom said. "Then we're all set. Thyme, Mrs. Ravelli will walk you to school. We're dropping Cori off on our way to the hospital. See you here this afternoon, okay?" She didn't wait for me to answer. Instead, she went to get Val and Dad because they were taking too long.

Everyone gathered by the front door to put their coats on. When Val was all bundled up in his matching blue coat and hat, he wrapped his arms around Cori, who hugged him back. Then he reached out to hug me.

I leaned in close to his face, pressing our foreheads together. "Her name sounds like *ravioli*," he whispered, with a sneaky smile.

I laughed. "You got this?"

His smile faded. "I want to take the train, but Mom says we have to take a taxi."

"Well, I think she just wants to make sure you get there on time, Captain America."

He fingered his new superhero costume. Before Val got sick, he wasn't really into costumes or dressing up. He was just a normal, annoying little brother who stuck Legos in the cracks between our kitchen cabinets. But the first time he stayed in the hospital, he saw a kid dressed as Spider-Man and decided he wanted to dress up, too. After that, Mom and Dad got him one new costume for each round of chemo. That made six. This new costume for his first round of 3F8 would make seven.

"I wanted Iron Man," he said softly. There was a tremble in his voice. He knew that Mom had spent all weekend trying to find the right costume, but the stores were out of stock and there wasn't time to order one.

"It's going to be okay." I rubbed his back to make him feel better, but he started crying anyway.

Mom gave me an annoyed look, but Dad just stepped in and lifted Val up, swooping him through the air until he started laughing. Meanwhile, Cori slouched next to the door in her hat and coat, looking bored until Mom tossed her Val's book bag, which he used to carry his stuffed animal lovies back and forth to the hospital. "I can walk to the subway on my own, you know," she said to Mom.

I looked at her. "You're taking the subway?"

"She is," Dad said. "But we're still walking you there," he told Cori, "because when you're on your own, you do things like this." He pulled off her hat to reveal her braids.

"Dad!" Cori shouted. Dad made Cori jump to get her hat back, while Mom yelled at them to get it together and Val laughed. Then they left, and I was alone with Mrs. Ravelli.

Someone I'd only just met.

"*Ay!*" she said, unwinding her shawl. "Quiet, is good, yes? After that, we need some tea."

೦⁄೦

Mrs. Ravelli got straight to work in the kitchen, digging through drawers for the things she needed, clamoring on about what she found and didn't find. I liked the way she exclaimed, like it was okay to shout whenever you wanted, but I wasn't sure about the giant quilted bag that she set on the counter. There could be all kinds of stuff in there. Had Mom and Dad searched her for weapons or mind-altering substances? Not likely. They were too busy getting Val out the door, as usual. I had to look out for myself.

So, while Mrs. Ravelli filled our kettle and set it to boil on the stove, I sat on one of the stools at the breakfast bar and watched closely to make sure she wasn't going to poison me and stuff me in the closet. Her hands never stopped moving. They darted over the counter and the sink, leaving a trail of order and neatness behind. I wondered what she thought of us, with all of our drama and rushing around. And I wondered what she thought of me, being there alone with her.

Suddenly, I wished I'd gone with my family. They were loud and annoying, but they were mine. I didn't want to be left behind, especially not on Val's first day of treatment. A sick feeling rushed through my stomach, the same way it did every time they left me, whether I was spending the night with Shani or staying with a helper like Mrs. Ravelli. It wasn't the same as homesickness, but close to it. I was familysick.

Mrs. Ravelli rummaged around inside her bag and pulled out a packet of tea bags held together with a green rubber band. "You like milk or lemon?" she asked, and my stomach tightened. I liked it when my parents were home with me. I liked it when I went with them to the hospital so I didn't have to worry about what was happening to Val.

She set the tea bags on the counter and dug through her bag again. This time, she offered me a tin with a picture of cocoa beans on the front. "Or maybe you like hot chocolate?"

A smile snuck onto my face.

She nodded like I'd said something and pulled a white paperboard box from her bag, the kind that was tied with bright red string and came from bakeries. "Now, you do me a favor," she said. "*Ay!* What was I thinking? I could feed an army."

She whipped open the box to reveal two shining rows of doughnuts.

Well, that did it.

The tightness left my stomach, and I realized how hungry I really was. I wondered if Mrs. Ravelli had done this before. Were we her first cancer family, or had she watched over others? She sure seemed like she knew what she was doing. Even Mom couldn't resist getting doughnuts every once in a while.

She pointed at a doughnut coated with red and green candy. "You like the sprinkles?"

"Not really." I reached for a regular glazed. "I like the plain ones the best. With all those sprinkles, you can't even taste the doughnut."

"Smart girl," Mrs. Ravelli said, and I noticed how her eyes crinkled up at the corners. "Eat up. We don't want to be late on our first day."

She set a steaming mug of hot chocolate in front of me, and I stuffed the doughnut in my mouth, wondering how I was going to slurp the cocoa down in time. Then Mrs. Ravelli came back and dropped an ice cube in my mug with a wink.

9

PAIN

THE MAIN SIDE EFFECT OF VAL'S NEW CANCER DRUG WAS pain. I read that online. Mom and Dad didn't like to dwell on the "downside," as they called it. I wished they trusted me enough to tell me what was going on, but they didn't. I had to look up what was happening with Val on my own, although there wasn't as much information as you might expect. Not many kids got neuroblastoma. More people won the lottery.

The 3F8 antibodies, the ones from mice, would travel through Val's body and attach to the cancer cells to help his body kill them. Which sounds great, right?

But there's a *but*—a big one.

Because neuroblastoma is nerve cancer, the cancer cells look just like regular nerve cells. During the drug infusion, the antibodies would attack the healthy nerve cells in Val's body, too. Like pins and needles, only millions of needles stabbing him all over, all at the same time.

That's where the pain came in.

So, while Mrs. Harris went on about prime factoring in math, I thought about what was happening to Val at the hospital, and how much it hurt, and if he would get through it okay. I wished he didn't have to do the treatments at all. It seemed wrong to give him a medicine that would hurt him, though all cancer treatments came with a price—the chemo stole Val's hearing, and the stem cell transplant left his immune system weak. With 3F8, the price was pain.

It was hard to accept, but Grandma Kay said sometimes the enemy of your enemy is your friend. That's why she added ladybugs to her garden in the springtime. The ladybugs always chewed up her favorite rosebushes, but they also killed off all of the aphids in the garden, and the aphids destroyed ten times as many plants as the ladybugs.

According to the hospital's website, Val would get the 3F8 infusion through his MediPort, which was a special plug the doctors put in his chest back in San Diego. That way he wasn't getting stuck with needles all the time. He just plugged in to get his meds, the way other kids plugged in their headphones.

"I'm like Cyborg," he'd said the day he got the MediPort. Later, his nurse had taught Mom and Dad how to flush the port. Which sounds gross, but really just means rinsing out the connection to keep it clear. Not like flushing a toilet.

"Thyme," Mrs. Harris said, loudly enough to make me jump.

My attention snapped back to class. Mrs. Harris was standing at the front of the room, staring at me, like everyone else. She waved. "I said, Thyme Owens, come on *down!*"

Face burning, I stood up, searching the whiteboard for

clues, but Mrs. Harris was blocking what was already written there. I had no idea what I was supposed to do.

I grabbed a black dry-erase marker from my desk—at MS 221, all students were required to carry them due to their green policy—and as I turned back to the front of the room, Jake's eyes caught mine. I froze. Just for a second. But it was long enough for Darien from homeroom to notice.

"What's wrong, California? Forget to pack your brains?" He laughed, and a few other kids joined in, but not Jake. He twisted around in his seat and threw an eraser at Darien's head.

Mrs. Harris's voice cut the laughter short. "Boys! Is there a problem back there?"

Darien's grin vanished, replaced by wide, innocent eyes. "I was just helping Thyme."

"You can help *everyone* by paying attention. Now." She sounded just like Mom, with her "no arguments" voice. Judging by her outfit of the day—a skirt with pink poodles and a matching bow in her hair—I wouldn't have thought she had it in her.

"Yes, Mrs. Harris," Darien said, but he rolled his eyes, too.

Seven, Jake mouthed as I turned away, and I thought, *Seven what?*

By the time I got up to the board, I could see what he meant.

Mrs. Harris had written different numbers across the board. Some of them had lines drawn beneath them, like legs. Below the legs were more numbers, like *eleven* and *two* below *twenty-two*. Eleven and two were the prime factors for twenty-two. A prime factor is a basic building block in math. A prime number can't be divided by any number other than one and itself—like three, five, or eleven. I was supposed to write my number's prime factors. My number was seven, which was already a prime number. So . . . the answer was also seven.

Great, I thought as I squeaked the answer onto the whiteboard. Maybe Jake thought I was too dumb to factor a prime number? I glanced at him, and there was that funny feeling in my stomach again.

"Well done," Mrs. Harris said. Then she called another girl up to the board.

On the way back to my desk, Darien pointed at Jake and made a kissy face at me. I wanted to jam my dry-erase marker right down his throat. Instead, I sat down and counted the minutes until lunch.

◎◎

On the way to the cafeteria, Darien snuck up behind me. Standing, he was at least an inch shorter than me. But what he lacked in height, he made up for with nastiness. "Hey, California. Looks like when it comes to math, you need more *time*, right?" He said it loud enough for everyone to hear. Then he laughed really loud, right next to my ear.

I cut away and hung back near the wall so he would leave me alone. Which he did, thankfully, following his goon friends down the hall to the cafeteria.

Emily's friend Lizzie stopped next to me. "You okay?"

Thanks to her glasses, her eyes looked extra big and worried.

"He's so original," I joked, and she laughed.

"Darien is as dense as a bag of rocks," she said. "I bet he doesn't even know what a homophone is. In third grade, he stuck his tongue to a flagpole like in *A Christmas Story*."

"Only an idiot would do that."

"Precisely," she said, and we both laughed. Her blond hair was pulled back with a plastic hairband. Not as goofy as the pigtails, but still more of a little-kid style. "Mom says my brother dared me to do that when I was five years old, but I was already too smart for him."

"Nice brother."

"I have *three*. Can you imagine?"

I couldn't. When Val was feeling good, he had more energy than three boys put together. At the thought of him, all my worries came rushing back, and I felt even lamer for worrying about a pole-licking doofus like Darien.

On our way to the cafeteria, Lizzie talked about other kids at school and who was dense and who wasn't. When we got to the doors, Emily came rushing up to us.

"Where have you been?" she asked Lizzie. "You were supposed to help me with the copies for Mr. C."

Lizzie flushed pink. "Sorry, I was talking to Thyme."

Emily glanced at my outfit: a long-sleeved shirt from my old school and jeans that were all of a sudden too short. Mom hadn't had time to buy me new ones. "Hey, Thyme," she said, with zero degrees of warmth. She probably thought I was a total jerk for the way I'd acted when she bought me lunch.

"Sorry about last week," I said. "I have a twenty-dollar bill for emergencies, so I can pay you back. I just have to get the money from my bag."

"What happened last week?" Lizzie asked.

"Nothing." Emily waved it off, but I didn't want her to think I was clueless.

"I should have said thank you."

"Totally not necessary," she said, although I thought maybe she sounded pleased. "It would be a crime to let you eat the free lunch. They leave those sandwiches out until they grow beards." She grinned. "Tell you what. You can make it up to me right now. I could use your help."

⊚⊚

Helping Emily meant spending my lunch break in the teacher's lounge. Back home, there were rumors of reclining sofas and televisions in the lounge. One kid even swore he saw rainbow-colored disco lights flashing inside. But here, there were just a bunch of tired-looking grown-ups sitting around a cheap folding table with their lunches, like normal people.

One of the teachers frowned when we walked in. She pointed at us with her triangle of tuna sandwich. "Can I help you?" By "help," she looked like she meant "remove" or "extinguish." Then she caught sight of Emily. "Oh, hi, Emily. Do you need something?"

Emily held up a sheet of paper. "Hi, Mrs. Peterson. I'm making flyers for Mr. Calhoun. We're doing *The Wizard of Oz* for the Spring Fling!"

Mrs. Peterson smiled. "Just keep it down, please."

"Yes, ma'am." Emily ducked her head close to us. "Mrs. Peterson likes to read *Architectural Digest* at her desk during tests. I brought her my mom's old copies." She laughed and flipped her ponytail over her shoulder, like she had absolutely everything under control.

The photocopier was on the other side of the room. We got our lunches out to eat while we worked. Emily said she didn't usually bring a bag lunch, but she'd made an exception for Mr. C. She had a little plastic container filled with rice balls that her mom ordered especially for her. Lizzie had a regular PB&J with a pack of chocolate chip cookies, the kind Mom never let me buy in stores. Mom preferred her own, which would have been fine if she had time to bake them.

Emily set up for the flyers on a table next to the copier. "Lizzie, you copy." She handed Lizzie a pack of bright, lemon-colored paper. "Mr. C got this on special order. It's perfect for the yellow brick road, right? We need parent volunteers to help with the show." She grinned. "Soon, we'll get audition sheets! I'm not supposed to say anything but I saw them on Mr. C's desk."

"Are you his assistant or something?" I asked.

"No. I just like to help out. Here, you can help me count the flyers for each classroom." She handed me a list of head counts.

"She wants to be an actress," Lizzie said.

"Or a dancer!"

They laughed, and we got to work. Emily said we had to

make almost four hundred copies, so there was no time to waste. Lizzie fed paper into the copier, Emily piled the finished copies on the table next to the machine, and I counted, sorting the copies into piles according to Emily's list. It was a little weird how we all just did exactly what Emily told us to do, but she worked just as hard as us, double-checking my piles to make sure the count was just right.

I was halfway through a stack of copies when I noticed a smudge in the top right corner. It looked almost like a fingerprint. I checked the next page. The mark was there, too.

"Emily, there's something on the flyer."

She took the paper. Then she pawed through the copies, messing up the stacks. "Oh, no."

"What's wrong?" Lizzie asked.

"Oh no oh no oh no!" Emily spun around. "They're all messed up!"

Lizzie looked at the sheet. Then she looked at her fingers. "I must have gotten chocolate on my fingers," she said. "I was just checking the sheet, to make sure it was perfect—"

"Well it's not perfect, is it?" Emily said. "Mr. C's going to kill me! He bought this paper *special*." Her face was red, like she was about to cry.

"Do you have a potato?" I asked.

"What?" Emily stared at me like I was crazy, but I had an idea.

"My dad made a stamp with a potato once. We could find some paint and stamp over the mark. Mr. Calhoun wouldn't even know."

Lizzie ran over to the counter next to the fridge. "Will this work?" She held up an apple.

"I think so. Now we just need paint." Where were we going to find paint?

I looked around the lounge. The teachers were eyeing us with suspicion. Then Emily finally snapped out of it. "I think I have nail polish," she said with a small, hopeful smile.

We found a plastic knife, and I cut triangles into the apple to make a star shape. Then Emily poured sparkly purple nail polish onto a paper plate. We stamped the paper. The star covered the thumbprint completely. It was going to take us forever to fix all the copies, but at least the sparkles looked pretty.

Emily held up the flyer and squealed so loud the teachers gave us warning looks. "Oh my gosh, it looks great! Thank you so much," she said, squeezing me with a sudden hug.

"No problem," I said. "It was fun." As soon as the words left my mouth, I realized they were true. I missed Shani, but I also just missed having friends around—even if this friend made me count four hundred flyers for her. Twice.

Lizzie adjusted her glasses. "It must be a pain to move in the middle of the year."

"It's not easy," I admitted.

"I've always been here," Emily said, "but my cousin just moved to Long Island. She says all the girls there make fun of her if she doesn't wear her jeans rolled up at the bottom. How dumb is that?"

"Pretty dumb," I said, thinking of Darien and what happened in math. Was he going to keep picking on me?

"You know what?" Emily said. "I'll fix it for you, Thyme."

"How's that?" Lizzie asked.

Emily turned away from me, toward Lizzie. "I can, you know, just . . . help her settle in."

Lizzie frowned. "People aren't projects." They were talking about me like I wasn't even there.

"Thyme doesn't mind," Emily answered. They both turned back to me. "Do you?" Lizzie didn't look happy, but Emily had her big smile on.

Maybe it would be nice to have friends. Just for now.

"No," I said. "I guess I don't mind."

10

SIDE EFFECTS

AFTER SCHOOL, MRS. RAVELLI WAS WAITING FOR ME AT THE bottom of the steps. We stopped to get groceries on the way home, which required trudging three full blocks away from school, past the subway and the peanut vendor on the corner. I wondered how New Yorkers ever got used to that sweet, burnt smell. It didn't seem like something I would ever like.

Mrs. Ravelli had a little metal cart on wheels, which we filled with the most carefully selected items our refrigerator would ever see. Fresh asparagus and arugula from the grocer on 89th, a pound of sopressata from A & S Market, plus the only brand of crushed tomatoes Mrs. Ravelli found accept-able. She must have caught wind of Mom's super-healthy food plan.

"Now, the anchovy paste," Mrs. Ravelli said as she pushed the cart along the sidewalk. She kept one hand on the cart at all times, like it might run away from her.

"Can we go to the apartment now?" I didn't see the point of all this shopping when Val was probably feeling awful and miserable after his first day of treatment.

Mrs. Ravelli stopped. Checked her watch. And my stomach knotted up.

"Mom and Dad don't want me there, do they?" I said. They'd done that before. Kept me out of the way while they were busy with Val. Like when I went to a sleepaway camp with Shani over the summer, only to find out that Val had a stem cell harvest while I was gone. If they were keeping me away, that meant things were bad.

Mrs. Ravelli touched my cheek. "Is okay," she said. "We go back now."

◎◎

Back at the apartment, we pulled the cart up the stairs together. I pushed while Mrs. Ravelli pulled. With each *thump*, the knot in my stomach tightened. Even when I knew Val was going to feel terrible, the side effects were hard to take. During chemo, everything had seemed normal until he was suddenly hunched over the toilet, crying and sick. With 3F8, I wasn't even sure what to expect.

On our way past apartment 3B, I spotted Mr. Lipinsky spying on us from his door again.

Mrs. Ravelli must have noticed him, too, because she stopped and waved. His door swung open a little wider, enough to see that he was wearing a tattered purple robe. "Good afternoon," she called, but Mr. Lipinsky just looked at her. He didn't even blink. His hard gray eyes just stayed open, staring, like one of the creepy metal statues in the park. Then he shut his door without a word.

Right before the door closed, I heard a sound from inside. A whistling, flutelike sound.

"Did you hear that?"

Mrs. Ravelli nodded. "Maybe is a bird, yes?"

I thought about Mr. Lipinsky having a pet. "Not a chance. He's way too mean. He left a note on our door that said we were terrible human beings."

Mrs. Ravelli chuckled. "Maybe he is like you say. Maybe not. Sometimes, people need time to adjust." She started up the stairs again. "My papa, he did not like change, either. He always say the city is no place for nice people. When I tell him I go to America, he stop talking to me. Every day before I left, I go to him, and he ask if I change my mind. Every day, I say no, and he tell me to go away."

She shook her head, huffing as we moved the cart up another step. "For weeks, I try. And for weeks, he refuse to see me. *Ay!* But when I go to the train, there he is. He no want me to leave, but still he kiss me good-bye. That is the way my papa was—*capo tosto!*"

She winked. "Stubborn. Like me. But sometimes, is good to have a hard head, no?"

I wondered whether it was stubborn or just plain insane to drag a grocery cart up four flights of stairs. Then I thought of Dad. He hadn't been able to crack the dog food ad yet, but he kept trying, even though the freelance work was really different from the work he did at home. Apparently, making ads for magazines was much more complicated, but he wasn't giving up. He said it was good to have a little stubborn streak.

But I was pretty sure Mr. Lipinsky was way more stubborn than that.

⊙⊙

Inside, Dad was sitting at the dining table, working. "They're in our bedroom," he said as soon as I walked in.

Mrs. Ravelli pulled the cart from my hand. "I do this," she said. "You go."

I swallowed and headed down the hall. There's nothing like walking into a room when you don't know what you're going to find. But I had to know.

Mom and Dad's door was shut. I knocked. "Hello? Can I come in?"

"It's okay," Mom answered. "Val's awake now."

I took a deep breath and slipped inside, stepping onto Mom's patchwork rug like it was made of eggshells. Val was nestled deep in the pillows, glued to the iPad while *Transformers* flickered across Mom and Dad's TV screen.

"How was it?"

"It went well," Mom said, but her cheeks were blotchy. And her eyes were puffy. I could tell Val's first day of treatment hadn't gone as well as she'd hoped.

She got up. "Keep your brother company while I check with Mrs. Ravelli about dinner."

"I'm not hungry," Val said.

"I know, honey. That's normal. But it won't hurt to have some bread or a little plain pasta. Dr. Everett said it's important to keep up your energy, even if you do get sick."

"It's not fair," Val grumbled. Then he reached for his arm.

"Don't scratch," Mom warned, and Val stopped, although he looked like he was two seconds from crying. She left, and I climbed onto the bed next to him. That's when I noticed the little red bumps on his skin.

"You got a rash, huh?"

Val nodded miserably, and I patted his fuzzy head as gently as possible. After pain, the most common side effect of the antibody treatment was a rash. Like hives, only the itching was supposed to be much worse. I'd never had hives, but I'd caught poison ivy from the woods at Grandma Kay's house, and the idea of itching like that made me shudder.

"Was it bad today?"

Val shrugged, eyes fixed on the iPad again.

"Like, flu shot bad or when you jumped off the slide and broke your arm? Do you remember that? You were three. Mom totally freaked out."

"It wasn't that bad," he mumbled, but he never had much to say about the hospital. It was like he wanted to forget as soon as possible. I didn't blame him.

I reached for the iPad. "How about if I show you the new app I downloaded? It's called Math Mysteries. You get to go treasure hunting."

He perked up. "Really?"

"Yep. You get a new hunt with every level you finish. The first one's a maze in the jungle."

He squirmed closer. "Like Indiana Jones?"

"Yeah. Just like Indy."

I clicked open the game and cranked up the volume so Val

could hear it better. We settled into Mom and Dad's pillows, and before I knew it, we'd worked though eight levels of Math Mysteries and my arm was falling asleep from Val leaning against me. He was nodding off, but if I moved, he would wake up again. So I stayed put until Mom stuck her head in the door.

"Come on," she said. "You need to get your homework done, plus I owe you an hour for helping Mrs. Ravelli with the groceries."

I kissed Val on the cheek and crawled off the bed. Mom gave me the time she owed me, and I added it to the Thyme Jar. Then I went into the kitchen, and Mrs. Ravelli showed me how to roll gnocchi. Little dough balls that were actually pasta. Each one had its own funny shape. Not one of them was perfect. What mattered, she said, was that they were just right on the inside. Which made me hope that Val's insides were doing better than his outsides, too.

11

SURPRISE!

THE NEXT DAY, I HEADED TOWARD MY USUAL TABLE TO MEET Celia and Delia. Only they weren't there.

"Thyme! Over here!" An arm flailed from the middle of the cafeteria, over by Emily's table. It was Delia. The twins always dressed alike, but if you looked closely, Delia's face was a little rounder than her sister's. Then Celia and Emily stood and waved as well. Which made three people waving and calling my name in front of the entire cafeteria. Suddenly, agreeing to let Emily help me didn't seem like the best idea after all. What was she doing?

I walked over and tried to ignore the fact that Jake was sitting at the very next table, but his attention was on his fries, not my slow march across the cafeteria.

"You lost, California?" Darien called over to me from another table full of boys.

Emily stood up. "Shut it, Darien. You're just jealous of anyone who's ever been on an airplane."

The girls at Emily's table laughed, and Darien turned red.

"Thanks," I said to Emily.

She smiled. "No problem. He's a loser, anyway. Move

over for Thyme, ladies." The other girls shifted so I could squeeze into a narrow opening next to Lizzie. There was barely enough space to fit my arms. I was trapped, only my cage was made of popular kids instead of bars.

On the other side of the table, the twins were grinning like they'd won the lottery.

"Emily invited us to switch," Celia said. She was sitting next to a redhead who looked less than thrilled.

"Everyone, this is Thyme," Emily said. "Thyme, this is everyone." Then she went around the table, pointing out everyone's names. There were two girls from my classes. The rest I didn't know, including the redhead, whose name was Rebeccah. She beamed when Emily introduced her, but she didn't say hello to me. She had a shiny black box in front of her, with colorful bites of food arranged in each pocket. A bento box. I'd seen them before in Japanese restaurants, but never at school.

Rebeccah caught me staring at her, so I put my eyes on my own lunch and found a surprise in the bag: chocolate milk. Mom used to buy it for me sometimes in San Diego, but only the organic, grass-fed, hormone-free kind. I wondered how Mrs. Ravelli knew.

"Thyme," Emily said loudly. I jumped and almost spilled the milk. "Can you believe Mrs. Harris's crazy cat vests? Everyone says she and Mr. Calhoun are totally together, but I think there's no way. Mr. C's *way* too cool for her. What do you think?"

The other girls paused, as though whatever Emily said was

super important. She gave me the big smile, like she was really interested in my answer, so I played along.

"I, uh . . . I don't know? I mean, Mrs. Harris is kind of strange. But the teachers here are okay. Although I'm still getting used to Mr. Ellison's love of Céline Dion."

Celia and Delia tittered.

"I mean, I understood the James Brown. And the Michael Jackson. But Céline's taking it too far, right?"

All the girls laughed, except for Rebeccah. "Where did you come from?" she asked, like she wished I would go back there.

"San Diego."

"I just love California," Emily said. "My dad took me to L.A. last summer. We went to Grauman's Chinese Theatre, where they have all the celebrity handprints and footprints." She grinned. "I was a perfect match for Judy Garland."

"I wish I could go to California," Lizzie said. "We never go *anywhere*."

She was about to say something else but Emily cut her off. "That reminds me! Thyme helped us make the flyers for Mr. C. Didn't you guys love the sparkle stars?"

The girls all said *yes* and *ooh* and *I loved them.*

Rebeccah looked at me with suspicion. "Are you going out for the show, too?"

"I don't think so."

"Well, do you sing?" she asked.

"Not if I can help it."

"Me neither," Lizzie said quietly, although I think I was the only one who heard her.

"I've taken lessons since I was five," Emily said. "I've been practicing for the Spring Fling all month. My vocal coach says I'm doing great."

"Ooh, what song are you practicing?" Rebeccah asked, with way too much excitement. Other girls used to act that way around Shani. She was pretty and talented, and that made people want to be her friend. Only Shani didn't like it when people kissed up to her, not the way Emily seemed to.

Emily went on about the songs she'd been rehearsing. Then her face brightened. "I know! Should I show you my favorite song?"

The other girls said *yes* and *sure* and *wow*.

Then Emily stood up, right there in front of everyone, straightened her sweaterdress, and started singing with a big grin on her face like she was on a stage. It was a song from *The Wizard of Oz*—the one where Dorothy sings with the Lion and the Tin Man about going to see the wizard. Her voice cut right through the chatter in the cafeteria. All around us, kids stopped and stared. Emily waved at us to join her. Lizzie blushed so hard her freckles disappeared, but Rebeccah hopped right up.

"*We're off to see the wizard,*" Emily and Rebeccah sang, "*the wonderful wizard of Ozzz!*" I couldn't believe what I was seeing. They had completely lost their minds.

Then they clasped their hands and bowed, and we clapped, although plenty of other kids laughed, especially the boys. I looked over at Jake's table. He raised his eyebrows, like he was surprised to see me at Emily's table, and I nearly died of embarrassment. I'd only bargained for a lunch, but I'd ended up smack in the middle of a talent show.

�◉◉

When I got home, Val was in Mom and Dad's room again. I hoped he was doing better, and that the second day of treatment had been easier than the first.

"He's resting," Mom warned when I turned down the hall.

"Can I just peek at him?"

She rubbed her temples in small circles. "If you're very quiet, Thyme."

I crept up to my parents' bedroom door and listened. There was a faint sniffling sound from the other side, so I turned the knob at the speed of a snail until the door swung open. Val was on the bed. But he wasn't resting. He was crying.

"Oh, Val." I hurried to the bed, but he turned away from me. I understood. I'd be mad, too, if I spent all day being tortured by people who were supposed to be helping me.

I tried to touch his back, but he wiggled away from me.

"Val."

No response. Maybe he had his hearing aids turned down. Or else he was just ignoring me.

I scooted closer, but he sat up and scurried to the end of the bed, where he had a pile of stuffed animals and model subway cars. The toys were all in a jumble. He grabbed one of the subway cars and rammed it into the side of his favorite stuffed triceratops.

"What's going on over here?" I asked loudly, hoping he'd talk to me.

12

ALL BARK AND NO BITE

AT THE END OF THE WEEK, MRS. RAVELLI WAS IN A RUSH to get back to the apartment. It was Val's last day of treatment for December, and she was in the middle of making him a celebratory cake—an Italian cream cake with all natural ingredients including almonds and coconut, which were full of healthy oils. She even used low-fat cream cheese in the frosting despite her dislike of low-fat foods.

When we walked in, there was no one there. Cori wasn't home from school yet, and Mrs. Ravelli said Mom and Dad were still at the hospital with Val. He had a party with his support group. I wondered what a party for cancer patients was like. It had to be kind of sad and happy at the same time.

I didn't have much homework, so I checked the list of chores Mom had left for me so I could earn time while she was gone.

"Ay! *Mio dio*," Mrs. Ravelli exclaimed. She popped into the room. "We forget the mail. Thyme, you run down for me, *d'accordo*?"

"*Si!*" I left the list next to the phone and grabbed the keys from the counter.

"*Grazie,*" she called as the door slammed shut behind me.

Downstairs, I collected the mail from our box and sat on the bottom step. Credit-card offers. Bills. Two pieces of mail for a Jerry Richards. He must have been the previous tenant in our apartment. But there was nothing from Grandma Kay. She hadn't written me yet, even though she'd promised to send me a letter every week. I was beginning to think she hadn't meant it.

On my way upstairs, I stubbed my sneakers against the steps, trying to make the loudest squeak possible. When I got to the third-floor landing, Mr. Lipinsky's door flew open.

He barged into the hall in his tattered purple robe, shouting, "What's all the racket out here?" Which was sudden, but not surprising. The real surprise was the gigantic bird sitting on his shoulder. It was white with a crest of yellow feathers, pebble eyes, and a hooked black beak—the kind of bird I'd only seen in pet stores before.

"I was just getting our mail," I said. "I live upstairs."

"Isn't that the unfortunate truth." His voice was rough as gravel, like he hadn't used it in a long, long time. Either that or he spent his days breathing fire at small children.

But Dad had said Mr. Lipinsky was harmless, and that I should try not to bug him, so I just said, "Bye," and started to walk past them. Then the bird squawked, and I jumped back.

"Calm down," Mr. Lipinsky said. "There's nothing to be scared of."

I wasn't so sure about that. I'd never liked birds much,

especially since our fourth-grade field trip to a bird sanctuary, where fifty songbirds swarmed me all at once. Apparently, you're supposed to drop the feed on the ground, not clutch it in your fists and scream.

Then Mr. Lipinsky murmured something to the bird, and I noticed how it crouched close to him. How its wings trembled. The tail feathers were as long as my arm, but thin and tattered at the ends, just like Mr. Lipinsky's messy white hair.

"How old is he?" I asked.

"*She.*"

"Sorry. How old is she?"

"Forty-six."

"Forty-six? That's older than my dad!"

"Congratulations. Maybe you can use that brain of yours to calculate a reasonable bedtime so I can get some sleep again." He went back in his apartment and slammed his door, and I wondered what could make someone so completely rotten that they spent their days being mean to everyone. Then I thought about how he always wore that old robe and how it looked like he could really use some shampoo for his hair. It had to be lonely, being mean all the time. Suddenly Mr. Lipinsky didn't seem so scary after all. He was all bark and no bite, as Grandma would say.

@@

When I got back inside, Mrs. Ravelli was finishing Val's cake. It was impossibly tall, with thick white icing and chopped nuts sprinkled on top. It looked like something out of a magazine. I couldn't remember the last time Mom had made a cake. She used to bake a lot before Val got sick. Cookies. Muffins. But that hadn't happened in months.

Soon, the front door opened, and Mom and Dad walked in with Val, who looked happier than he had all week. Cori was with them, too, although she looked much less happy. Her eyeliner was all smudged, like she'd been wiping at her eyes. Or maybe even crying.

Val ran up and wrapped his arms around me. "We had ice cream at the hospital! Then I got to ride the 5 train to 125th Street to get Cori, and now I only need the 4 to finish the green line." He grinned up at me, blue eyes gleaming, and I rubbed his fuzzy head. His skin looked a lot less pink. The hives were fading. And he was certainly less worn out. I hoped that meant things were getting easier for him.

"I'm going to my room," Cori announced.

"Wait right there." Dad went over to her and said something quietly, but I could tell she was in trouble by the way her shoulders slumped.

I turned to Mom. "What happened?"

She tucked her scarf onto her hook. "Just a misunderstanding at school. Nothing for you to worry about." She sounded annoyed, like I was bugging her, which stung a little.

Mrs. Ravelli popped into the room and said good-bye. Mom thanked her for such a beautiful cake, which Mrs. Ravelli insisted was no problem at all. She gave me a wink on her way out. Then Cori came back to the dining table with Dad, and we cut into the cake. It was as delicious as it looked—creamy and rich and fluffy. Val scarfed down his slice and went straight to his Lego table. It was hard to believe this was the same boy who'd spent the last four days huddled in Mom and Dad's bed every afternoon.

"He looks good," I said, and Mom smiled. "Does that mean the treatment's working?"

Her smile evaporated. She didn't answer.

"Can I go now? Please?" Cori asked, and Dad nodded a weary yes. She left the table. Our bedroom door slammed. It felt like a bomb had gone off in the room.

"Let's just enjoy today," Mom finally said. "Finishing this first week of treatment is a big deal for Val."

I looked at Dad.

"It's complicated, Thyme," he said.

"But it's working, right?"

He glanced at Mom. "We hope so," he said carefully.

I could tell there was something they weren't telling me. Was there some reason to think that the medicine wasn't working?

Dad stood up. "Now, how about you help me clean up? You can earn some time, and I can start burning off some of this cake." He patted his belly, which wasn't round at all.

I got up to clear our plates. When I took Mom's, she wouldn't meet my eyes. But I didn't ask any more questions, and I tried to act like I wasn't worried, even though that's not how I felt at all.

13

EUROPE WHO?

I DIDN'T GET TO TALK TO SHANI THAT WEEKEND. OR THE NEXT week. We finally managed a call the following Saturday, twenty-four days since we'd last laid eyes on each other in person, according to the Calendar of Us. It was December fifteenth, and there were fifty-five hours of time in my jar. I dumped them out on the bed to show her how much I'd saved, even if I didn't have as many hours as I'd hoped.

"That's more than two days," she said. "That has to be enough." I had the tablet propped against my pillow so we could talk while I counted. It looked like Shani's familiar face was sticking out from beneath my comforter, as though the rest of her was hidden under there.

"I don't know. Dad said I need two hundred hours to get a cell phone, but the most I've ever saved was eighty hours for our camping trip. That took me forever."

"You could always make some extra slips yourself," she said, sitting back against her pillows, which were a strange shade of . . . green?

"Did you change your room?" I asked.

"What? Oh, this? Yeah." She leaned back so I could see and lifted a pillow to show me the cute pattern of leaves and circles on the fabric. "They're lime trees! Mom got them for me as an early Christmas present. I was so over those pink stars."

"Oh." I looked back at the Calendar of Us. I'd been so focused on counting the days since we left San Diego that I hadn't realized Christmas was so close. I hadn't even made a Christmas list yet. "What about the stars on your ceiling?"

"Oh, those are staying. Gotta have my glow-in-the-dark universe."

I smiled, but it was beyond weird that I didn't recognize Shani's room anymore. While she told me all about this new boy at school and how all the girls liked him even though he was a total jerk, I searched the screen for more evidence of change. There was a set of books on her shelf that I didn't recognize. And a new picture tacked to her mirror. I couldn't really tell, but it looked like her with a group of girls at the winter carnival our neighborhood held every December.

"At least you don't have to stay with my idiot cousins for winter break," she said. "You know Jeremy still thinks chocolate milk comes from brown cows? You'd swear he was in kindergarten instead of fifth grade."

"You remember last summer, when I told him that knock-knock joke—"

She grinned. "Europe who!"

"You're a poo, too!" I said automatically.

Shani fell back on her bed, laughing, and when she caught

her breath, she said, "He never got it, you know. Even though we kept saying it again and again. I told him the joke went over his head, and he actually looked up."

We burst into a fresh wave of giggles, laughing until our sides ached. I told her how Emily was the queen of the lunch table at MS 221 and how I felt weird every time I looked at Jake. While we talked, it was like I stopped being there, in New York. Instead, I was home again.

Then Shani said, "Mrs. Bellweather gave us a new project. We have to research the Paleolithic era and write a report with an annotated bibliography! But Jenny's actually pretty good at that stuff. Who knew?" She smiled, and my stomach turned hollow.

"You're working with her on another project?"

"Well, yeah. We got a great grade on the pyramid model. She made little signs for all our facts about the desert. Mrs. Bellweather loved it."

I couldn't believe what I was hearing. "How can you stand her? She's so gross."

"Actually, she's not like that anymore. She hasn't chewed on her hair once."

"No way! She does it all the time. It's like . . . an addiction or something."

"That was third grade! You'd like her now, I swear." Shani was talking like this was a good thing. Like I was supposed to be happy about Jenny Hargrove taking my place with my best friend.

"It's been fifteen minutes!" Cori shouted from outside the

bedroom door. Dad had ordered her to let me use our room alone to call Shani. Cori was timing me.

"I have to go," I told Shani.

"It's okay. Mom's waiting to take us to the library." By us, she meant her and Jenny, so when she crossed her finger over her heart the way we usually did, I just turned my screen off.

When I opened the door, Cori barged right past me. "It's about time, loser bait."

She plopped down on the floor and opened her big, glittery drama club binder. She was working on a project proposal, something to do with making people-sized horse costumes and walking beneath them. The old Cori wasn't obsessed with clubs. She'd actually enjoyed spending time with us. But ever since Val got sick, Cori had found excuses to be somewhere else. Over the summer, she'd started volunteering at the zoo. Then she'd joined the high school's Green Team in the fall and spent all of her time with them before we left. Now drama club was all she seemed to care about.

I kicked her binder. "You don't have to be such a jerk about sharing a room, you know."

She glared up at me with her owl eyes. She was wearing a bright pink shirt with the words *I Believe* across the front, and her hair was twisted into loops tied with yellow rubber bands. "Maybe if you stop moping around the apartment and talking to your *old* friend, you'll make some new ones, and you won't be such a loser," she said in a flat voice.

"I am *not* a loser."

"Let's see . . . you spend your whole weekend waiting for

Shani to call, you do whatever Mom says, and you run around doing every little chore possible. Sounds like a loser to me!"

"I'm doing those chores for a reason!" I blurted out.

"Oh yeah?" Her eyes narrowed. "What reason would that be?"

"None of your business."

She laughed. "I bet you're saving all that time for something really lame. Like a hermit crab or a goldfish."

"You think you're so cool because you have all of these friends, but they don't know you! They're not *really* your friends," I shouted, and she stopped laughing. Her owl eyes blinked. I knew I shouldn't have let her get to me, but I was just so angry. Angry at Cori. At stupid Jenny Hargrove. At Shani.

I ran out of the room.

"Oh, come on, T! I was just kidding," Cori called after me, but I didn't stop. I ran past Dad at his computer and Mom and Val reading on the couch, out of the apartment, and into the hall. It was strangely quiet and shadowy compared to the apartment. But at least out there, I didn't have to listen to anyone telling me things I didn't want to hear.

ꙮ

Monday at school, there was news. Mr. Calhoun had started giving out audition sheets for the Spring Fling. Anyone who wanted to try out could pick up a sheet to practice over winter break. There were songs to learn and lines to memorize, depending on the part. Not that I was interested.

Normally, the Spring Fling was Emily's favorite topic,

but at lunch, she was quieter than usual. Her hair was in a perky ponytail, but her normally smiling mouth was stuck in a frown. While the other girls talked about which parts they wanted, Lizzie told me about her parents' store, Take Two. They fixed old things and sold them again. I said it sounded cool, and Lizzie told me she'd come up with the name herself. The whole time she was talking, I kept catching Emily watching us. Finally, she interrupted.

"I have a question for you, Thyme," she said loudly. The other girls hushed. "Say you were afraid of something—like, I don't know, heights—do you think getting on an airplane would be a good idea?"

It was a weird question, so I just said, "Probably not."

"Exactly!" Emily nodded like I'd said something really important.

I shrugged and unwrapped my sandwich. Mrs. Ravelli used exactly three slices of turkey spread out in a fan shape, just the way I liked it. She was some kind of mind reader when it came to food.

"But if you don't try, you never get to fly anywhere," Lizzie said quietly.

Emily glared at her. "That's the point, isn't it? You don't go on a stupid airplane if you know you're going to freak out!"

The table went dead silent. It was a weird thing to argue about, but middle school made people argue about everything. Every fight was a challenge to see who came out on top, only no one seemed to know what the problem was between Emily and Lizzie.

Delia giggled nervously. "I love flying," she said, "but we've only been once—"

"—to visit Grandma in Florida," Celia finished.

Emily slapped her hands on the table. "I don't care about your stupid grandmother!" she shouted. Then she stormed out of the cafeteria with Rebeccah close on her heels. As she stomped off, Lizzie stared at the table. Something had definitely gone down between them.

"What was that all about?" I asked.

Lizzie didn't say anything for a minute. Then she pushed her glasses into place and tucked her hair behind her ears, smoothing it down on the sides of her head. "She's just mad at me." I could barely hear her over the cafeteria noise.

"For what?" Lizzie just sat there, so I said, "Personally, I think going into outer space would be way scarier. I like oxygen, you know?"

She smiled a little, and I nudged her shoulder. "Come on. It can't be that bad."

Then I told her about the time Shani had stopped talking to me for a whole week in fifth grade. I'd left her clay model of the Colosseum on our deck, and it had melted in a surprise rainstorm. But I'd rebuilt the model from scratch and we were fine again, like always. Remembering that made me feel silly for worrying about Jenny Hargrove. What was one hair-chewing girl in the face of a lifelong friendship? Nothing, I hoped.

Finally, Lizzie said, "Thyme, can you keep a secret?"

I thought of Val and nodded.

"When Emily and I went to Mr. Calhoun's office this morning, I took the audition sheets for Dorothy, too."

"Oh." I was surprised. Practically everyone at MS 221 knew that Emily wanted to be Dorothy in the Spring Fling, especially Lizzie.

"Yeah." Lizzie stared at her sandwich some more.

"Well, I'm sure everything will be okay," I said, though I kind of understood where Emily was coming from. I felt bad for Lizzie. It was never fun to fight with your best friend, but Emily had a reason to be mad.

"That's the thing," Lizzie said. "I don't know if it will be."

14

PROOF

MRS. RAVELLI INSISTED ON WAVING AT MR. LIPINSKY IN THE
hall. Since my run-in with him and his bird, I preferred to
walk by his door like he wasn't there. But if she saw his door
open even the tiniest bit, she stopped. Just like she did that
afternoon, on the day Lizzie told me her secret.

"*Ciao,*" Mrs. Ravelli called, waving her little gloved hand.

Mr. Lipinsky's door opened a little wider, but I didn't
stop. He wasn't going to say anything, anyway. He was just
going to stare at us. That's what he always did when I was
with Mrs. Ravelli.

Then I heard him clear his throat. "That cart of yours is a
nuisance," he said.

I turned around just in time to see him shut his door.

Mrs. Ravelli stood there for a minute, and I felt terrible,
like I should go bang on his door and demand an apology.
But then she clapped her hands and said, "*Capo tosto!*" just
like she had when she'd told me the story about her dad.
As though Mr. Lipinsky's brand of stubbornness was a true
achievement.

"You know how we heard a bird in there?" I said. "He has one. I saw it."

"So it seems," Mrs. Ravelli said. "Is a cockatoo, yes? White, with a bit of yellow?" She splayed her fingers over her forehead like the bird's crest.

"You saw it, too?"

"*Ay!* I see many things. Cockatoos are beautiful songbirds. They repeat what they hear."

"Really? It just squawked at me."

"Of course," Mrs. Ravelli said. "In Italy, we have a saying: Old birds are not caught with new nets." Then she winked, like she had given me a great piece of wisdom. Mr. Lipinsky's bird *was* old. So I guess that made me the new net. I thought of the bird's beady eyes and hooked beak. I figured I was just fine with not catching it.

ᐇ

Upstairs, the apartment was quiet. No Val running around in a Batman cape, waiting to hug me when I walked through the door. No Dad working at the table. "Does Val have a playdate?" He and Mom had been spending time with his support group ever since his party at the hospital.

"No, *bambina*," Mrs. Ravelli said as she untied her scarf. "They'll be back soon. They took little Val for his blood test."

"What blood test?"

She hung her scarf with her coat and squeezed my shoulder.

"Don't worry," she said. "Little Val will be fine. God willing."

Then she disappeared into the kitchen, humming a tune, while I wondered if this was the big secret Mom and Dad weren't telling me. Had something gone wrong? Or was this just a regular test, like the scans?

Cori got home a little while later. "What?" she said when she saw me watching her. She'd changed her hair again. Today she was wearing bright blue and pink strands woven through her dark waves. She looked like a rock star.

"I thought you were Mom."

"As if." She looked around. "They're not here?"

"They took Val for some kind of blood test."

She scowled. "This is what I'm talking about," she said, and stomped off to our room, which made no sense because she hadn't been talking about anything at all. I almost followed her back there, but I knew she'd just find something mean to say to me.

Instead, I finished my homework and folded the laundry, pairing the socks and stacking them in the bins just the way Mom liked. It actually made me angry, folding socks for Mom while she was keeping things from me, but I told myself I was earning time. That was what mattered.

It was dark outside when the door to the apartment swung open and Val burst in, wearing his Captain America costume and carrying a huge stuffed dinosaur. "Rawr!" he yelled, running at me with what looked to be a T. rex, his favorite dinosaur after triceratops. Mom and Dad trailed after him.

"Watch your boots!" Mom shouted over the roaring.

Dad scooped Val up, dino and all, and carried him back to the boot trough in front of our coat hooks. "Come on, buddy. Let's get those wet galoshes off your stinky feet." Val giggled as Dad set him down on the bench and started working the boots off his feet.

Cori walked into the room with an anxious look on her face.

"Are you girls ready to eat?" Mom asked. "Your brother's hungry."

"*Right*," Cori said. She started spreading the place mats on the dining table, slapping each one down with a big clapping noise. Mom didn't even seem to notice her attitude, but Dad sure did. I saw his head snap in Cori's direction, but he didn't say a word. He just went over to his albums and slid a record into the player. As the low thrum of Louis Armstrong filled the room, Mrs. Ravelli emerged from the kitchen with a pan of meat loaf, and my stomach growled. She set the pan on the table, along with mashed potatoes and green beans. Everything smelled delicious.

"Bye, bye, then," she said as she pulled her scarf over her head.

"Won't you stay?" Dad asked. Like he did every night.

"No, no. You eat. I see you in the morning." Then she left, like she did every night.

"Ravioli sure knows how to cook," Cori said, shoveling a huge bite into her mouth.

Mom frowned. "Cori. It's Mrs. *Ravelli*. Show some respect."

"Ravioli is the best," Val said. "So it's a nice nickname. Not like Ralph-ioli."

"Or Rav-smelly," I said around my mouthful of food.

"Or—" Cori started, but Dad cut her off with a wave of his hand.

"Seriously. That's enough." He was struggling to keep a straight face. He didn't want to get in trouble with Mom, either. Cori was the only one who challenged her anymore. I wondered if Cori would be the one to ask about the blood test, but then she started complaining about her drama club and how the school wouldn't pay for spring projects due to budget cuts.

"They can't just do that," she said. "It's total bull."

"Don't talk like that," Mom said, and Cori slumped back in her chair, muttering something about the system and how they obviously didn't understand.

"You think I don't get it?" Dad said. "These big advertising companies are all politics. I almost lost this freelance job because I didn't use purple in the dog food ads. Guess what? The client's kid loves purple. It was completely unreasonable, but that's the way life is sometimes. You have to pick your battles, kiddo. You can't win them all."

"Well, my friends think we should protest," Cori said.

Mom frowned. "I don't think that sounds like a very good idea."

"What do you want me to do? Just sit there and take it?"

"Sometimes that's the only choice you have," Mom said.

Cori sat there, stewing, and I had to admit I felt pretty sorry for her. Even if she was a jerk half the time, Mom and Dad weren't being fair. It wasn't like she wanted to join a biker gang or something.

Then, right when we'd gotten back to eating, Cori turned to Mom and said, "Why should I listen to you? You never tell me what's going on anymore. You take Val for a blood test, and you don't say a single word to me about it. You don't even care that I *exist!*" It was like she was reading my mind.

The table went quiet.

Mom looked stunned, her face still as a statue.

Val reached over to pat Cori's hand. "It's okay, C," he said, and she started crying into her napkin.

"How about some Legos, buddy," Dad suggested. "You have that new set of subway cars to build, remember?"

Val took the bait.

After he hopped down, Dad turned to Cori. "You owe your mother an apology," he said quietly. "But I think we also owe you girls an explanation."

Mom started to object, but Dad said, "No. We need to tell them. It's time."

I couldn't believe my ears. Dad had taken the controls.

"Cori, you first," he said.

Cori apologized, and Mom thanked her.

Then Dad explained that Val's blood test was to check for

HAMA. HAMA stood for "human anti-mouse antibodies." Because 3F8 came from mice, Val's body would eventually fight back against it. When that happened, he would test positive for HAMA. Then the 3F8 would stop working . . . and we needed the 3F8 to keep working, to keep the cancer from coming back. If Val spiked a fever, that could be a sign of rejection. Or a fever could also be a sign of infection, or even a relapse . . .

"The goal is to get enough antibodies into Val before he becomes resistant." Dad looked at Mom. "Which we will."

Mom's mouth pursed up. I hadn't seen her cry in ages.

"What happens if he doesn't get enough antibodies?" Cori asked.

Dad took a deep breath. "Then the cancer could come back." The way he said it sounded like we would be out of options.

"But he could try something else," I said. "There are other trials, right?" There had always been one more thing to do for Val.

Mom shook her head. "This is the best treatment available for him."

"If the cancer comes back, there's always chemo," Dad added. "We'll never stop fighting, but there are limits to what his body can take." His voice broke on the last words.

I felt like I couldn't breathe. With chemo, there had been no talk of rejection. Val just took the medicine and it killed the cancer. But this was so much worse than that. Val could reject the 3F8. The trial could fail. He could *die*.

"We didn't want you girls to worry about the blood tests," Mom said. Her voice sounded hoarse, like it was hard to talk.

"Jesus, Mom!" Cori exclaimed, her eyes full of tears just like mine.

"Cori," Dad said, but all the fight was gone from his voice, too.

"What do we do now?" I asked.

Dad gripped Mom's hand and gave it a squeeze. "Now we wait for the test results."

⚭

After dinner, I helped clear the table. Then I collected my time and went into my room to add the slips to the Thyme Jar. That made sixty-one hours. I sat on my bed and pulled Mr. Knuckles into my lap. Grandma Kay gave him to me when I was just a baby, though why she chose a stuffed Hulk hand was beyond me—maybe she'd been expecting a boy. Weird or not, Mr. Knuckles was always there for me.

"You think Val's going to be okay, right?"

Mr. Knuckles gave me a thumbs-up. Well, not really because his thumb was permanently tucked, but in my mind that's what he did.

I looked at the Thyme Jar. I wondered how long it would take to get Val's test results. I wondered if it was even worth saving my time anymore, with how serious everything had gotten. I couldn't help missing home, but wanting to leave felt wrong. I wasn't sure how those two things could ever work out. And then a terrible thought crept into my mind: If Val's treatment stopped working, there would be no reason to stay in New York. No reason at all. Because Val would be out of options.

"Stop it," I cried, burying my face in my pillow. I couldn't think like that. I was a terrible sister to think something like that—of course Val's treatment would work. It was going to *work*.

There was no other option.

15

YOU'RE INVITED

"DID YOU HEAR THAT EMILY GAVE REBECCAH A RIDE TO school today?" Delia said as I fumbled with my locker in the morning. The twins' lockers happened to be on either side of mine—twin bookends for the new girl. They were wearing dresses with red and white checkers, like picnic blankets. Their entire wardrobe matched, like they shopped at some kind of twins-only store where everything came in pairs.

"What about Lizzie?" Celia asked.

"She *walked*," Delia said, like walking to school was the worst fate ever. The twins rode the bus.

"Lizzie should have stepped up her game for middle school," Celia said.

"Emily has better fashion sense," Delia agreed.

I could feel them waiting for me to comment on the Emily and Lizzie situation, but I wasn't going to spill the beans about the Dorothy trouble. I just hoped Lizzie was doing okay. I'd meant to catch up with her before homeroom, but I hadn't slept much the night before, and my fingers were being even clumsier than usual. I couldn't get my locker open to save my life.

After a few minutes of watching me yank at the latch, Delia asked for my combination and spun the numbers with three quick movements. "There ya go, sweets," she said.

As the door swung free, something red and sparkly fell out of my locker.

"Ooh!" Delia exclaimed, snatching the envelope off the floor before I could react.

"Ohmigosh! You totally got invited to Emily's holiday party," Celia said as Delia pulled a card from the envelope and held it up for me to see.

You're Invited!

to

a special holiday celebration

at

7pm sharp

on

December 21st

with

your host,

Emily Anderson

at

90 East 92nd Street, Penthouse Floor

(rsvp by phone or e-mail by Dec 18th)

A note was written across the bottom in Emily's bubbly handwriting: Sorry for the short notice! I really hope you can make it!

"Score," Delia said as she handed over the shiny invitation. "Are you excited?"

I nodded, but honestly I didn't know how I felt about the invitation. With everything going on at home, I didn't feel like going to a party. We usually spent Christmas at Grandma Kay's with just our family, unless my cousins came to visit. It was nice of Emily, though. She'd kept her promise from the copy room, but did that really mean she was my friend? Or was I just a project, like Lizzie had said?

"We're totally going," Celia said.

"We go every year," Delia added. "Our dad works with Emily's dad."

I thought about how much Emily must love having the twins invade her house every year.

"You should come," Celia insisted. "Your family can come, too. They have this huge apartment. It's a whole floor at the top of the building, and they have a Christmas tree in every single room and waiters with trays of fancy food. It's the best party *ever*."

"I believe you," I said, "and that sounds awesome. It just . . ." I searched the invitation, as though it might give m an answer. I wasn't going to get my usual Christmas, anyw With her bad hip, Grandma Kay couldn't fly all the way ac the country. Maybe going to the party would be a nice dist tion. But if my family came with me to the party, ever

would find out about Val, and the drug trial, and everything . . .

"I don't know if my family can make it," I blurted out. My cheeks burned with a hot mixture of shame and panic.

"That's totally okay," Celia said.

Delia patted my arm. "We'll all be there, so you won't be alone."

Alone. Was that what I really wanted?

Celia and Delia walked away with their arms linked together. After a minute, I slid the invitation between my books, clicked my locker shut, and headed down the hall after them.

⊗⊘

Halfway to homeroom, I slowed down. My head hurt from crying the night before. I didn't feel like listening to gossip about the Spring Fling. Plus, now that Emily was mad at Lizzie, there was bound to be drama at lunch. Maybe I would go to the nurse and tell her my stomach felt sick. That I needed to go home. At the thought of home, my stomach really did clench.

I spun around and started weaving down the hall in the opposite direction. Mom was sure to be annoyed when I called, but Mrs. Ravelli wouldn't mind coming to get me. She'd probably even make me one of her hot chocolates and tell me stories about skipping school in Italy.

By the time I hit the front hall, I was running. I turned the corner at full speed, ready to leave MS 221 behind forever, and smacked right into Jake Reese.

My books went flying, and so did Emily's invitation.

For a second, we both stood there, staring at each other. Then I bent down to get the books at the same moment he did, and our heads smacked together, too.

"S-sorry," I stammered as Jake rubbed at a spot on his forehead. He was wearing a dark wool jacket with metal buckles. His hair looked even curlier than usual. I'd been trying not to stare in class, but up close, it was impossible not to look. He was just so *noticeable*.

"You okay?" he asked.

"Yeah." Great. Just perfect, Thyme.

I grabbed my books, trying to stack them so they wouldn't slide, and Jake handed over the invitation. He looked past me like he wanted to leave, then kind of stood there like he was waiting for something instead, only I didn't know what. Was I just supposed to leave first? Or was he waiting for *me* to say something?

That's when I noticed his earbuds were hanging from the collar of his jacket, like he'd just been listening to music on his way to school.

"I listened to that song," I said. "The one by Simon and Garfunkel."

He scuffed his boot against the floor. "Oh yeah? What did you think?"

"It was nice . . . but I thought it was weird, too, how they sang in those whisper voices."

As soon as I said it, I wished I could take it back. I didn't want him to think I was making fun of him. It's just that the song really was strange. Dad had played it for me twice.

He nodded. "Me too," he said, and I smiled with relief, which made me blush. It felt good to talk about a normal thing like music.

"My dad has their record," I said. "He has a really big collection. I mean, too big to bring them all here. He had to leave a lot of them in storage when we moved."

"Cool," he said. "My grandma listens to their stuff all the time."

"Does she live nearby?"

"You could say that," he said. "I moved here this summer. We're living with her now, just until we get back on our feet. Mom and me." He looked less than happy when he said it, and I wondered what had knocked them off their feet. Then I realized that meant he was new, too. Which was nice. I was trying to think of what to say next when the late bell rang.

"You got invited to Emily's party?" he asked, looking right at me all of a sudden.

I felt a flutter in my stomach. "Yeah."

"Me too. Are you gonna go?"

That's when I made up my mind. "Yeah. I think I will."

He grinned. "Me too."

16

VIP

OUR CAB PULLED UP OUTSIDE OF EMILY'S BUILDING ON East 92nd Street at six thirty, half an hour before the party was supposed to start. I wanted to avoid running into anyone else on the off chance that Dad would start blabbing about hospitals and cancer. At home, he'd given us a special poster to celebrate the beginning of winter break. It was a to-do list for all of us, with things like *sleep*, *eat good food*, and *family time* on it. The list part had made Mom smile. Cori had rolled her eyes. I guess Dad was just trying to make things easier while we waited for the results from Val's blood test.

"You're sure you don't want me to go in with you?" Dad asked as a doorman approached the cab.

"No, I'm okay on my own."

He squeezed my hand. "I'll see you at ten sharp, like we talked about. All right?"

I leaned across the vinyl seat to hug him. "Thanks, Dad."

"Have fun, but not too much fun," he said with a goofy look on his face. I think he was happier about the party than I was. He was the one who had always invited his old college buddies over for barbecues and football games, back when we still did that kind of thing.

Amazingly, Mom hadn't objected to me going alone. I think the fight with Cori had fried her wires. But it was Cori who had surprised me the most. As soon as she heard I was going to an actual party, with actual friends, she vetoed the sweater I was planning to wear and dragged me into our room to look through her clothes, which were all colorful and flashy, like her. I was afraid she would make fun of me for being lame or tell me I should be super grateful for her help, but she just pulled a pretty pink dress from the closet and held it up.

"You're taller than I was when I wore this to Cousin Marisa's wedding. Do you remember that? It rained for hours, and we had to hide under that big white tent in her backyard. When they cut the cake, Val wouldn't come out from under the table. He said it was his fort." She stopped talking, and her eyes got far away. I wondered if some small part of her missed being normal, too.

"You know what?" she said, blinking fast. "You can borrow my cashmere sweater to go over this. It'll be perfect."

"But the sleeves are too long."

"We'll roll them up! Come on, get changed. Then we'll curl your hair."

And I did, because it felt nice not to argue with her for once.

෨෧

Inside Emily's building, there was a uniformed man waiting in the elevator. "Your name, miss?" he asked, holding the doors for me.

"Thyme Owens. I'm here for Emily Anderson's party."

He checked a list and nodded. "The penthouse it is."

Then he pressed a button, and the elevator zoomed up while my stomach dipped. The doors had a mirror finish. I blinked, and someone else blinked back: a girl in a puffy black jacket and a pink party dress, with dark, wavy hair. Thanks to Cori's curling iron, I looked more like her than ever before. But that was nice, somehow. It made me feel like maybe I could be more like her—have fun and be cool, even if it was only for one night.

The elevator stopped, and the doors parted, revealing a huge vaulted foyer with a super-tall Christmas tree. The air smelled like evergreen and freshly torn mint from Grandma's garden.

"Here you are, miss."

I stepped out of the elevator onto a white marble floor. My fancy black shoes clicked against the stone. They also pinched my toes, but Cori had claimed they looked best with the dress.

The elevator doors whispered shut, leaving me alone with the glittering tree. A thousand tiny white lights sparkled among the branches, which were packed with ornaments of every shape and size. I wondered if Emily collected ornaments the way Grandma Kay did. My heart sunk at the thought of Grandma, alone in her house at home, decorating her tree by herself.

"Thyme?"

Emily was standing at the other end of the foyer. As soon

as I saw the surprised look on her face, I knew it was a mistake to come so early. She must have thought I was some kind of stalker.

"Sorry I'm early."

She smiled. "It's no problem. Come on, I'll show you my room."

I hoped that it really wasn't a problem, but now I felt lame being there at all.

We stopped by a coatroom, and I hung my jacket on a long metal rack. Then Emily led me down the hall and through a living room the size of our apartment. There was another fancy Christmas tree in front of the windows, next to a row of long tables dressed in white cloths. We turned down another hall, and Emily opened a door. Inside was a plush white carpet, a couch, and even a fireplace—but no bed.

"Want some water?" Emily asked.

"Sure."

"Sparkling or flat?"

"Um . . . I guess flat?"

She disappeared through another door, and I caught a glimpse of a tall white canopy bed inside. So this was just her sitting room?

A minute later, she came back with a bottle of water for me and a Perrier for herself. She plopped down on the couch and I perched on the other end, careful not to drip water on the shiny pillows. Being alone with Emily in her bedroom was a lot different than sharing a lunch table. I wondered what she thought of my dress and my hair. She had on a sparkly black dress that looked like something a model would wear—the sequins shimmered every time she moved. She must have felt awkward, too, because she kept fussing with her hem. Maybe she was having second thoughts about inviting me.

"I like your fireplace," I said, because Grandma Kay always said to open a conversation with a compliment.

Emily smiled. "Here. I'll turn it on." With the flip of a switch, small orange and blue flames flickered to life on the logs. "It's gas," she said. "My mom says a live flame adds ambience to a room, like, the way fresh flowers make people happy? But I don't know." She glanced at the tiny blue flames. "It doesn't look that real to me. Right?"

I thought fire was fire, but I agreed with her anyway, because that was Grandma's other conversation tip: Don't cause a fuss.

Above the fireplace, brightly colored paper stars hung from the ceiling. They looked sort of like origami, but not. There were dozens of careful cuts in each folded star. They were beautiful, even though they were only made of paper.

"Did you make those?" I asked, and Emily nodded.

"They're called *parols*," she said. "We make them every year at Christmas. Only this year I have to make them twice. My nana's coming from the Philippines for her birthday, and Mom wants to surprise her . . . not that Mom gets stuck making the decorations."

"They must be really hard to cut out."

Emily quirked her lips. "Yeah, but you get faster the more you practice. They're supposed to bring hope. Faith. Good stuff like that." She looked at me like she was deciding something. Then she shrugged. "I can show you if you want."

She got her scissors and I watched her cut slits in the paper. Then we twisted each sheet and stapled them together to form elegant stars. Grandma Kay would have loved them. I decided to make one for her when I got back to the apartment, even though it wouldn't get to San Diego by Christmas.

While we worked, Emily told me how her mother wanted her nana to move to New York, but she would only visit. I told her my grandma didn't want to come with us, either, but that I didn't blame her because I'd rather be back in California, too—though I was careful not to say too much about my family or Val. I just told her how the avocados in San Diego were nearly as big as my head, and the strawberries tasted better than candy, and how the breeze came in off the ocean, all the way across the city, carrying that tangy, fresh smell right into our house.

"I wish I could go to California with my dad again," Emily said. "He travels a lot for his job. But usually he goes by himself, or my mom goes with him."

"They just leave you here alone?"

She held a curl of paper for me to staple. "No, I have an au pair. She's from France. My parents have this thing about me not missing school. They don't want me getting a big head or something. That's why I go to public school."

"Oh. I wondered, you know, with all of this." She blushed,

and I said, "Not that I don't like it. You're just a little fancier around here than I'm used to."

Emily laughed. "You know what? I'm glad you came early." I lifted up the finished star, and she clapped. She was being so nice, not bossy at all like at school. It didn't make sense.

She got some string, and we hung my star with the others above the fireplace. That's when I noticed that the mantel was lined with photographs. Emily in fancy dresses, standing in front of theaters, at parties. Lizzie was in almost every picture, even the older ones.

"What's going on with you and Lizzie?" I asked.

Emily's face froze up. "Why? Did she say something to you?"

"Just that she wants to try out for Dorothy, too. And you're mad at her for it."

"It's just a misunderstanding," Emily said, smiling her big, toothy smile from school, the fake one she gave the twins when they were annoying her.

"You could have fooled me."

"I've known Lizzie since kindergarten. She'll be fine." She turned away, shutting me out, exactly the way Mom did when she didn't want to talk about the hard stuff.

"If you say so." Why was I so annoyed? If Emily wanted to lose her best friend over something as stupid as a play, that was up to her.

She turned back, paper clenched in her hands. "Look, I just don't think it's a good idea for her to audition. But that's all I can say about it, okay?"

"Okay."

Super-awkward silence filled the air. Then a knock sounded at the door, and a tall, beautiful woman with Emily's same dark hair leaned inside. She looked like a movie star.

"It's time, *Ly-ly*," she said. Her voice lifted up at the end of each word.

"Yes, Mother. We'll be right there."

The door clicked shut.

"We'd better go," Emily said. "My mom means business."

◎◎

In Emily's living room, things were different. There was music, and fancy people, and waiters in white shirts with little black bow ties. Most of the girls from school were there. Rebeccah was standing with an older redheaded girl who must have been her sister. They were both wearing black, like Emily. In fact, lots of people were wearing black. No one else was wearing a bright pink dress like mine.

Rebeccah walked up, and I plastered a smile on my face, but she just brushed past me to talk to Emily. An uneasy feeling washed over me as I stood there, wondering what to do next.

I turned around to go look at the Christmas tree and ran straight into a little blond boy no older than Val.

"Ow! Why'd you do that?" He scowled up at me.

I started to say I was sorry but I didn't get to finish because Lizzie rushed up to us, looking worried.

"There you are!" she said. "Mom said no running, Jamie."

The little boy pointed at me. "She's mean! She stepped on my foot!"

I put my hands up. "I didn't mean to. I swear."

Lizzie laughed. "I'm sure you didn't. My brother just likes to tell stories sometimes. Don't you, Jamie?"

Jamie stuck his tongue out at me, and Lizzie and I both laughed. Her dress was pale purple, which matched the frames of her glasses perfectly.

"I like your dress," I said, and Lizzie said, "Really?"

I nodded. I was glad to see at least one other person wearing color.

"Mom! Over here!" Lizzie waved, and a woman hurried over to us with two little boys trailing after her. She was pretty, with Lizzie's same blond hair.

"Is everything okay over here?" she asked, crouching in front of Jamie. "Or has some great injustice befallen my littlest man?"

"Jamie ran off without hanging up his coat," Lizzie said, while her brother gave me the stink eye. "This is Thyme."

Her mother smiled and said that she'd heard so much about me from Lizzie. "You two look adorable," she said as she wrestled Jamie out of his coat. "And here Lizzie was convinced she'd be the only girl wearing color!"

Lizzie flushed pink. "Want to go get some punch? It tastes just like Hi-C, but with *sparkle*." She fanned her fingers out when she said the word.

"My mom says I shouldn't drink anything with food dyes in it," I said, and immediately felt like a huge dork.

But Lizzie just laughed. "Food dyes? Really?"

"Yeah, sort of." I couldn't explain that I knew all that stuff

115

because of Val. That because of Mom, I knew way too much about what was healthy and what wasn't.

Lizzie's mom asked if my parents were there. "It's always so hard when you're adjusting to a big move. I'd love to meet them."

"They couldn't make it," I said, and my neck got hot and my face, too. Then I started to feel like I couldn't breathe. I'd thought the party would be more fun on my own, but being there without my family just made me feel *more* alone.

Lizzie's mom was still holding Jamie's jacket.

"I can hang that up for you," I said.

Her eyebrows rose in surprise. "You don't have to—"

"It's no problem," I said. Then I grabbed the jacket and took off. When I got to the coat closet, the racks were all full. I tried to stuff Jamie's coat between two other jackets, but it wouldn't slide in, and when I pushed too hard, the rack almost fell over. Which made me want cry for some crazy reason.

"You've got problems with coats, huh?"

I jumped away from the coatrack and brushed the loose bangs out of my eyes.

Jake Reese was standing in the doorway to the closet, white earbuds in place, staring at me.

17

EMERGENCY

"I DON'T KNOW WHAT HAPPENED," I SAID AS A WAITER dabbed at a big, wet stain on my pretty pink dress. But the truth was, I knew exactly what had happened. Jake had caught me wrestling with the coatrack, and I was so embarrassed that I said something that made no sense and rushed past him, straight into a waiter carrying a tray full of champagne.

"Don't worry," Lizzie said. "Soda will get it out for sure. The carbonation helps."

Emily made a face. "Not always. If that dress was silk, it'd be ruined." *If* the dress was silk. I wondered if she was mad at me for bugging her about their fight. She wasn't giving me the fake smile, though, so maybe she was trying to be helpful, in her own way.

I caught a glimpse of Jake's springy hair hovering behind them. He was wearing a dress shirt and a skinny black tie. I thought he'd never looked nicer, which made me feel even dumber about making a fool of myself. I wished he would just disappear. In fact, I wished they would all just disappear. Leave it to me to find a way to look stupid at every opportunity.

Rebeccah came to my rescue by ignoring me entirely. "I asked Mr. Calhoun about the audition dates again," she told Emily. "He said it looks like the day after we get back."

Emily looked at Lizzie. "Plenty of time to practice. Or, you know, change your mind."

Lizzie's cheeks pinked up. She turned to me. "Are you going out for a part?"

She and Emily both looked at me. Great. Exactly what I didn't want to get caught up in—the Spring Fling and their fight. I wished the stupid waiter would stop dabbing at my dress so I could get out of there. "Probably not."

"Well, I think you should if you want to," Lizzie said, which made Emily frown and Rebeccah roll her eyes. Of course they thought I couldn't sing or dance. I couldn't manage to walk through a room without wrecking my dress!

The waiter finally stood up. "That should do," he said.

As soon as he moved out of the way, I shot out of my chair. I didn't even wait for Lizzie when she called after me. I'd thought the party would be fun, a way to pretend everything was fine for a night. But kids were so different here. More grown-up. They brought bento boxes with sushi for lunch and wore sparkly black dresses. Why couldn't just one thing feel normal?

Grandma Kay said there was no such thing as normal. She and Grandpa grew up in Lancaster, Pennsylvania. They got married there, but then they moved to San Diego for his job with the navy. According to Grandma, she spent a lot of time eating canned tuna and waiting for life to go back to normal after they moved, and that's when she discovered that there was no normal—just normal for now. And normal for now meant that things were always changing. Cancer had changed everything: the things I ate, the place I lived . . . what kind of normal would we find when we got back to San Diego?

I ended up in front of a table packed with fancy treats: neat rows of salmon rolled up with cream cheese, asparagus spears, and, at the end, a fountain—a *chocolate* fountain. I stabbed a chunk of cake with a skewer, then thought better of dipping in the chocolate. The last thing I needed was a big brown stain next to the big wet stain on my dress.

I groaned and stuffed the plain piece of cake into my mouth.

"The food's pretty good, huh?" Jake stepped up to the table next to me. His arm brushed mine, and I felt weird, like I wanted to talk to him and run away from him at the same time.

I took a bite of a strawberry so I could unstick the cake that was glued to the roof of my mouth. Chewing frantically, I watched Jake coat a chunk of cake in chocolate and eat it without a drop of mess.

"Did you try the black stuff on those crackers down there?" he asked.

Finally, I swallowed my last lump of cake and managed to say no.

He leaned closer. "Don't. It's fish eggs."

"Gross," I said, giggling. "But I know what caviar is." Of course he wouldn't think so. Seeing as I'd been nothing but stupid in front of him. The girl who didn't know prime numbers and dropped her books on the floor and wrestled with coats.

"Cool." He stabbed a cube of cheddar cheese and offered it to me.

"No, thanks." I could just imagine orange bits stuck between my teeth.

He popped the cheese into his mouth and chewed.

"What do you call cheese that's not yours?" he asked.

"Stolen?"

He grinned. "Nacho cheese."

We laughed, and I tried not to stare at the way his springy hair bounced like it was full of laughter, too, or how he got a dimple next to his mouth when he smiled.

"What are you listening to?" I asked, pointing at his headphones.

He ducked his head and mumbled something, but I couldn't hear him.

"What?" I stepped closer. He smelled like coconuts.

"It's a song my dad wrote," he said quietly. "He died last year. Heart attack."

"I'm sorry," I said, stunned by what he'd said. I didn't know what else to say, so I just put my hand on his sleeve. He peeked up at me, sheepish, and our noses got way too close, so close that I could see little bits of green mixed into his brown eyes.

Right then, a waiter cut between us to load more food onto the table.

Jake made a face behind his back and I laughed, but the way he smiled back made me feel totally inside out, like I needed to focus on my breathing again. That and the news about his father, which I hadn't expected. And yet here Jake was, alive and smiling. It was hard to imagine how that would be possible if anything ever happened to Val.

"I'd better get back," I said, even though I'd much rather have stayed there talking to him instead of gossiping with the girls.

"Sorry about your dress," he said. "It's a nice color. Everyone else is so boring." Then he grinned and disappeared into the crowd, leaving me with a smile on my face.

◎◎

When I got back to the corner with the chairs, the girls were circling like sharks, waiting for me.

"There you are," Lizzie said. "I was looking all over for you."

"You were?"

Emily stepped between us. "Thyme, you've got to come quick."

She latched onto my arm and dragged me to the foyer with the gigantic Christmas tree. The other girls trailed us, talking in hushed voices, which freaked me out. When we got to the tree, Emily pointed. A man was standing next to the elevator in his fancy tuxedo. He had his back to us. Then he shifted, revealing the person he was talking to: my father.

"Your dad just showed up," Emily said. "He said there was some kind of an emergency."

My breath caught.

The only reason Dad would come early was if something was wrong with Val.

I pushed Emily's arm away.

All I could think was that Jake had lost his father. Jake's father had *died*.

Dad saw me coming and reached his arms out.

I rushed into him, trying not to cry.

"It's all right," he said softly. He rubbed a circle over my back. "Val just has a little fever. We have to stop by the hospital. I'm sorry you have to leave early."

"It's okay," I said. "Let's go."

18

LUCK

AFTER THREE LONG HOURS AT THE HOSPITAL, WE GOT TO bring Val home. His chest films had been clear, and his fever had broken with antibiotics. But even with that good news, the doctors were worried that he might be rejecting the 3F8. They wouldn't know until they got the results from Val's HAMA test, which we were still waiting on. There had been some trouble with his blood sample.

Val spent the weekend resting while we waited for Dr. Everett to call. He'd said we'd hear from him by Monday, December 24—otherwise known as Christmas Eve, in normal households. If Val was positive for HAMA, then he couldn't stay in the drug trial.

And if that happened . . . well, I didn't want to think about that. All weekend, I couldn't even look at the Thyme Jar, in case I jinxed Val by thinking the wrong thing. All I could do was cross my fingers and pray. I was skeptical that praying or crossing fingers did much but Grandma Kay believed in those things, so I crossed my fingers for good luck anyway.

Waiting was the worst. Mom spent Monday morning cleaning while Val watched videos on the couch and Dad used the living room floor to reorganize his record collection. Meanwhile, Cori holed up in our room, making T-shirts for her drama club. She'd spread newspapers over the floor and borrowed a set of Dad's super-thick paint pens, the ones that smelled so sharp, Mom made her crack the window even though it was freezing outside.

First, Cori traced the letters onto the shirts using a paper template. Then she colored each letter in carefully. I kept expecting her to kick me out of our room, but she didn't. Maybe she'd caught some kind of holiday spirit. Or maybe she was just being nice because we were all thinking about Val.

After her second shirt, she pulled her headphones loose and looked up. "Want to help?"

"Really?"

She nodded, so I sat next to her while she traced a set of letters onto an old yellow shirt of Dad's. The fabric was turned inside out, but I remembered it had a picture of a pyramid on the front with a rainbow coming out of the top. When I'd made fun of him for wearing a rainbow, he'd said that it was an album cover from the greatest band ever: Pink Floyd.

"Dad let you have this?"

Cori nodded. She was biting her lip from concentrating so hard.

"There," she said, sitting back again. The shirt read: *ART IS LIFE.* It looked cool, but I didn't understand how she could focus on her drama club with everything else that was going on.

"Do you really care about drama this much?"

She shrugged. "I don't know. I guess it's just fun to work on."

"That's not what I mean. You never used to like clubs. You didn't even belong to one until Val got sick, and now it's all you do."

"I guess I'd rather stay busy."

Back home, she'd been so busy that I'd barely seen her for months—until she got in trouble. In October, she'd run a mannequin head up the flagpole to attract new members to the Green Team and had gotten suspended. Then I'd gotten to see her a lot.

"What happened that night Mom and Dad brought you home with Val?" I asked. "Did you get in trouble again?"

She grinned. "That was nothing. Mom was just mad that I skipped math with my friends." Then she got more serious. "This is something I can do, T. Something I *can* change, you know?" She stared hard at me, like she really meant it, but it sounded like an excuse to me.

"Aren't you worried about Val?" I asked.

She put the cap on her marker and set it down very carefully next to the shirt. "Of course I am," she said quietly. "It just helps to think about other things sometimes."

"Or *all* the time."

She made a face. "Think what you want, doofus. I've got a

buttload of T-shirts to make. Are you going to help me color this in or what?"

"Or what," I said, and she groaned.

But I guess I'd caught the holiday spirit, too, because I picked up a paint pen and let Cori show me how to color in the letters. I had to start in the middle so the paint didn't bleed over the edges. But I'd never been very good at staying inside the lines. As I colored in the *A* from *ART IS LIFE*, the hole in the middle of the letter got smaller and smaller until you could barely see it.

"Sorry," I said as Cori stared at the shirt. I thought for sure she would yell at me, and that all this "working together" stuff would vanish back to wherever it came from.

But she just took the pen and colored the *A* in the rest of the way.

"Whatever," she said. "It looks better like this anyway."

◎◎

An hour later, the phone rang, and Cori and I waited while time stood still. After several seconds that felt like years, Mom walked into our room.

"It's for you, Thyme," she said, handing me the phone. For me? Shani leapt into my mind. Had she found a way to call during her vacation after all?

"Hello?"

"Hey! It's Emily."

"Oh. Hey." I wondered if she was calling to ask why I'd run out of her party like my hair was on fire. But I couldn't explain about Val. And I couldn't make up some other excuse with Mom listening in. "Hold on." I clapped my hand over the phone. Cori and Mom both looked at me. "It's my friend from school. She needs to talk for a minute."

"Well, I'm busy in here," Cori said, hunching over a T-shirt like it would take a bulldozer to make her move. So much for being buddies.

"Then I'll use the hall."

Mom frowned. "Well . . . just come right back if you get another call, okay?" She didn't sound mad at all. She even smiled at me a little bit, like she understood.

In the hall, I pressed the phone to my ear. "Hey, Emily."

"I wasn't sure you were coming back," she said.

"Sorry, I was just changing rooms. How'd you get my number, anyway?"

"From the school directory. Is that a problem?"

"No. No problem," I said, because she was starting to sound irritated. "Things have just been crazy at home."

"Is that why you had to leave early? Your dad looked worried." Of course he had, with Val running a fever. And Emily had noticed.

"We just had to take care of something. But everything's fine now. I think." I winced at my own stupid words. I felt like I was back in her room, saying all the wrong things again and sounding like a total dork. Hopefully she wouldn't ask me to explain.

After a short silence, Emily said, "Well, if you're not busy,

I was wondering if you wanted to go to *The Nutcracker* with me this afternoon?"

"What?" The last thing I had expected was an invitation.

She laughed. "You know, the famous ballet? It's about a girl who's dreaming of Christmas morning. They have a Christmas tree that grows as high as the ceiling, right in front of you. It's kind of goofy but I go every year, only my cousin caught the barf bug, so she can't go with me. I have an extra ticket, with backstage passes and everything."

"Wow. That sounds fun—I mean the show, not the barf bug."

"So you'll come? I mean, I know it's short notice but I can give you a ride if that helps."

I cracked the apartment door and peeked inside. Val was on the couch, eating crackers in a nest of stuffed animals. His cheeks were still flushed, his body limp with exhaustion. On the way home from the hospital Friday night, he'd slept with his head in my lap. Part of me wanted to go see the show, but I knew I couldn't leave him while he was still feeling so bad—or before we got his test results.

"I don't think I can go," I said, and there was an awkward silence. "I want to. It's just, well, it's Christmas Eve."

"Oh. Totally. I understand." Emily didn't sound snappy at all, just let down. I wondered if she'd asked Lizzie. Maybe not, if they were still fighting.

"What about Rebeccah?" I said.

"She's out of town. Anyway, I just thought you might appreciate it. It's a New York tradition."

"I'm really sorry," I said, more to myself than to Emily. I felt kind of let down, too. Cori had her shirts. Dad had his records. Mom had Val. What did I have? Not much. Not even Shani. She was on vacation. She wasn't going to call.

"It's fine," Emily said. The chirp was back in her voice. "I'll see you at school—don't forget, Spring Fling tryouts! I'm so excited."

"Me too," I said automatically, although I didn't feel excited at all.

◎◎

When I went back inside, Dad had pushed his records to the side. There was a stack of board games on the rug instead. "I thought maybe we could use a Champions Tournament before we do lunch. Ready to go down in flames?" he asked, and all my bad feelings took a step back.

We had invented the Champions Tournament the first time Val was in the hospital. Dad brought stacks of games to the waiting room, and he and I played mancala and Jenga and checkers until one of us won three different games. Which was usually me.

I sat on the rug while Dad set up the mancala board. The *clink clink* sound was nice to hear, though at home we would have played on our screened porch instead of right in the middle of the living room. This time, Dad won. Then we set up checkers. Halfway through our match, Mom signaled Dad from the couch, where she was sitting with Val.

"Can you call Dr. Everett again?" she asked.

"We're almost done," he answered as I hopped one of his

129

black checkers with my red one. I added another chip on top of mine to make it a king, and he groaned.

"Honey." There was an edge to Mom's voice. "He said to call back if we didn't hear from the lab within an hour."

"I thought they said to call by noon."

"They said they *close* at noon," Mom said, clearly irritated now.

"Right." Dad ruffled my hair. "I'll be right back."

He left to call the lab, and I forced myself to study the board. I could win, as long as Dad took the bait and jumped my checker. Then I'd scoop up his last two players with my new king. I rehearsed the moves in my head, but it was hard to concentrate with Dad making such an important call. I listened for his voice over the blare of the TV, but Val had the volume cranked way up.

"Mom, can you turn it down?"

"I can barely hear it!" Val said, making a pouty face at me. I knew he was just cranky and worn out from having had a fever, but I felt so frustrated all of a sudden.

"Maybe you should turn your ears up," I said, like I was saying something perfectly reasonable instead of being mean.

Mom cut her eyes at me. "Thyme. That's not very nice." Something snapped inside me. It was like all my frustrated feelings poured out at once.

"He *can* turn them up, you know. Then the rest of us don't have to go deaf, too."

"Thyme!"

"What?" I knew I shouldn't have said it, but sometimes, it was all too much—the noise from the TV, the waiting, the missing out. I was tired of not counting.

Dad came back into the room, and my crabby feelings drowned in a fresh wave of guilt.

"No news yet," he told us. Then he glanced at the TV. "Can we turn that down?"

"Really, Michael?" Mom said. "Val, you're going to have to adjust your hearing aids. Apparently, the TV *must* be turned down."

Dad put his hands up. "What did I do now?"

"*Nothing,*" Mom and I said at the same time.

Of course, Mr. Lipinsky chose that exact moment to bang on the ceiling from below. I wanted to reach through the floorboards and smack him. Instead, I tried to focus on the game. If I won, then everything was going to be okay. Val would get better, and I would get to go back home. Somehow, it would all magically work out the way I wanted it to.

Dad's hand wavered over one of his pieces. Then he spotted the bait. "Looks like I got you this time." He hopped my piece, and I swooped in with my king, hopping his two remaining players in a flash. "Or not," he said, and we laughed.

Then the phone rang, and the color drained out of his face.

"I'll get it!" Cori shouted from our bedroom.

"No!" Dad called. "I've got it." He left the room, and Mom stared hard at the TV like she wasn't listening for Dad's voice with every fiber of her being. Val seemed oblivious, cheering for his beloved Transformers as they crashed into planets on the screen. Cori came in and joined them on the couch, snuggling next to Val.

As the seconds ticked by, I stacked the checkers into two neat rows. Three even stacks of black. Three stacks of red. I centered each stack perfectly on a single black square. Like soldiers lined up for battle, but hovering, unsure if they were really going to war or not.

Then Dad walked back into the room. We all looked at him. My heart beat faster. "The HAMA test was negative," he said. "It's just an infection. He's okay."

Mom burst into tears, and Val crawled into her lap and patted her face.

"Don't worry, Mommy. I'll get better. Promise," he said, and she just wrapped her arms around him. Then she reached for Dad, too, and they clung to each other like their lives depended on it. Mom made a little choking noise, and Dad squeezed her harder. Then he waved for me and Cori to join in, and we all just clumped up together in a big, sappy group hug.

When we broke apart, Val pointed at the screen and laughed. "That guy's died like ten times already! How can he *do* that?"

"He's just really lucky," I said. But not as lucky as my brother. That afternoon, he was the luckiest kid in the world. He could continue his treatment. He still had a shot. And just like that, all the frustrations I'd been feeling melted away.

"Is it time for presents yet?" Val asked, for the hundredth time that day.

Mom's shoulders started shaking. When we pulled away from her, she wasn't crying anymore—she was laughing. "What the heck! We'll all open one, for Christmas Eve. You too, girls!"

I went over to our little fake tree (because ironically, a real tree could increase Val's chance of infection if he didn't have one already), oddly decorated with construction-paper loops and popcorn (because all of our other ornaments were in storage), and scanned the small pile of presents circling the tree skirt (because there wasn't so much money for presents this year), and Mom called out, "Who wants cookies? I feel like baking!"

That's when I knew Christmas wasn't going to be so bad after all.

19

FAVORITE THINGS

WHEN GOOD THINGS HAPPENED WITH VAL, THE HAPPY FEELINGS stuck to us for days, like a coating of invisible fairy dust—but even fairy dust runs out of power eventually.

By halfway through winter break, we were all tired of each other. Dad ended up going to a meeting for his freelance work, but Mom was playing it safe with Val, keeping him home so he didn't pick up another bug. Which meant Cori and I were stuck there with them.

"I'm so sick of this apartment," Cori said, flinging the remote into the couch cushions. She was impatient to hang out with her friends. They were planning a sleepover for New Year's Eve.

Mom made a hushing sound. "Keep it down." Val was having quiet time in his room. His fever was gone, but Mom said he still needed rest.

Cori snatched up her cell phone and started texting with quick, furious clicks.

"Maybe when your father gets back we can go ice-skating," Mom said. She was in the kitchen, scrubbing a cookie sheet in the sink. She'd been on a baking streak since Christmas. "That is, as long as you can stop texting that boy long enough to finish your thank-you notes." Thank-you notes were a big deal with Mom. Every birthday, every holiday, no matter what—we sent thank-you notes.

Cori moaned. "I don't want to go ice-skating."

"I do!" My cards were spread out across the dining table. Letters, envelopes, stamps: an assembly line to get the job done quickly.

Mom smiled at me. She'd given me time for Christmas— two fresh slips of paper, wrapped in a pretty painted box. Two whole *days* of me time that she said I could use for something special, like a day at the zoo or the circus. "Something fun, something we can do together," she'd said. But I'd just added them to the Thyme Jar and thought, *Well, going back to San Diego definitely qualifies as something we'll have to do together.*

"For your information, Liam is in charge of the posters for our protest," Cori told Mom. "We have, like, thirty-three signs we need to make, and zero time to get them done. I should be at his place right now helping with everyone else. Not that anyone cares."

"We've talked about this. You can't go by yourself. When Dad gets back—"

"Why not?" Cori said. "I've been taking the subway on my own every day."

"This isn't every day," Mom said.

"It's the *exact same train*," Cori shouted, and I cringed.

Mom stopped scrubbing her cookie sheet. "That can easily change. If you'd like, I can ask Mrs. Ravelli to take you to school from now on, before she takes Thyme."

"I don't want to take the subway," I said, but they both ignored me.

"It's not *fair*," Cori said.

"Your brother is still *recovering*," Mom said.

Cori stood up and faced Mom. "I shouldn't have to stay here just because he does. I'm not the one catching germs and getting fevers and ruining everyone's lives."

"Coriander Owens, you better fix that attitude fast or you'll be on house arrest for real. I mean it. No New Year's Eve sleepover, no drama club, no *nothing*."

Cori's face went this way and that, like different parts of her were fighting for control over her mouth. But she must have really wanted to go to that sleepover, because she finally swallowed, her cheeks flaming, and muttered, "Fine."

"Good," Mom said. "Now go finish your thank-you notes."

Cori caught my eye. Normally, she would've taken a crack at me or rolled her eyes, but this time she just stomped off without another word. Which was actually pretty nice for a change.

A few minutes later, Mom walked up to me with a stack of pretty red-and-white cookie boxes in her arms. "Thyme, can you take a break and run these to the neighbors for me?"

She set the boxes on the table. The top one was addressed to Mr. Lipinsky.

"Why are we giving cookies to him?"

"Everyone likes homemade cookies," Mom said. "And some people need them more than others. It's the right thing to do." That was what Grandma Kay said when we spent Christmas Eve working at the soup kitchen instead of playing games and watching movies like everyone else. According to Grandma, nothing worth doing was easy, and that was why we *had* to come to New York, even though she was spending Christmas alone for the first time ever.

"But Christmas is over."

"Christmas isn't over till I say it's over! I'll give you an hour of time, okay? Now get your butt out that door before I make your sister go with you."

It was no use arguing. Plus, it was another hour added to the pile. I decided to start at the bottom of the building and work my way up.

First was our landlord, who looked so surprised to get a gift that I felt like Santa Claus. Then the family in 2A with their little baby who never cried because he was the best baby on earth—I know, because that's what the mom said when I handed her the cookies. "Look at the pretty cookies, Henry!" she said, and the baby cracked a grin, sending a river of drool down his shirt. The mom beamed at me. "Isn't he just the best baby in the whole wide world?" Then the woman in 2B, who was some kind of actress. She had a voice like a frog. When she took her box, she croaked a raspy *thank you*, like the frog was especially stuck that morning.

Then it was time for the third floor.

The man in apartment 3A didn't answer. I'd only seen him once. Cori had Val convinced that he was a ghost. I left the ghost's cookies in front of his door and looked at apartment 3B, debating whether or not to knock. I could just drop the cookies and run. But Mom would ask if everyone had been home.

I knocked.

No answer.

I tried again, smacking the door hard with my fist.

Still no answer, so I dropped the cookies in front of Mr. Lipinsky's door and turned for the stairs, relieved that I wouldn't have to face him after all. But then his door creaked open, and I stopped.

"That's littering, you know. You can't leave things in the hall like that."

I turned around. Mr. Lipinsky was spying through the crack in the door like usual.

"They're cookies. For Christmas. Or the holidays, or whatever."

He opened his door a bit wider and eyed the box like it was full of candied rats. "Any *hamantaschen* in there?"

I shrugged, confused. He sighed. "Little triangle-shaped cookies with jam."

"No. Sorry."

He looked up. "You believe that, Ada?" he asked the ceiling. "She doesn't even know what a *hamantaschen* is." He picked up the box and looked at me. "Stay there," he ordered in a no-nonsense voice. Then he disappeared inside his apartment, while I wondered if he was not just weird, but completely crazy. Who was this Ada person? And why was he looking at the ceiling to talk to her?

With his door open, I could see the posters on his wall: *Evita*, *The Wiz*, *Peter Pan* . . . all Broadway musicals. Despite the horrible cooking smells coming from inside, I crept a little closer to see what the rest of his apartment looked like. When I peeked through the door, a burst of whistling made me jump. His bird was right there in the living room, perched on a metal stand.

That's when Mr. Lipinsky reappeared, carrying a small, square casserole dish. He shuffled up to the door and shoved the dish into my hands. "*Chag Semeach.*"

The edges of the white ceramic were coated in burnt black smears, and whatever was filling the inside didn't look much better: squiggly and green and charred in places.

"I was planning to take that to the potluck at the VA, but I can make another," he said gruffly. Then he started to shut the door.

"Wait. What is it?" I held the dish as far away from my body as possible, in case it turned out that the casserole really was full of overcooked brains. It definitely reeked badly enough to be something gross like that.

"It's a kugel."

"A what?"

He huffed. "Don't you know anything?" He glanced at the ceiling again and murmured something about *stupid* this and *moron* that, but then he seemed to come to some kind of a decision. "A kugel brings luck. Share it with your family on the holiday, and you will be blessed." He cleared his throat and stared at me, his gray eyes piercing, but not angry. Not like the day we moved in. "Back in my day, we used to say thank you when someone gave us a gift."

My skin flushed hot, even though I didn't think his definition of the word *gift* matched with mine. I preferred gifts wrapped in crisp, colorful paper that smelled, well, not rotten.

"Thank you," I said, putting on my best thank-you smile.

"And thank you. Now do me a favor and stay off your heels on the stairs. You walk like an elephant." I must've looked confused again, because he said, "A proper step involves the ball of the foot as well as the heel. You people seem to have forgotten how to use your toes. You thump around like elephants all day, making it impossible for the decent people in this building to take a nap."

With that, he shut his door, and I went upstairs, walking on my toes the whole way.

◉◉

A few minutes after I got back from delivering cookies, the locks turned on our apartment door.

"I'm home!" Dad called as the door sprung open. There was a huge box on the floor in front of him, just outside. Val came running from his room, and Dad handed him an armful of mail from on top of the box, which Val carried inside and dumped on the floor.

"Avalanche!" he shouted, diving into the pile.

"Looks like someone's feeling better," Dad said. He picked

up the enormous box and tried to angle it through the door, but one tattered corner kept catching on the door frame. I grabbed the other side, and together we managed to get the box inside.

"Thanks," Dad puffed.

Mom popped in from the kitchen. "What's this, a mail explosion? I'd help, but I'm in the middle of cookies for Val's support group." She looked at Dad. "How was the meeting?"

He gave her a thumbs-up. "Don't worry about the mail. I've got it covered." He handed me an envelope from his back pocket—a letter from Grandma Kay! "When you're done reading that, you can take care of this box, too."

"Why me?" I wanted to go skating, like Mom had said.

Then I saw the label on the box. The address was in Shani's handwriting! I'd sent her a collection of cool metal hair clips shaped like ladybugs and dragonflies, but when nothing came for Christmas, I'd figured she was so busy with her family trip that she'd forgotten about me. But she hadn't.

An hour later, she surprised me again with a FaceTime request. So I didn't get to go ice-skating after all, but spending time with Shani was worth the trade.

"How did you find a box of strawberries this time of year?"

"Duh. It's California," she said, crossing her eyes at me on the iPad.

"Oh. Yeah." We laughed.

"I can't believe you got me all of my favorite things," I said, unwrapping an ear of chocolate corn. The chocolate was from Hans and Harry's, our favorite bakery back home. I peeled the gold label off the plastic and stuck it to my sweater.

"*When the dog bites,*" Shani sang. "*When the bee stings—*"

"*When I'm feeling sad,*" I joined. "*I simply remember my* favorite *things, and then I don't feeeeeeeeeeeeeeeeel—*" I squeaked.

"*So bad!*" Shani sang, laughing as I flopped back on my bed and bit into the chocolate.

"So did you talk to that Jake guy again?" she asked, and I choked a little on the chocolate. "Wait a minute," she said, "You like him!"

"No I don't! I mean, I don't know." I knew what it meant to like someone, but I'd never liked anyone before. Before Shani could say anything else about Jake, I changed the subject. "My mom made me take cookies to the annoying neighbor with the giant bird."

"Did he tell you to get lost?"

"Close. He acted like I was trying to poison him. He's totally crazy. He gave us this disgusting burnt casserole and Mom was like, *what?*"

"Old people are crazy. My grams keeps putting her slippers in the oven to warm them up. Mom swears she'll burn the house down one day."

Then I told her about Emily and Lizzie, and how they were so competitive about the Spring Fling. "Lizzie said I should try out for something. But I can't sing. And we both know I *shouldn't* dance."

Shani cracked up. "You could do it as a joke," she said.

I picked at a nail. "Well, the show's in March."

"Oh." Her eyes fell.

"I'm coming back before then, duh. Mom gave me two days of time for Christmas. I have over a hundred hours now. I'm not missing our birthdays again."

Shani grinned. "Well, you could just do it for now. It'll be fun!"

I knew she was just saying that because she loved projects more than I loved Coke floats, but hearing her tell me to do it felt weird, and kind of wrong. Suddenly all I could think about was how Shani was doing things without me, too.

"Is that what you're doing with Jenny Hargrove? Having fun?"

She blinked. "That's just for school."

"But you guys have been hanging out, too," I said, letting all my worries break free. "What's next, sleeping over and making her calendars?" I felt terrible saying that, but it was the truth.

"Why are you giving me such a hard time?"

A long minute passed where I didn't say anything. What was I supposed to say? *I miss you and I wish I was home instead of sitting around this tiny apartment with my family all week? I wish I felt like I actually belonged somewhere, instead of living in between?*

Shani tapped the screen. "Look, we both wish you were here. But you're not, and Mom doesn't want me sitting around the house"—she made air quotes—"'*wasting away.*' It's hard when you're not there in the morning. And at lunch. But I don't blame you." Her voice trembled a little. I'd hurt her feelings, and she didn't deserve it. She wasn't the one acting like a big baby.

"I'm sorry," I said. "I'm going to stop being stupid now, okay?"

She smiled.

"As long as you promise to call me next week," I added.

"Deal," she said. Then she stuck her tongue out, and I leaned so close to the camera that my eyeball filled the screen.

"Cut it out, or the eyeball of doom will suck you into its gooey center!"

She squealed, and I leaned back. "Look, I gotta run," she said. "Mom's making me go to the mall with my idiot cousins. But I'll e-mail you later. Promise."

We said good-bye, and a familiar empty spot opened up in my heart again.

I flopped back against my pillows and grabbed Mr. Knuckles.

"What do you think?" I asked the fuzzy green hand. The color had faded over the years, the fabric more gray than green. "Should I do the Spring Fling?"

Mr. Knuckles pumped his fist at me.

"You say yes to everything," I scolded, and Mr. Knuckles bounced from side to side. With his fingers curled up, the move didn't look much like a wave, but I got the message.

20

MAZEL TOV

THE NEW YEAR ARRIVED WITH A BANG, AND NOT JUST FROM THE fireworks that I missed when I passed out on the couch at ten o'clock. This bang was from below us, in Mr. Lipinsky's apartment, and it was so loud that Mom jumped halfway across the kitchen.

Cori was still at her sleepover, and Dad was trying to get some work done on his laptop while Val watched a show. Meanwhile, Mom and I were attempting to cook Grandma's Kay's traditional New Year's Day dinner of black-eyed peas and collard greens, only it wasn't going so well. But Mom was determined, because collard greens weren't just tradition—they were a superfood, packed full of vitamins and other good stuff. We'd been on the phone with Grandma for an hour, trying to get Mom's greens to hurry up and cook so we wouldn't be stuck chewing on grass-flavored leather for dinner. When the bang happened, Mom told Grandma she'd have to call her back, because apparently our neighbor was blowing something up downstairs.

"Do you think he's okay?" I asked, following her into the living room.

"No," she said with an eye roll just like one of Cori's. "I mean, yes. But I caught him stuffing old grocery flyers in Val's stroller when I left it downstairs yesterday, so anything's possible."

"Maybe he's trying to be nice."

"Really? You think he's nice?"

"No." I just thought there was a chance—a very small one—that maybe Mr. Lipinsky was actually trying to help us with the flyers in his own weird way. But Mom obviously didn't agree.

She tapped Dad's headphones to get his attention and told him Mr. Lipinsky was blowing things up downstairs, in case he wanted to do anything about it.

"Are you serious?" Dad said. "Maybe it's just his TV."

"A couple of skeptics, both of you," Mom said, looking at me and Dad. "Fine. I'll go down there myself and get to the bottom of this."

"That's not what I meant," Dad said, but Mom just shook her head.

"Oh no. Don't change your tune now that I'm going."

Dad held his hands up in surrender.

"I want to go," Val said, hopping up from the couch.

"Not this time, honey."

Val pouted. "I'm not scared of him," he said, crossing his arms to show us how tough he was. "I can do things, too, you know."

Mom dropped to one knee. "I know." She gave him a

squeeze. "We'll be right back." She looked at me. "Thyme, you're coming with me."

"Why me?"

Mom gave Dad a look. "You're my witness."

☙❧

On the way downstairs, Mom was kind of mumbling to herself, like she was practicing what she was going to say. Then, when she knocked on the door to apartment 3B, her face looked paler than usual, and I realized she might actually be nervous about confronting Mr. Lipinsky face-to-face.

When he pulled open the door in his purple robe and his crazy this-way-and-that hair, I stepped right in front of Mom and said, "There's a building code, you know. You can't just blow stuff up inside your apartment. It's dangerous!"

"Thyme!" Mom exclaimed, while Mr. Lipinsky stared at me, his gray eyes as piercing as usual.

Then he did the weirdest thing.

He shouted, "Mazel tov," clapped his hands, and slammed the door right in our faces.

"What on *earth*," Mom said. Then she knocked again, and when Mr. Lipinsky opened the door with absolutely no sign that he was sorry in the least, Mom let him have it.

"Excuse me, *sir*, but if you think you can treat us so rudely after we have been nothing but understanding about your endless stream of complaints, you are sadly mistaken! Believe me, I'd rather shut my finger in a door than come down here, but you can't expect us to just sit up there and wait for you to blow a hole in our floor. Now, what exactly is going on in there?"

Oh wow! I couldn't wait to hear what Mr. Lipinsky would say to that.

But he didn't say anything at all. Not for a whole minute at least, while Mom stood there with her arms crossed and her perfect bangs all out of shape and her pale face blotched with red.

Finally, she said, "Don't you have anything to say?" That was Mom's cue to apologize. *Thyme, do you have anything to say to your sister? Cori, what do you have to say to Val?* The answer was always supposed to be *I'm sorry*, though I usually wanted to say "nope."

Mr. Lipinsky cocked his head to the side and jiggled his ear lobe. "I'm a bit hard of hearing," he said. "I'm afraid you'll have to speak up."

Mom's face got so red, I thought she'd explode. "You're crazy," she said.

He actually smiled. "What other people think of me is none of my business."

"Are you blowing things up in there?" she demanded, and the old man's mouth twitched. Then she brought out the big guns. "I'm happy to call the police if that's what's required."

"No need," Mr. Lipinsky said. "No need at all." Then he turned around and left us there.

Mom looked at me with her mouth hanging open like a fish, so I just said, "He does that sometimes," because he did have a habit of cutting you off mid-conversation, but he usually shut the door when he did it.

Mr. Lipinsky came back with an open bottle of champagne in his hands, and Mom just said, "Oh," very small, like she wished she could disappear, because that must've been what we heard upstairs. Champagne pops when you open it. I remembered when Dad brought some home the night Val got into the 3F8 trial. The cork from Mr. Lipinsky's bottle must've nailed the ceiling beneath our kitchen floor.

"It's my late wife's birthday," he said, glancing at the ceiling, like he had when I gave him the cookies, only now it made sense. Ada was his wife, and she was dead.

Mr. Lipinsky looked back at Mom. "You people must be celebrating the New Year." He extended the champagne bottle, but Mom backed away like he was offering a used hankie.

"No, thank you," she said. "Though I am sorry for your loss." She almost sounded sorry, too. Mr. Lipinsky had really thrown her for a loop.

"Suit yourself." He tipped the bottle back, and just as he took a swig, a short figure barreled between me and Mom and flung himself around Mr. Lipinsky's legs.

Then three things happened very fast:

1. Mr. Lipinsky spit his champagne all over us.

2. Mom screamed, "Val!"

3. Val shot into Mom's arms like a real-life flying superhero.

"Why you little—" Mr. Lipinsky said, wagging his trembling fingers at Val like he wanted to strangle the life out of him. Then he slammed the door in our faces again, only this time Mom didn't knock to make him apologize. She just ordered us upstairs immediately, with instructions not to touch a *thing* until we'd washed ourselves off in the bathroom.

"This is why we don't hug strangers," she told Val, who just nodded miserably.

I nudged Val's shoulder. "If it makes you feel better, I'm pretty sure you scared him to death, too."

"Don't encourage your brother," Mom said, but I swear I also heard her say, "Serves the old fool right," under her breath.

☙◙

After Dad picked Cori up from her sleepover, we called Grandma again to say happy New Year from the dining table. The traditional meal had started with her and Grandpa. There were pictures of him feeding me black-eyed peas for good luck in the New Year when I was little. He looked so nice, with his round cheeks and giant hands, that I wished I remembered him, but he died before Val was born. Mom said Grandpa's laugh had been the best. That he'd made everyone else laugh, no matter how they felt.

Mom had given Grandma a tablet for Christmas, and she was doing her best to video-chat with us, though she kept leaning too close to the screen every time she spoke. "I got your thank-you note just yesterday, Thyme," she said, her wrinkled mouth filling the screen, which made Val giggle. "Such lovely handwriting."

"Thank you, Grandma."

"I wish I could say the same for you, Rosemary," Grandma scolded.

"*Mom,*" Mom said, which made me and Cori laugh. It was so weird hearing Mom say that word in that way.

"In other news," Dad said with a wink for Mom, "I think we're ready to dig in. Shall we start with the greens?"

Dad raised his fork, and Grandma raised hers. She was sitting at her table in San Diego with a plate of greens and black-eyed peas, just like us, only she also had a thick slice of her homemade bread. It looked so good, I could practically taste the butter.

We all took a bite, except for Val, who was eating regular green beans instead.

Then we chewed.

And chewed.

Finally, Grandma asked how the greens turned out, and we all smiled and nodded, although no one swallowed a thing because Mom and I must have really messed up. The greens were way too salty. But with Grandma watching, none of us were about to spit our food out. Somehow, I got my bite down, and lucky for us, Grandma didn't seem to notice that we barely ate anything for the rest of the meal. It turned out that we hadn't soaked the black-eyed peas properly after all, so they tasted like little chips of cardboard, hard and chalky and even yuckier than the greens.

"This was just lovely, Rosemary," Grandma said when we were finishing up.

Our food had been so far from lovely, I had to fight the

urge to giggle. Mom must have felt the same way, because she just smiled and made an *mm-hmm* noise with her lips sealed shut.

Then Grandma said, "Oh, I almost forgot. That nice woman from the real estate agency called. I'm just going to give her my set of keys for now. That should take care of her for you. I didn't want you worrying, with everything else you have going on."

"What real estate lady?" Cori asked.

Mom coughed, grabbed her water, and washed her food down in a hurry. "That's fine, Mom, thanks," she said to Grandma. "It's nothing," she said to us. "We were just short a set of keys. How about you kids say good-bye. We'll talk to Grandma again soon."

Cori looked at me, and I shrugged. I didn't know what Grandma was talking about. Maybe it had something to do with renting our house while we were gone. But Mom's face had gone really red, so I couldn't imagine that was it. Maybe they'd found a renter, and Mom just didn't want to tell us about it. I hoped whoever they were, they wouldn't mess up my room.

We all said good-bye to Grandma Kay, though I didn't want to. In just an hour, I'd gotten used to having her there again. Val even sang the good-bye song from his old pre-school, with Dad joining in using a goofy voice. When we finally signed off, the room felt strangely empty.

Then Cori pushed her plate away and groaned. "That was the worst," she said. "I can't wait until Mrs. Ravelli's back."

I looked at Mom, expecting her to get mad. But she just sighed and said, "Me either."

Then Dad burst out laughing, and so did I, which was such a relief.

But when I looked over at Val, his little blue eyes looked so big and sad all of a sudden.

"I miss Grandma," he said, and the air went out of the room. For a second, I thought Mom would agree with him, too. But then she started talking about all of the super-fun things they were going to do in New York once he was better, as though that made up for Grandma not being there. Only it didn't, not really. Of course Val missed Grandma. We all did.

When Mom went to get the dessert, I didn't tell Val things would get better. I just squeezed his hand and said, "I miss her, too."

21

SNOW DAY

THE NIGHT BEFORE SCHOOL STARTED BACK, SNOW FELL THICK AND heavy over the city. I woke up early to a strange kind of quiet. No beeping horns. No rattling trucks. No sirens. It sounded like the world had stopped. For five solid minutes, I lay in my bed, staring at the bluish light filtering through the curtains. As time ticked by in silence, a tiny glow of hope built in my chest. Maybe we wouldn't go back to school that morning after all. I was nervous about seeing Jake again. What did you say to a boy who told you he liked your dress? And shared all his secrets? Or was he like that with everyone because he was a nice guy, and I was crazy to think that maybe he liked me? Shani would have known what to say.

BUZZZZ! Cori's alarm clock shattered the silence.

"Stop it," she said, whacking at the alarm clock and knocking everything else off her bedside table in the process. A split second later, a dull scraping noise erupted outside the window. A plow. The sound grew until the screech was so loud it felt like the plow was scraping the inside of my skull.

CRASH! Muffled shouting drifted in from the street. After a few high-pitched beeps, the plow's scraping picked up again, and I slipped my head beneath my pillow to pretend for five more minutes that I didn't have to get up, though I had a sneaking suspicion that there were no such things as snow days in New York City. In San Diego, even the threat of ice guaranteed at least a delay, but in this place, people didn't seem to let anything get in their way.

I must have drifted off again, because the next thing I knew, our door popped open with a bang. The frame was so thickly painted that the wood tended to stick.

"Girls, time to get up," Mom said. Pause. "*Now.*"

"I'm coming already!" Cori shouted.

"You better be. Your alarm went off twenty minutes ago. Now hurry up, or you're going to be late. You're on your own starting today. Thyme, Mrs. Ravelli will be here any minute. Get moving."

"Okay, okay." I stuck one leg into the icy air to prove I was moving. But as soon as Mom left, I pulled my leg back beneath my comforter. Then her words registered. Cori was walking to the subway on her own? What about Dad? He always went with her.

I jumped out of bed and hustled my freezing skin into a set of fresh clothes. When I got to the breakfast bar, Dad wasn't in his usual spot at the dining table, in front of his laptop.

"Where's Dad?"

Mom slid a whole-grain toaster pastry onto my plate, the organic kind with the frosting that didn't really taste sweet. "He starts full-time at the ad agency this week," she said, moving on to Val's plate. "From now on, he'll be out of here first thing in the morning." She poked Val's side. "And soon, you'll be off to school just like your sisters, buckaroo!"

Val giggled, and bits of pastry sprinkled from his mouth to the floor.

"Dad didn't tell me that," I said.

Mom hurried back into the kitchen. "What?"

"I didn't know," I said, more loudly this time. If they'd told me Dad had taken a full-time job, I would have remembered. And why was he taking a job? I thought he was just working freelance so it would be no problem when we moved back to California.

"Sorry," Mom said. "Things came together last week. We're lucky a position opened up. We couldn't get by on freelance projects forever. It was perfect timing, really." She turned away, and a sinking feeling came over me. Ever since Mom and Dad told us about Val's blood test, I'd thought maybe they were being straight with me. But I was stupid to think they weren't hiding things anymore.

"Eat up," Mom warned. "Mrs. Ravelli will be here any minute. And you still need to brush your teeth *and* your hair. Maybe you can get up on time tomorrow, okay?"

"Fine." I took a bite of my breakfast, but the pastry turned to sawdust in my mouth.

Cori rushed by, stuffed her arms in her jacket, and shouted good-bye to Mom, who came around the corner to give her a quick hug. "Don't make me regret giving you your freedom," Mom said. Cori smiled and left, looking like she was on top of the world. Of course she was. She was getting exactly what she wanted, while I was just stumbling to keep up. Suddenly, I had to get out of the apartment, away from Mom, who didn't think twice about hiding things from me.

When Mrs. Ravelli showed up a few minutes later, I was ready to go in my scarf, gloves, boots, and puffy jacket. "Can we just leave?" I said.

"In a minute, *bambina*. First, let me get your lunch." She walked past me and said hello to Mom and Val and took her time in the kitchen while I sweated by the door.

"Here you go," she said, handing me a lunch bag. I stuffed it in my bookbag while she tied her scarf over her curly gray hair, and finally, we were off.

"I'm sure you're happy to see your friends," she said on our way to school.

You have no idea, I thought. At least the girls at school didn't forget to tell me about major important life-changing news. Sure, they went a little overboard when it came to gossip, but being overinformed was better than being left out completely.

Thanks to the fresh snow, the walk that morning was hard. Some of the sidewalks were fully shoveled, while others were impossible. More often than not, we had to worm single file down wandering, slippery paths that were closer to sledding runs than walkways. By the time we reached MS 221, Mrs. Ravelli was panting and my stomach was twisting. How could Dad have taken a full-time job? That didn't make it sound like we were going home in March.

My back was all sweaty under my heavy coat. I had to get

inside before I combusted. I said bye to Ravioli and darted up the steps to the red double doors. A gust of warm, musty air greeted me—the smell of books and piping hot radiators. I shrugged off my coat, and the tightness in my throat started to ease, then let up entirely when my locker popped open after only two tries. I told myself it was going to be okay. There were one hundred and twenty hours in my Thyme Jar. More than I'd ever earned before. One way or the other, I was going to get back home.

๑๑

At lunch, everyone was buzzing about the Spring Fling again. Tryouts were at the end of the week. According to Emily, Mr. Calhoun said she had a "great shot" at the lead role. Of course she looked right at Lizzie when she said it, and Lizzie looked away. So they were still fighting, then.

"You'll make an awesome Dorothy," Rebeccah said to Emily.

"I know." Emily grinned, and everyone else exploded into chatter about the show, everyone except for Lizzie, so I asked her if she'd had a fun vacation.

"It was okay," she said. "I had to work at my parents' store. Last-minute shoppers and all that." Then her eyes brightened behind her glasses. "I almost forgot! I brought something from the store." She rummaged in the pocket of her overalls, which looked like something Val would've worn when he was three. The pigtails were back, too. I liked how she wore what she wanted, even if it was a little goofy.

"I found this in an old dresser," she said, pulling out a wad of yellowed newspaper. "I thought it was just trash, but wait till you see what's inside!"

"What's that?" Emily asked.

Lizzie hesitated, the paper nearly unfolded. "It's just something I found at my parents' store."

At the mention of Lizzie's family store, Emily rolled her eyes. "Not old stuff again."

"Old stuff can be cool," I said, thinking maybe Emily would take my hint to lighten up, but she just glared at me like we hadn't spent all that time together at her party and she hadn't asked me to go to *The Nutcracker* with her. Maybe those things meant less than I'd thought.

"Well, are you going to show all of us or just Thyme?" she asked Lizzie.

A pink blush crept over Lizzie's cheeks as she unfolded the paper while the whole table watched. Inside was a pile of flat, dull green leaves. She plucked one from the top. "They're four-leaf clovers."

The four matching leaves were perfectly spaced and perfectly smooth.

"That isn't real," Rebeccah said.

Lizzie just sat there, so I took a clover and felt the leaves. They were paper thin, but they had ridges and veins like real leaves. They were just old and dry. "It's real," I said, and everyone else leaned in for a better look, picking up clovers and holding them to the light. Everyone except for Emily.

"Look at how old that newspaper is," she said. "Who knows where it came from."

Rebeccah leaned back. "She's right. They're probably covered in germs. We shouldn't touch them."

Celia had a clover in her hand. Slowly, she put it back on Lizzie's pile. So did Delia and all the other girls.

"Sorry," Lizzie said as she folded up the newspaper. "I thought you guys might want them, for good luck at tryouts."

Emily frowned, and Rebeccah said, "You keep them. You need all the luck you can get."

Lizzie's face closed up. Then she crammed the clovers in her pocket and rushed away from the table. The whole time, Emily just sat there, letting it all happen.

I balled up the end of my turkey and Swiss and stood to go after Lizzie.

"Where are you going?" Emily asked.

"To talk to her." For a second, Emily looked like she regretted everything that had happened. I leaned across the table. "You could go talk to her, too, you know. Right now." For a second, Emily's eyes widened. Maybe I'd said exactly what she was thinking. Or maybe she was just plain annoyed, because the next thing I knew, she was glaring at me again.

"You have no idea what you're talking about. This is none of your business."

"You're right," I said. "It's not." I didn't know why I gave two hoots about these girls and their stupid fight. I guess I just didn't like watching Lizzie get dumped on.

"Run along after your little friend," Rebeccah said, clearly enjoying her new place at Emily's side.

I waited for Emily to say something else. When she didn't, I left.

✪

I caught up to Lizzie in the hall. She wasn't crying, but she was close to it. When I tried to talk to her, she ran into the girls' bathroom and hid in one of the stalls.

"Don't listen to them," I said from the other side of the door. "They're just being jerks."

She sniffled. "That's not it."

"Look, they can be mad all they want, but it's not like Mr. Calhoun already gave Emily the part. He just said she had a great shot. Maybe he says that to everyone."

There was a long pause. Then Lizzie said, "They're right, you know. Emily's the one who belongs onstage. I can't sing like her."

"Who says you can't?"

"Well, Rebeccah, for one."

"She's just kissing up to Emily. She'll make the best Wicked Witch of all time, but trust me, she's a total jerk. She'd say anything to make Emily happy."

I heard Lizzie sigh. "She didn't go to school with us before. But when we got here, everything changed. She's around all the time now. This is so stupid. I should just tell them I'm not doing it. I can't sing in front of other people like that, anyway."

There was no one else in the bathroom, which gave me an idea. "Try it," I said. "Sing something for me right now."

"Are you crazy?"

"Well, you can't just hide in there all day. Let me hear what you can do. I bet you're great." I hadn't planned on saying any of that. It just came out.

The door opened slowly. Lizzie pushed her glasses into place. "Are you serious?"

"Why not?" I walked over to the bathroom door and leaned against it so that no one could come in. "It's just us. Go for it, and I'll tell you if you should try out for the show."

She tucked her hair behind her ears and pressed her hands against the sides of her head for a second. Then she shut her eyes and started singing. It was the same song that Emily and Rebeccah had sung in the cafeteria—"We're Off to See the Wizard"—and yet it wasn't the same song at all. Lizzie started out quiet, but when she hit the word *because*—*because, because, because . . . because of the wonderful things he does*—the notes stretched out and filled up. Her voice turned the bathroom into a concert hall. I could see Dorothy skipping down the yellow brick road. It was like I was there.

She sang the final line, and the word *Oz* hung in the air. Then she opened her eyes. Her hands were shaking as she adjusted her glasses.

"That was amazing," I said, and she blushed so hard, her freckles disappeared.

She shook her head. "It's just the acoustics in here. The way the ceiling curves would make anyone sound great."

I laughed. "That is so not true. Forget Emily and Rebeccah. I think you should do it."

"I want to," she said, although she looked almost sick at the idea.

"Then it's settled. You're trying out."

She finally smiled, and we walked back to class together.

22

SOMETHING NEW

ON MY WAY OUT OF THE BUILDING THAT AFTERNOON, I FELT A tap on my shoulder. It was Jake. "Hey," he said as kids streamed past us.

"Hey." I'd seen him during the day, but I hadn't known what to say after our talk at Emily's party.

"Can I show you something?" he asked.

"Yeah, sure."

He led me back around the corner and opened the door to the music room. It was empty, except for the rows of chairs circling the piano. Our footsteps echoed, which reminded me of walking into a hospital late at night. Big and open and strangely quiet without people around.

"Hold on," he said. Then he ran to the back of the room, opened a storage locker, and came back with a sleek black case under his arm. Inside was a glossy guitar with a swirly red-and-brown body. He lifted the guitar.

"Hold on," he said again, as though I might vanish any second. Little did he know, I was so nervous, my feet felt glued to the floor, like I was in one of those dreams where you can't walk no matter how hard you try.

He strummed once. Twice. Then he played a short song, no longer than a minute. The notes were soft, the rhythm quick and even. It made me think of Dad playing blues records back home.

When Jake finished, he set the guitar back in the case.

"That was great," I said, because obviously I should say something. He'd played a song for me. It occurred to me that maybe he had *written* the song for me, and my mouth dried up.

"You think?"

"Yeah, I really do."

He smiled. "Cool. It's a cover of a famous song. Well, a cover of a cover, technically. My dad used to play this song a lot, too. This is his guitar. I brought it in so I could practice to surprise my mom."

His mom. The truth was a mix of relief and disappointment, along with a fresh wave of embarrassment at being disappointed. Luckily, Jake didn't seem to notice me blushing away. He was running his fingers over the guitar. As I watched him, I thought of how his father had probably touched that same wood a million times. It seemed impossible that someone could just die one day and never come back.

"She's going to love it," I said. "My mom loves homemade gifts, and that's way better than any clay dish I've ever made."

"I bet you do all right," he said, and I explained how I really had absolutely no touch when it came to forming clay into useful objects. Mine always came out tortured.

He put the guitar away, and we walked out together.

Thankfully, when Mrs. Ravelli saw us, she became very interested in the bushes next to the steps.

"See ya," Jake said. Then he bounded down the steps and headed in the opposite direction. But at the corner, he turned around and waved good-bye.

◎◎

On the way home, Mrs. Ravelli fixed a sharp eye on me. "I see you have a new friend, yes?"

"Sort of." I dodged a pile of flattened cardboard outside of a bodega, which I'd learned meant corner market. They were like grocery stores combined with delis, only in a fraction of the space. We were on our way to a drugstore near the subway. Mom had asked Mrs. Ravelli to grab some toilet paper. Leave it to Ravioli to have a favorite place to buy *toilet paper*, specifically.

"*Vai, bambina,*" Mrs. Ravelli said, and I slowed down. She placed her gloved hand on my arm. "It is not easy, being new," she said. "Many years ago, when I was a girl, not as young as you, but still a girl, I was new. New to New York. To the country."

She waved her hand at the stores, the street, the sky. "All of this, it was new. And so I know what I am talking about, you see. I know." She patted my arm. "You do good, Thyme. Is important to make friends. And a handsome one at that." Her eyes twinkled, and I thought I would die of embarrassment.

"Soon, new friends are old friends," she said. "Then you are not so new anymore."

She meant well, but the idea settled strangely in my mind.

With every person I helped, with every conversation I had, I was making ties. Ties to school. To New York. That wasn't what I wanted, but it was happening anyway.

We walked past a smooth mound of untouched snow. There were little patches like that here and there along the streets, perfectly intact, as though everyone in the city had agreed to save them. The sun cut through the clouds, and the snow transformed into a beautiful, diamond-crusted slope. I ran my mitten across the surface, leaving a blobby trail behind.

"Wow. It's so sparkly."

"New York, she is beautiful in the winter," Mrs. Ravelli said, and I looked at the street. Though the road was gray with tire tracks and slush, the trees above were still edged in white. The streetlights, the signs, the awnings lining the storefronts—everything was dusted with a fine coating of snow, like powdered sugar. As though New York had transformed into Candy Land overnight.

"It's hard. Everything is so different here," I said. Although I could've said everything is so different *now*. Things hadn't really been the same since Val's diagnosis. Everything had changed. Not just where I lived.

"Yes. Yes, it is all very, very different," Mrs. Ravelli said. "For me, it was the food. No one knows how to cook a good *paste* here!" She winged her arms this way and that, as though this was the biggest travesty ever. *Paste* was Italian for pasta. It sounded like *poss-tay*. And Mrs. Ravelli took her *paste* seriously. "Still. I tell you. The people, they told me, go to Little Italy. You will see. There, they make good *paste*. But no! Is no good. That is why I make for you," she said, touching her finger to my cheek. "You must make for your own, Thyme. Don't wait for nobody else. You make for yourself, and it will be the best."

That sounded nice, but I wondered if it was possible. Could I really just make life the way I wanted it to be? Did that mean cashing in my time slips and heading home? Or could it mean something else, like the warm feeling that tugged at my heart when Lizzie smiled at me. That wasn't a feeling I wanted. But it was there, beneath everything else— the promise of something new.

We turned the corner, and the sweet, burnt smell of nuts greeted us. That's when I saw the purple robe up ahead. As we got closer, I knew it was him.

Mr. Lipinsky was on the sidewalk, looking up at the bus sign. And he wasn't wearing a coat, even though it was so cold, my hands were going numb inside my mittens. Mrs. Ravelli spotted him, too, and made a beeline to the bus stop. She touched his arm to get his attention.

"I was looking for the 101," Mr. Lipinsky said. But according to the map on the sign, the M15 stopped on our block, not the M101. "Jerry's not doing so hot." I thought of all the mail we got, for a Jerry Richards.

"They said to take the 101 . . . I swear it stopped here." He waved a hand dismissively at the sign. "They didn't make this all so confounding back in my day."

"Let us help you home," Mrs. Ravelli said, reaching for his arm.

He pulled back. "I don't need your help. I need to see my friend." He looked around like he was confused about where he was.

"I see." Mrs. Ravelli lifted her bags. "Then perhaps you help me, yes?"

Mr. Lipinsky's brows pinched together, but he couldn't say no. Not to Mrs. Ravelli.

We walked to our building together, with Mr. Lipinsky grumbling about bus schedules the whole way. But when we got to his apartment, he unlocked the door and led us inside without another word.

◎◎

Mr. Lipinsky's apartment was like a museum. In addition to the Broadway posters, the walls were covered with framed Playbills and tickets stubs. There was even a feathered head-dress in a big glass case. His floor plan was exactly the same as our apartment upstairs, but with all of the theater stuff everywhere, it was a whole other world.

Mrs. Ravelli got him settled into a worn leather chair in the living room and waved me over. "Talk to him while I fix the tea. It will make him happy."

I wasn't so sure about that, but I sat on the edge of a wooden chair opposite Mr. Lipinsky anyway and listened to him complain about his home being invaded, while his bird squawked in response. She was sitting on a perch inside a giant domed cage in front of the windows. The cage had to be at least five feet across, with bells and toys tied to the bars here and there. When Mr. Lipinsky stopped talking for a minute, the bird flew across the cage, wrapped its talons around the brass bars, and stared at me like she was waiting for something.

"Let her out," he ordered.

"What?"

He waved his hand at the cage. "It's a simple lever, on the door there."

I looked at the door, which was two feet tall and easy enough to open. If you wanted to.

"Don't be a ninny," Mr. Lipinsky said. "She needs her exercise." Then he looked right at me, his gray eyes sharp again, though his white hair was as messy as ever. "Please," he said. Or at least I think that's what he said. The word was so soft, I might've imagined it, but the idea that he may have asked nicely was enough.

I walked over to the cage. "Easy, girl."

Mr. Lipinsky grunted. "Her name is Sylvie."

"Hey, Sylvie," I said, and the bird surprised me by whistling, loud and clear.

"Where did she learn to whistle like that?"

"My wife taught her. Now quit stalling and let her out."

I pulled the latch, and the bird launched through the door. I ducked on reflex, like that could possibly save me from being attacked. Next to me, Mr. Lipinsky made a weird coughing sound. I opened my eyes and saw that he was laughing.

"Sylvie," he called, and the bird landed on his arm. "Sylvie, this is . . ." He raised his eyebrows at me.

"Thyme. With an H-Y."

He nodded. "This is Thyme," he said to the bird, who cocked her head at the sound of his voice. He looked at me. "Thyme, this is Sylvie. If you hold out your arm, she'll fly to you."

"Maybe next time."

"Fair enough. Usually I let her out before you all get home. The noise makes her nervous." Sylvie squawked again, and I found it hard to believe that we bothered her at all.

Mrs. Ravelli popped back into the room with a tray full of cookies and tea. She set it on the coffee table and said, "Help yourself. I just going to tidy up a bit." Then she disappeared back into the kitchen.

Mr. Lipinsky grumbled about her touching his stuff, but he also took a cookie. Then he did something new. He asked me a question. "Are you any good at checkers?"

"Maybe."

He pulled out a worn playing set from beneath the table. "How about a wager? You win, and I'll give you all the mail that ended up in my box."

"You've been taking our mail?"

"I haven't taken anything! The mailman put it in there." His mouth twitched. "So what do you say? Shall we?"

"What do you get if you win?"

"Nothing more than the pleasure of your company. And sweet victory, of course."

"Yeah, right. And I bet you want to sell me a piece of the Brooklyn Bridge, too."

"Suit yourself. Everybody's got the right to be wrong."

"Fine," I said. "I'll play."

I set up the pieces while Mr. Lipinsky poured two cups of tea. Meanwhile, Sylvie started whistling again. He patted her, and she sang louder, which sounds noisy but was actually nice, like listening to Grandma Kay whistle while she gardened. "It was Ada's idea to get a bird," he said. "She needed something to love—something other than me, I guess. Can you imagine that?"

I didn't answer, because it seemed like the kind of question you don't answer.

"We tried to have a family for a long time, but it wasn't meant to be. Poor Ada, bless her heart . . . she ran out one day and came back from the pet shop with this tiny white speck of a thing. The shopkeeper said the critter wouldn't last the week, but he didn't count on Ada. That woman made everyone want to live, just to be around her for another day—birds included. Forty-six years later, here we are. We sure showed him, didn't we, Sylvie?"

Sylvie trilled a high note, and the way he smiled at her, I could see that she was his friend. He needed her as much as she needed him. Maybe he'd just had a bad day, getting confused about the bus. Val had good days and bad days, too. We all did, one way or the other.

"Can that guy believe how old she is now?" I asked.

"I have no idea," Mr. Lipinsky said with a straight face. "He's been dead ten years."

I covered my mouth in shock, but Mr. Lipinsky just grinned. Then he started laughing for real. His chuckle turned into big, round belly laughs that made me laugh, too, even though laughing about a dead person was terrible. Then I thought about what he'd said outside, about his friend Jerry and how he wasn't doing so hot. Jerry, who used to live in our apartment, who now lived far away.

"I'm sorry about your friend," I said.

Mr. Lipinsky nodded. "I appreciate that," he said. And he sounded like he really meant it.

23

SECRETS

ON THURSDAY AFTERNOON, CORI CAME HOME LATE FROM SCHOOL. Mom was still out with Val at a support group playdate, and Dad hadn't gotten home from work yet. With the new job, his hours had been later.

"Don't tell Mom, but I got detention," Cori said as she ripped her coat off and tossed it on the floor. Her *ART IS LIFE* shirt was on inside out. She'd been wearing the protest shirts to school every day.

"What did you do?"

She thought for a second. Then she flopped into the chair across from me and said, "It's not fair. We were just trying to make them explain why there's no money for drama when they still have basketball and cheerleading and *chess*."

"I like chess," I said, and she shot me a look.

"Duh. You like anything boring. But sometimes, you have to stick your neck out, T. All we did was stand up during the assembly for, like, five minutes. That's all. They said we were disruptive, that we made a scene, and now we aren't allowed to wear our shirts anymore. *Augh!*" She buried her head in her arms. Part of me wanted to point out that disrupting an assembly *was* making a scene, but I couldn't believe she was telling me any of this stuff in the first place.

"Maybe you should just lie low for a while," I said.

She sat up. "You know what? You're exactly right."

That night, Cori didn't say a word to Mom and Dad about detention. And in the morning, she acted totally normal. You wouldn't have thought she'd gotten in trouble in the first place, or that she was hiding it from our parents. She wasn't wearing one of her drama shirts, either. But as she zipped up her book bag, I caught a glimpse of painted fabric inside.

"I thought you weren't supposed to wear those shirts?" I whispered. "What if you get detention again?"

"Shh!" Cori leaned closer. "What Mom doesn't know won't kill her."

I almost said, *But when she finds out, it might kill you.* Then I thought about Dad taking his new job without telling me, and I figured Cori could do what she wanted. She wasn't the only one in our family keeping secrets.

෴

Friday was audition day at MS 221. In sixth-period PE, everyone lined up outside the locker rooms instead of going to class.

"Listen up, sixth graders!" Our teacher, Mrs. Emery, marched past us. "If you're going out for the Spring Fling, line up on this side of the hall." She pointed with both hands like an air-traffic controller. "Once the other classes line up, Mr. Calhoun will escort you to the auditorium. If you're not trying out, get your be-hinds changed and meet me in the gym in five minutes. Understood?"

"Yes, Mrs. Emery!"

The hall erupted into chatter as nearly half of our class bolted for the other side of the hall. "Go on," I told Lizzie, but she just stood there, looking scared.

"I don't think I can," she said.

Everyone else was lining up. It was the moment of truth for anyone who wanted a part. I didn't want a part, but I didn't want Lizzie to miss out.

"What if I go with you?" I said, and she finally smiled.

◎◎

The auditorium was one place I hadn't been. It was one of those quiet places, like the hospital. I thought of waiting for Val on his first day of chemo, listening to the silence in the waiting room. I told myself to be happy that I wasn't doing that again, but there were still a million butterflies in my stomach as we sat down in the auditorium seats. Which was dumb. I wasn't doing the Spring Fling. Right?

"Emily tries out next period," Lizzie said.

"Don't worry about her," I said with a smile.

Lizzie's brow creased as she worried about it anyway.

Rebeccah was in the row behind us. She had her red hair in a big, puffy ponytail that bounced every time she turned her head. She saw me looking and leaned over the chairs. "What are you going out for, Thyme?" Her eyes flicked over my sweater, a soft cable-knit that Cori had loaned me.

"I'm just here to watch Lizzie."

"Too bad. I bet you'd make a great Munchkin. You're the

right height, you know." She held her hand above my head. "They give Munchkin parts to the people who don't get anything else. Just wait. Maybe you and Lizzie will end up being Munchkins together!"

Rebeccah laughed and flopped back into her chair, while Lizzie blushed bright pink.

"Maybe if we throw some water on her, she'll melt," I joked, but Lizzie didn't laugh.

"Okay, people. Listen up!" Mr. Calhoun stood in front of the stage, next to a long row of folding tables, and called for attention. He looked the way I imagined college professors must look—smart, in a blazer and bow tie, with bushy eyebrows that wiggled as he waited for everyone to quiet down. "All right. As you all know, this year we're staging a production of *The Wizard of Oz.*"

Applause broke out, and he raised his hand for silence. "There are many, many parts in the production. You'll find the audition sheets right up here, in case you've forgotten yours." He pointed at the papers lining the tables. "You may only audition for two stage parts. Crew positions may sign up on the sheets provided. Orchestra auditions are tomorrow. Final cast and crew selections will be posted Monday morning. Any questions?"

It got quiet, like we were all holding our breath. I know I was. Which didn't make sense, because I wasn't there to sign up for anything.

"Good," he said. "Take the next few minutes to sign up,

and remember, you may only audition for two parts today. If you're signing up for a crew position, please do so and return to the gym for the remainder of the period."

He stepped back, and kids rushed the tables. I gave Lizzie a little push and she went, too. A minute later, she came back with a neatly stapled packet in her hands.

"You okay?" I asked.

She nodded, her face pale. "Now it's your turn."

"What?"

"I can't do this by myself! Do it with me, please."

"I am *not* trying out for anything."

"Just go look," she said. Her eyes were so big behind her glasses, I thought she might cry if I didn't say yes, so I said okay and walked to the tables, head swimming. What was I doing? I knew nothing about plays. I'd only ever been in a real theater once, to see *Peter Pan* with Shani. I remembered watching Peter soar into the air, like magic, and wishing I could fly, too. At the time, I hadn't realized that there was some kind of trick holding him up—something the stage crew had put together to fool the audience. But once I knew, it made perfect sense. Could I do something like that?

There were four options on the sign-up sheets for the crew positions: set design, lighting crew, prop masters, sound production. And under sound production, a familiar name: *Jake Reese*. My hand hovered over the sheet. There were only two other names with Jake's. Plenty of room for more sound producers. Whatever that meant.

Mr. Calhoun stepped onto the stage. "All right, people.

First up, Dorothy. Can I get all of my Dorothys over here?" he asked, pointing to the first row of chairs. "Mrs. Smith will show you where to sit. And next, my Lions, Tin Men, and over here, the Witches . . ."

I scrawled my name beneath Jake's and jetted over to the first row, heart pounding as I slid into the seat next to Lizzie. I was planning to wish her good luck and get out of there before I died of mortification—I mean, who signs up to work with a boy who says nice things about her dress and plays guitar for her unless she likes him, too?—but then I noticed Lizzie's face was even paler than before, so I stayed in my seat and hoped Mr. Calhoun wouldn't notice.

"Jemma Halstead," he called, and the willowy girl next to Lizzie climbed the steps to the stage. Everyone got quiet as Jemma read off a few lines, her voice barely audible. Then Mr. Calhoun asked her to sing a portion of "Somewhere Over the Rainbow," which didn't go much better, with mumbled words and mouse-like squeaks on the high notes.

"One down, one to go," I said to Lizzie, but her eyes were slammed shut. "Lizzie?"

She bent forward, pressing her hands over her ears. "I can't," she said. "I can't." Her breath was whistling in and out of her mouth way too fast.

"What's wrong?" I whispered, but she didn't say anything, so I rubbed her back like I did for Val, only it didn't seem to help.

Mr. Calhoun called the next girl up to the stage. Lizzie was the last girl left in the Dorothy group, but with the way she was breathing and the way her foot was *tap-tap-tapping* against the floor, it didn't look like she would make it onstage.

Then someone slid into the seat on Lizzie's other side. I looked up, right into Emily's oval face.

"What are you doing here?" I asked.

"Hall pass," she said, her attention fixed on Lizzie. She pulled a brown paper bag out of her pocket, unfolded it, and held it over Lizzie's nose and mouth.

"Breathe into this," she said, brushing Lizzie's blond hair away from her face. "You're okay," she said. "You're okay." She said it the way Mom told Val he was okay, even when he wasn't. That's when I finally saw the truth about them. Emily and Lizzie may have been on the outs, but they were just like me and Shani. They were best friends. They needed each other.

After a few more breaths, Lizzie sat up and looked at Emily. And smiled.

"You're okay," Emily said one last time. Then she shook her head. "I've been waiting back there for fifteen minutes. I told you not to do this to yourself."

"I know it's stupid," Lizzie said, "but I'm tired of practicing all the time in class and never being in the show. I want to sing."

"If she wants to sing, she should sing," I said, and Emily's eyes flashed.

"She has stage fright, duh. You can't sing if you can't breathe!"

We both looked at Lizzie, who was breathing into the

brown paper bag again, more slowly now. Mr. Calhoun called her name, and she pulled the bag away. "I can do it," she said. Then she counted to ten with her eyes shut. Calming herself down.

Emily stood up. "Do what you want. I have to get back before Mr. Wocjio notices I've been in the bathroom for a million years." Then she ran off. But right before she went through the auditorium doors, she looked back. Just once, like she wanted to stay.

"I'm sorry I didn't tell you," Lizzie said to me. Then Mr. Calhoun called her name again, and she clenched her hands. "This is stupid. Everyone will be staring at me."

"It'll be okay. Just don't look at them."

"I can't *not* look at them," she said, her eyes wide behind her purple glasses.

Her *glasses*.

"You can if take these off," I said, sliding her glasses free.

Then I pointed her in the direction of the stage and watched as she recited her lines, quietly at first, then with more feeling. When she finished the lines, she shut her eyes and sang, and every single person in the auditorium stopped and stared because what we heard wasn't just a girl singing a song, but a song coming to life. I could see Dorothy winding her way along the yellow brick road, searching for home.

When Lizzie finished, she opened her eyes, and everyone applauded. And even though she couldn't see it, I gave her two thumbs up.

24

NO FITS

THE SATURDAY AFTER TRYOUTS, SHANI AND I TALKED JUST LIKE we'd planned. She mentioned Jenny three times and I pretended not to notice. Then I told her that I'd signed up for the Spring Fling, and it seemed like she was happy to hear the news. It was weird talking about our separate lives, but that was better than not talking at all. At least that's what I told myself.

In the afternoon, Cori went with Dad to buy supplies for a project she and her drama friends were doing on their own. Val didn't want to go anywhere, so I stayed with him to read books on the couch, but he was acting fussy. He kept picking at his stuffed triceratops while I read, and I wondered if he was worried about starting 3F8 again. He was going back to the hospital on Monday morning for his second round of treatment.

I held up the book we'd just finished. "Want to read it again?"

Val nodded. He was obsessed with this story about a girl whose pet monster kept having fits. Everywhere they went, the monster got mad about sharing toys or people talking loudly on the bus, and she would scold him and tell him not to act up. Val scolded the monster right along with her. But his favorite part was at the end, when the girl has a fit herself. And the monster helps her calm down. I liked how that was the last thing you expected from a monster, but that's exactly what he did. I was just getting to the good part, where you find out that the monster is really the little girl's stuffed toy, when Val said, "Sara doesn't have any hair, either."

I stopped reading. "Who's Sara?"

"She's at the hospital, too."

"Oh." He and Mom had been spending a lot of time with their support group. "Is she part of your playgroup in the mornings?"

"Uh-huh." He picked at the triceratops's horns, pulling the threads loose. "She got the medicine at the same time as me."

"Oh." I rubbed my hand over his patchy brown hair, which had grown from fuzz into something like scruff. He was wearing a brand-new Iron Man costume. It had come in the mail for his second round of treatment. That brought his count up to eight costumes in all.

"What if Sara's not there anymore?" he asked.

"Where? At the hospital?"

He nodded.

"She might not be. I mean, maybe she won't be on the same schedule as you this time."

He shook his head, frustrated. Triceratops suffered another yank. "Where is heaven?" he asked all of a sudden.

"Oh." I looked at the kitchen. Mom was out of sight. "Well, I think it doesn't matter *where* heaven is. The idea is just that it's a very nice place."

His little blue eyes got serious. "Can you visit there?"

My breath caught. "Do you mean . . ."

"If Sara went to heaven, I want to say good-bye."

I swallowed hard, and told myself I did *not* want to cry. "Well, in that case, all you have to do is shut your eyes. Then she would hear anything you said."

He looked hopeful. "Really?"

"Pinkie swear," I said, and we locked fingers.

Then I heard a throat clear behind us. Mom was standing there with a plate of snacks. "I thought you two might be hungry," she said, and I wondered how long she'd been listening.

"Yum, apples!" Val shouted, like he hadn't just been talking about visiting one of his sick friends in heaven. He jumped up to grab a slice, and Mom looked at me.

"Be careful what you promise him," she said, and a shiver ran over my skin. I felt like I'd done something wrong. I knew Mom didn't like us to talk about the hard stuff, not if we could help it. And I understood why. They don't call it the hard stuff for no reason. But Val trusted me, and I wasn't going to lie to him the way Mom and Dad lied to me, even if it made her mad.

@@

When Dad got back with Cori, I helped him gather Val's lovies for a trip to the Super Sudz Laundromat. We had to wash them before he took them to the hospital, just to be safe. Mom didn't want to bring a whole month's worth of germs with them.

"Got it?" Dad asked as I hefted a pillowcase full of stuffed animals over my shoulder. I gave him a thumbs-up, and we headed down the stairs. When we passed by Mr. Lipinsky's, his door stayed shut, even though I clomped my boots hard against the floor. I hadn't seen him since we'd sat together earlier in the week. Maybe he was busy with Sylvie. Or maybe he was too tired to spy on us that day. Mainly I just hoped he was doing okay, and that he wasn't out wandering the streets somewhere.

At the Super Sudz, Dad and I worked quickly, loading lovies into the washer by color so they didn't bleed all over each other. We did *not* want a rainbow massacre on our hands.

After the washers started up, Dad said, "Let's look for quarters." I was surprised, because Mom hated it when we did that. But Mom wasn't there. So, when the other people left our row, we dropped to our knees and looked beneath the machines, risking dust bunnies and old chewing gum to find lost quarters. Dad found zero. I found three.

"You smoked me," he said as we sat on the bench next to the washing machines. He brushed the dust off his knobby knees. He kind of sighed when he did it, and I noticed how his beard looked even grayer around the edges. Maybe it was just the awful fluorescent lighting, or maybe he was worn out. He had the new job. He had Val's treatment coming up. I felt bad for not noticing him much lately.

He looked at me. "You know what? That jar of yours sure has a lot of time in it."

I froze. What was Dad doing spying on my Thyme Jar?

"I bet I know what you're saving up for," he said with a grin. "I know it's hard. Your brother takes up a lot of Mom's time, and your sister . . . well, she's a handful. But I understand. Of course you want your own life, too." My heart thumped against my chest. Had he overheard me talking with Shani? Was he reading my mind?

He leaned closer. "Just remember, you can't have a cell phone until you're twelve, no matter how much time you save up. Those are the rules."

Relief washed over me. "Sure, Dad. No problem."

"That's my girl. It's going to get better. You'll see. You might even want to come see the Empire with me one day. It's right by my office."

I nodded, because going up to the top of the Empire State Building did sound kind of cool, but Dad had just said "one day" like we were going to stay in New York forever. Like Val's treatment wasn't going to be over in three months at all. Part of me wondered what that would be like. Would we keep living in the same tiny apartment? Would Val really go back to school one day? And if he did, what would it mean for me?

"Dad, when are we going back?" I asked, thinking of how we'd already been in New York for six weeks. "And don't say *in a while*."

"Well . . . after your brother finishes three rounds of 3F8,

he'll have a new set of scans. Then we'll see where we're at."
It sounded like a doctor's words coming out of his mouth.
Words that say things but don't promise much.

"Before we left, you said March."

He sighed. "I did. But that was before we knew if Val
would reject the medicine."

"But now we know, right?"

"Well, we know for *now*." He shook his head, and then his
shoulders dropped. "Look, Thyme. I know you and Shani
want to have your birthdays together like you always do. But
March is a long way away. We don't know what's going to
happen between now and then. We won't even know if the
3F8 is really working until Val has his scans."

"I thought that's what the blood test was for?"

Dad shook his head. "No, that just tells us if Val's rejecting
the medicine. There's a chance that even with the 3F8, the
neuroblastoma could come back. It's a small chance, but that's
why we're trying not to get ahead of ourselves, okay?"

"Okay," I said, even though I was not okay. Every time
it seemed like Val was on the road to success, things just got
more complicated.

Back at the apartment, Dad handed me a time slip for
helping with the laundry. I added the slip to my jar, and it
fluttered down to meet the others, like a feather on air. So
much time. Usually, it made me feel good to count the slips.
The jar meant home. It meant being in the same room with
Shani again and giving Grandma Kay a hug. But when I tried
to think of those things, my mind kept going back to Val's

friend Sara. How he was so worried about missing her if she was gone. I hoped that when Val went back to the hospital on Monday, she would still be there.

◎◎

Late Sunday night, I woke up to someone screaming. For a second, I didn't know where I was.

Then I heard Cori. "It's Val," she said, her voice tight with panic.

We ran into the hall. Mom and Dad were already in Val's room. "No pinchies!" he shouted, flailing at them. "No pinchies!" Pinchies were shots.

"You're okay, honey," Mom said. She stroked Val's face, but his eyes were only open a tiny bit. It didn't seem like he was really awake.

"He's all right," Dad said to me and Cori. "It's just a bad dream."

"He doesn't look all right," Cori said just as Val screeched again. My hands were hot, my feet freezing. Standing there in the darkened hallway, it felt like the world was ending.

"Go back to bed, girls," Mom ordered.

I couldn't move.

"They don't need to see this!" she shouted at Dad.

He raised his hands and dropped them again, helpless. He looked so broken, standing there while Val cried out. That's when I remembered Val's book.

I pushed past Cori.

"Thyme, don't," Dad said, but I slipped past him and leaned over the side of Val's Lightning McQueen bed.

"No fits, Val!" I shouted, because he always turned his hearing aids off when he slept.

Mom looked at me like I was a lunatic. "Michael, get her out of here!"

Dad reached for me.

"No fits, Val!" I shouted again, and his body stopped moving. I'd gotten through to him. "No fits," I repeated, a little quieter, but still loud enough for him to hear. His lips curved just the littlest bit, like he was about to laugh. Then he slumped back, arms limp, fast asleep.

Mom stared at me like she didn't know what to think. I wanted to tell her I was just trying to help, but the words wouldn't come out. I felt like I was in a dream, like none of this was real, and we were all trapped in it together, only the dream was a nightmare.

Dad's hand settled on my shoulder. "Let's go," he said, and I went.

25

NEWS

IN THE MORNING, WE WERE ALL EXHAUSTED, BLEARY FROM TOO little sleep and sore from snapping at each other. Mom barely looked at me, but Dad explained that what had happened to Val was called a night terror. That's a thing that can happen when you're really scared about something—in Val's case, that meant going back to the hospital to start 3F8 again. On some level, he was afraid of the pain.

Val didn't even remember what had happened during the night. He was the only one smiling and acting normal at breakfast, back to his usual brave self. I gave him a high five before I left with Mrs. Ravelli and promised I'd play games with him when he got home from the hospital.

"Pinkie swear?" he said.

"Pinkie swear."

When I walked into MS 221, kids were crowded around the trophy cases. That's when I remembered the casting announcements for the Spring Fling. I squeezed through the crowd and caught a glimpse of my name—on sound production, right next to Jake Reese's. I couldn't believe that I'd done it. Then I wondered if Jake had seen the list, too, and my face flushed. Suddenly, I felt like I was about to cry. I was just so tired from the night before.

I pushed my way out of the crowd and found Celia and Delia waiting at our lockers.

"Have you heard the news?" Delia squealed.

Celia grabbed my arm. "Thyme! Did you see the list?"

"Yeah. I'm on sound production. Yay!" The twins were always so dramatic. Like what I signed up for was a big deal.

"That's not what we're talking about." Delia circled closer to me. Celia wrapped her other arm around her sister, and they both bent forward, creating a little bubble of privacy in the middle of the hall. "It's *Emily*," Delia whispered. "Mr. Calhoun gave her the alternate! Lizzie got Dorothy! *Lizzie!*"

"What do you mean?" I'd been so busy thinking about me and Jake on sound production that I hadn't even checked the other sheets. "What's an alternate?"

Celia was practically panting. "The alternate gets to be a Munchkin, too. But she doesn't get to be Dorothy unless Lizzie can't do it!"

"Oh wow."

"I know, it's terrible," Delia said, her eyes glowing. Celia giggled. Obviously, the twins didn't think Emily's loss was all that terrible. More like exciting. Entertaining, even.

At lunch, Emily didn't have much to say about the Spring Fling. In fact, nobody had much to say about anything. Everyone was too busy stealing glances at Emily and Lizzie, waiting to see what would happen next. Then the twins brought up the science fair, which was in a few weeks, and Lizzie said she was going to build a battery out of a lemon.

"That's so stupid," Emily said. "You can't get electricity from a lemon."

The table hushed and Lizzie turned pink. "Actually, you can," she said quietly.

"I'm just kidding! I'm sure your experiment will be awesome," Emily said with her big fake smile. Then everyone went back to eating, even though we all knew Emily wasn't kidding.

"See you guys," Lizzie said a minute later, slipping away from the table early.

Rebeccah gave Emily a sympathetic look. "I can't believe she still *sat* with us."

Emily said, "I know," but her eyes followed Lizzie out of the cafeteria. I got up to follow Lizzie, too. After what Emily had done for her at the audition, I'd thought that maybe they could make up. But with Rebeccah spouting garbage in Emily's ear, that wasn't going to happen. I wished I didn't care, but the truth was, that bothered me.

On the way out of the cafeteria, Jake fell into step beside me. "Hey," he said.

"Hey." He was wearing a shirt with a drawing of a guitar on the front. It said *Keep Calm and Play Guitar*. "So they posted the Spring Fling assignments," I said. "I'm on sound production."

"Really? Do you play an instrument?"

"Not . . . exactly. I mean, I just thought I'd try it."

He smiled. "That's cool. I'll see you at the meeting?"

"Yeah." According to the morning announcements, we were supposed to report to the auditorium after school on Wednesday for our big orientation to all things *Wizard of Oz*.

"I'll save you a seat," he said. Then he bumped my shoulder with his, and my heart sped up. I wondered if his heart was speeding up, too, or if it was just me. I needed to ask Shani how this worked, liking someone. Was I supposed to tell him? Was he supposed to tell me? Is that what he was doing when he smiled like that and said nice things and—*augh*.

Then Jake pressed his earbud into place and started humming. He didn't seem like his heart was trying to jump out of his chest. But still. The more I thought about it, the more sound production sounded, well, exotic. Like working on a movie. Maybe there was a sound booth behind the stage. Or a fancy sound-effects machine. The possibilities were endless.

෨෨

After school, Mrs. Ravelli was waiting at the bottom of the steps with a small white box tied with red string. When she saw me, she lifted the box and wiggled it like a worm on a hook. She said pastries were *come il cacio sui maccheroni*, which meant "like cheese on macaroni."

"Did you get angel ears?" I asked.

"You tell me. Is the sky blue?"

She untied the box and produced a golden brown pastry made of a thousand crunchy layers. To be fair, they were really called elephant ears or angel wings, but Mrs. Ravelli had mashed the two names together, and I kind of liked the idea of angels flying around with giant pastry ears.

Back home, my favorite dessert was a cream horn from Hans and Harry's, a layered puff pastry with cream inside. They were too big to eat alone, so Shani and I had always shared. We split the horn right down the middle with a plastic knife and raced to finish. I never won, but I told Shani that was just because she had such a big mouth, which is the kind of thing best friends can say in a totally not-mean way. I'd meant to tell her about the angel ears, but I kept forgetting.

"Is Val home yet?" I asked.

"No, *bambina*," Mrs. Ravelli said. "Your mama say they will be a little late today."

"Oh." I wished I'd known that before I ran out of school after the final bell. Otherwise I might've looked for Lizzie before I left. She hadn't had much to say about what happened at lunch. I didn't understand why she wouldn't stick up for herself. Maybe she felt guilty for taking the Dorothy role from Emily, but she'd won the part fair and square.

Halfway to the apartment, Mrs. Ravelli tapped my nose. "Your face, it look so serious for a young girl! You tell me, was there trouble today?"

I took my time chewing the last bite of the angel ear. Lizzie was still on my mind. And signing up for sound production. And what working with Jake would be like. I had to ask my parents for permission to stay after school on Wednesday, too.

"*Vai!*" Mrs. Ravelli said, clapping her hands. "Come now. You wait too long, you have to talk to me at the Green-Wood," she said. Meaning, *Green-Wood Cemetery*. Where Mr. Ravelli was buried. And where Mrs. Ravelli planned to be buried, too. Apparently Italians thought that talking about where they were going to be buried was normal. Or maybe that was just Ravioli.

"There's this play," I said, my face flushing. I hadn't planned to tell anyone about the Spring Fling, because it was no big deal. Right? "And I signed up to work on it."

"What? You going to be in a play, and you say nothing?"

"No! No. I'm not going to be *in* the play. I'm just working on it."

She patted my arm. "Very good, Thyme. You make your own way, and that is good."

I thought back to what she'd said before, about making my own way. That's what was happening, but it still felt new. And private. I didn't want my family getting any ideas about me. They wouldn't understand that signing up for something at school didn't mean I wanted to stay in New York forever.

"Mrs. Ravelli? Would you mind, for now, if we didn't say anything about the play to my parents? It's just, the show isn't until March."

She studied my face for a moment. She had these creases that showed up on either side of her mouth when she was thinking, parentheses for her worries about undercooked *paste* or the lack of asparagus in our diets. She tapped my nose with her gloved finger. "I tell you what. You tell me about the play. And for now, it will be our secret, *bambina*. But not forever, *capisce*?" *Capisce* meant "do we have a deal?" Another of Mrs. Ravelli's favorite phrases. Because in Italian, they used fewer words to say the same thing. And that was better, in Mrs. Ravelli's book.

At the apartment building, we stopped by Mr. Lipinsky's to give him some angel ears, too. I still hadn't seen him since the week before. He didn't answer when we knocked, so I thought we would just leave them by his door, but Mrs. Ravelli dug in her big quilted bag and magically produced a key.

"You have his key now?"

"Just in case," she said with a wink, although I couldn't imagine how she'd talked him into it.

Inside, Mr. Lipinsky was nowhere to be seen. Mrs. Ravelli took the pastries to the kitchen and I went over to Sylvie's cage. She whistled when she saw me. For an old bird, she had a ton of personality.

Mr. Lipinsky shuffled into the living room. "Kicked out of my own kitchen," he grumbled, while I jiggled the bells on Sylvie's cage. She squawked and tapped them, too.

"If you whistle to her, she'll whistle back," he said. I tried whistling to Sylvie, and it worked. "She likes you," he said as he settled into his chair. For once, he wasn't wearing the purple robe. Instead, he had on a button-down shirt, but the sleeves were rolled way up. There were streaks of white flour on his forearms and across the fabric.

"What are you baking?" I asked, hoping it wasn't another

kugel. Mom had warned me never to accept anything like that from anyone ever again.

He gave me a quizzical look. "Who said I was baking?"

At first, I thought he was joking. As in, *Who said I like to be grumpy?* Duh! Everyone. I wanted him to tell me how baking was a science based on hundreds of years of innovation. How back in his day, there was some kind of honor to walking around with smears of flour on your forearms. But Mr. Lipinsky seemed confused again, like that day at the bus stop. Maybe it was a bad day.

"Never mind," I said. "Want to play checkers?" His expression softened, so I got out the checkers case. We set up the pieces. While I waited for my turn, I looked at all the theater stuff on Mr. Lipinsky's walls. Either he was a huge fan, or he'd had something to do with Broadway.

"Where'd you get all this theater stuff?" I asked.

He glanced at the Broadway posters. "My Ada was the top of the town in costuming. Everyone wanted her for their shows."

"Oh. Cool." That explained the headdress. There was also an Egyptian-looking mask hanging on the wall, and a pretty hat balanced on a stand over by Sylvie's cage. When I looked back at Mr. Lipinsky, he had a far-off look in his eyes, but he wasn't sad. His mouth was halfway to a smile.

"I'm working on a play at school," I said, and his eyebrows rose.

"So you like being onstage, then. Should've known it, from how you carry on up there."

"No, I'm backstage. On sound production."

He slapped his leg. "Imagine that. Never woulda thought you had it in you."

"Neither did I." I felt a mix of excitement and nerves, but mostly nerves.

"I was a stagehand, you know," he said. "All it takes is doing. You jump in, grab a brush, coil a rope. It's a team sport. As long as you do your part, the show goes on."

"I don't know how to do any of that stuff."

"Chin up," he said. "You'll be fine. Ada would tell you that I've forgotten more about theater than you'll ever know. You have any problems, you see me." With that, he fixed his attention on the checkers, but soon Mrs. Ravelli bustled into the room. She said dinner was "all taken care of" and that it was time for us to go, because Val and Mom might be back by now. I wondered when she'd started fixing his dinners. Was that how she'd gotten a copy of his key?

I stood up, and Mr. Lipinsky spread his hands wide. "What? In the middle of a game?"

"I have to check on my brother." It felt weird talking about Val with Mr. Lipinsky. I was afraid that he'd say something horrible.

"I've seen those contraptions on his head." He wiggled his hands by his ears where Val's hearing aids stuck out. "How bad is it?"

"Not great," I said, "but he's a fighter."

Mr. Lipinsky nodded. "I'll get you next time," he promised, and waved me out.

The living room was empty, so I went to Mom and Dad's room to see if she and Val were home yet. He'd done so much better at the end of his last week of 3F8, I guess I had hoped he would be fine this time. Sitting on the bed playing with his lovies, talking about which train they rode.

Instead, Val was lying in their bed, his eyes puffy and red. Mom raised a finger to her lips, and I stopped. Then she slipped off the bed and steered me into the hall. "He needs rest." Her voice was scratchy. "Your father went to the office to get some work done. Your sister should be here soon. She said she had something after school today." Mom looked skeptical about that. I thought of Cori sneaking her protest shirts to school and changed the subject.

"Is Val okay?" I asked, even though I hated that question. Asking if everything is okay pretty much guarantees that something is *not* okay.

Mom ran her hand through her hair. It was longer now, flopping into her eyes. She needed a trim. "Everything's fine. But the pain lasted longer today, so it's taking him longer to sleep it off." Her voice trembled as she spoke. I was just glad she was actually telling me what was going on. After talking to Mr. Lipinsky, I was even thinking I should just tell her about the Spring Fling. Plus, I had to ask about staying after school for the weekly production meetings.

Then she said, "Let's not talk about it anymore." She straightened up, pulling herself back into line. "What's new with you?" Her eyes were red-rimmed and bleary. She looked like the last thing she wanted was to listen to me blab about my day.

Suddenly, the Spring Fling, and Emily losing the part, and me getting on the stage crew seemed like the smallest news in the world.

"Nothing," I said. "Nothing much happened today."

26

GIVE IT TIME

THE DAY MOM GOT THE CALL THAT VAL MADE IT INTO THE CANCER trial at Sloan Kettering, she'd taken us all out to Chuck E. Cheese's, given us a hundred tokens each, and told us to do whatever we wanted. Cori had complained that she was way too old for Chuck E. Cheese's. Until I started beating her at Skee-Ball. Then she stopped whining and started putting some serious effort into winning. Back then, getting into the trial had seemed like a miracle. We didn't know about the pain and the hives and the way our lives would get jerked around, one week to the next. All we knew was that Val needed it.

"They didn't tell us it would be this *hard*, every time," Mom said on Tuesday night, after Val's second day of 3F8 for January. He was asleep in Mom and Dad's room again. Things had gone a little better, but he was still too exhausted to eat dinner with us.

"They said there could be a lot of side effects," Dad said. "I think this is within the range." He set the pot roast that Mrs. Ravelli had cooked on the table in front of him while Mom scooped fluffy mounds of potatoes onto our plates.

Mrs. Ravelli's potatoes. My mouth watered, but I forced my fork to wait until the gravy arrived.

Mom reached for the gravy boat but then stopped, her fingers resting on the handle. "I don't know," she said. "If he keeps this up, sleeping for hours and hours . . ." She frowned. "He can't go on like this. It's not right. Maybe we should try the therapist in SoHo, the one Sara's parents are using. She says the acupuncture helps with the pain."

"Val's friend Sara?"

Mom glanced at me. "Yes, actually. She's on the same cycle this week."

"Oh. Good," I said, relieved to hear that Sara was okay, but Mom had already drifted off again.

"If you want to try the guy in SoHo, we can try him," Dad said, attacking the roast with a carving knife. "I know it's hard, but we have to give it time."

He dumped a pile of meat on my plate and then Cori's, while Mom ran her finger back and forth along the gravy boat's ceramic handle, lost in thought.

"Mom?" Cori said.

Mom didn't answer. Dad rested a hand on her shoulder. "It's going to be fine, hon."

"I know—" Mom began, but Cori interrupted her again, louder this time.

"Mom!"

Mom looked up, eyes blazing. "What? What is it that's so important?"

Cori slumped back in her chair. Her hair wasn't in a fancy

style for once, but long and straight like mine. The eyeliner was still there, though. "I just wanted some gravy," she said.

"Me too," I added, and Mom's scowl melted.

"Sorry, girls. I'm sorry." She hustled thick puddles of gravy onto our plates. "It's just complicated right now, with your brother. We want the best for him."

"So do I," Cori and I said at the exact same time.

Cori stuck her tongue out at me. "Jinx, you owe me a soda!" A giggle forced its way out of my mouth, which I'd just overstuffed with gravy and mashed potatoes. I bent over, laughing as big, wet drops of brownish potatoes hit my plate.

"That's nasty, T!" Cori wailed, slapping at my arm. Which, of course, made me laugh even harder. Dad got in on the game, making faces as I tried to chew. Even Mom smiled.

Then Cori told us how she was planning a fund-raiser for her drama club, and Dad gave her a thumbs-up, and for a few minutes, dinner felt normal. Like it was okay to talk about other things besides cancer treatments and acupuncture and blood tests.

"So, Thyme," Dad said. "I hear you have something to tell us, too?"

I swallowed fast. "I do?"

"Well, we couldn't help noticing the change this week. Mrs. Ravelli said you could explain." My heart raced. Had Ravioli spilled the beans about the Spring Fling? "About Mr. Lipinsky?" Dad said with a knowing look. "He hasn't banged on the ceiling in days. No notes, either."

"Oh. Right." I was relieved they hadn't found out about

the Spring Fling, but also a little disappointed. It was hard to tell if I wanted them to know or not.

"I figured he was dead," Cori mumbled.

"Cori," Mom scolded, though she was smiling. Then she turned her smile on me. "So what happened? Tell us."

I told them how I'd gotten to know Mr. Lipinsky over the last week or so, and that he wasn't such a terrible neighbor after all. That he had a bird named Sylvie who liked to whistle, and that he was even sort of nice, in his own mean way. It was funny to hear myself say that. I wouldn't have thought that about Mr. Lipinsky just a couple of weeks earlier. But sometimes, people change. Or I guess the way you see them changes, and suddenly, they are someone else completely.

"Well it's good to hear that he's been nice to you, but I'm still reserving judgment," Mom said.

Dad smiled at me. "Kill 'em with kindness, right? That's my girl."

A sunny feeling swept through me, and before I'd even decided to ask, I told them I needed to stay after school for something. "You've been a busy bee," Dad said. "Tell us more about this 'something.' It doesn't have anything to do with a boy, does it? I've already lost one daughter to hormones. Don't think I'm ready to lose another."

Cori groaned. I almost fainted. "*No*, Dad. I just want to check out our theater group." It was embarrassing, admitting it to them, like I was shining a light on all my secrets.

"Really?" Cori said. "That's awesome, T."

"I think that sounds good, too," Dad said. A drop of gravy

had caught his chin. Mom reached with her napkin to wipe it, but he swatted her away. "I can clean my own messes, thank you very much." And with that, he added a huge blob of potatoes to his chin.

"Michael," Mom scolded, trying to hide her laughter. "Thyme, just let Mrs. Ravelli know what time to pick you up, okay?"

By then, Dad and Cori were competing to see who could fit the most potatoes on their chin.

Mom dug her fork into her own food. "That's enough, you two. We all know I've got you both beat." Her fork hovered in front of her chin, the potatoes piled so high, it was a miracle they balanced on the tines. Cori giggled, and Dad leaned forward, wiggling his eyebrows at Mom. Slowly, Mom's fork came to rest on her chin.

"No way," I whispered. It was like our old mom had shown up again, the one who'd started a food fight with Dad when he spilled pancake batter on the kitchen floor last year.

Mom's potatoes started to slide. But just when they were about to crash, she ducked her head and slurped the potatoes into her mouth.

"Aw!" Cori exclaimed. "You totally had that." She was right. Mom was back.

But soon enough, we heard a sound from Val in the bedroom, and it was over. Mom wiped off her face and folded up her napkin. And then she was gone again.

27

SOUND PRODUCTION

ON WEDNESDAY AFTERNOON, MR. CALHOUN WORKED HIS WAY across the stage, handing out packets of information to different groups of kids seated on the well-worn floor.

"Here you go—this is for sound production," he said, tossing me a stack of paper still warm from the photocopier. "Make sure each person in your group gets a copy."

I passed a packet to Jake and the two other kids sitting with us, a girl with a wispy nest of hair and a quiet dark-skinned boy who drummed his fingers against his jeans while Mr. Calhoun waited for everyone to finish. Satisfied, he stepped to the edge of the stage and raised his arms. His bow tie of the day was green with black polka dots.

"Good afternoon, everyone, and welcome to our production of *The Wizard of Oz*." Some of the kids clapped and whistled, but Mr. Calhoun raised a hand for silence. "I expect the show will be fantastic. But first, let me say that no matter what role you fill, the show will only be a success if we all work together."

A murmur of agreement rippled through the crowd.

Across the stage, Emily and Lizzie were sitting together,

but they weren't talking. Lizzie's eyes were on the floor, while Emily nodded at every word Mr. Calhoun uttered. She'd missed school the day before, but her bright eyes and glowing cheeks didn't look very sick. I guess she'd needed some time to get over losing Dorothy. I wondered if she'd ever find a way to forgive Lizzie for winning the part.

Mr. Calhoun continued. "While it may seem like the acting parts are the most important roles in a production, crew members are essential. Without sets, we cannot run down the yellow brick road. Without lights, we cannot see Dorothy escape the Wicked Witch. And without sound, there is no drama," he said, eyeing our small group. He paced back and forth as he spoke, his long fingers drumming the back of his clipboard.

"The stage crews will work with faculty advisers, whom you can find waiting with Mrs. Smith by the piano. Those of you with acting parts, please follow me for a brief orientation to the stage. After that, our parent volunteers will work with you in groups. Starting tomorrow, you'll report to the auditorium during your lunch period and your assigned music or theater elective, if you have one. Afternoon rehearsal schedules vary by role, but Wednesday production meetings are mandatory for everyone. All right. Let's move, people!"

Somebody shouted, "Break a leg!"

Mr. Calhoun's bushy eyebrows twitched, but he just said, "Save it for opening night."

Jake and the other kids stood up, so I grabbed my book bag and followed them to the piano. Mrs. Smith, the music teacher, waved us over to her side. Music wasn't one of my electives, but I'd spotted Mrs. Smith in the halls before. Lizzie said she was a real singer, that she'd even sung backup on old records like my dad's.

"Are you my sound team?" She punctuated her words with a flutter of piano keys.

"That's us, Mrs. Smith," the other girl said.

"Nice to see you, Amelia." Mrs. Smith smiled at the rest of us. "Hello, Davis. And Jake, my guitar player." Jake ducked his head, and Mrs. Smith's wide brown eyes settled on me. "What's your name, sweetheart? I don't believe we've met."

"It's Thyme. With an H-Y." And then, like I needed an explanation, I blurted out, "I'm new," and felt my cheeks growing redder, though maybe that was just because everyone was looking at me.

She nodded. "And do you play an instrument, Thyme with an H-Y?"

"No."

"That's fine. We'll get you all set up, don't worry." Which, of course, made me worry. What had I gotten myself into? Everyone else already knew Mrs. Smith. There were probably all musicians, and I hadn't even been able to play the plastic recorder in third grade.

Mrs. Smith flipped to the back of her packet, where Mr. Calhoun had included a diagram of the stage. "First things first. Let me show you where you'll be working." She waved for us to follow and headed across the stage.

Jake walked next to me. "Don't worry about the instrument

stuff, that's for the orchestra kids. We won't be playing regular instruments, anyway. That's what makes it so fun."

"Thanks," I said, but I still felt out of place.

"Here we are." Mrs. Smith led us behind the tall red stage curtains. "This is stage left, for those of you who don't know."

Amelia with the wispy hair frowned. "But it's on the right."

"Exactly. That's why I told you it's called *stage* left." Mrs. Smith tapped her finger against a copy of the stage diagram. She explained that stage directions are based on the actors, not the audience. So what seemed like the right side to someone in the seats was actually stage left to someone onstage. Then she ran through the other words on the diagram—*downstage*, which was closest to the audience, *center stage*, and *upstage*, which was at the rear.

Next to the curtains, ropes descended from the ceiling in thick bunches that hooked into metal levers along the wall. "These, you do not touch," Mrs. Smith said. "They hold up the lights, the scenic elements, the curtains—and we don't want any of that falling on our heads." She waved us over to a folding table next to the wall. "Our work space is here, next to the prop tables. This is where we'll organize our sound cues during the show."

She reached under the table and pulled out an enormous trunk. The brass-edged case was worn, its dark sides scuffed. As the lid creaked open, a cloud of dust puffed into the air.

Mrs. Smith coughed and fanned the dust away. "Everything we have from previous shows is in this box." She reached in and pulled out a set of long, ribbed sticks. They looked like croquet mallets to me, until she rubbed the sticks together, producing a rasping, rattling sound. "Some of these old props might work. But some of the sounds we need are new. So we'll have to make it work. I know there's something in here for thunder."

I breathed out with relief. We were all going to make it up as we went, musicians or not. That still sounded like a lot to figure out, but not impossible.

Just then, Mrs. Smith spun around holding a thin sheet of metal.

CRACK!

The metal popped back and forth between her hands, producing a sound so loud, it made me jump. I landed on something lumpy, only to discover it was Jake's foot.

He smiled, but my skin turned hot with embarrassment anyway. *Oh, here, Jake, let me crush your foot.* Brilliant, Thyme. Maybe next I could offer to smack him in the head with one of the wooden sticks! Then he'd like me for sure.

At the thought of Jake liking me, my face burned even hotter.

Mrs. Smith dropped the metal sheet back into the pile. "Why don't you all have a look at what's in the trunk, and then we'll go over the plan for the next seven weeks. I know it's only January now, but March will be here before you know it! Amelia, come with me to the music room. I set some drums aside for the show."

She and Amelia left through the doors to the hallway, and

Jake and Davis climbed into the prop trunk, which was easily big enough to hide several bodies. They picked out objects, shaking or striking them to make noise while I flipped through my information packet. There was a list of scenes for each act of the play, with little stars noting the sounds needed for each scene. A number written inside each star matched a key at the bottom of the page—like star five, which was the sound for lightning. As in, the lightning that strikes before the tornado sweeps Dorothy off to Oz. I remembered that part from the last time I'd seen the movie. Lightning flashed, gray clouds swirled, and then—the tornado.

Jake climbed out of the trunk and came over to look at my paper. His springy brown hair had bits of dust caught in it from rooting around in the trunk. "I'll never get it, you know. Dorothy had all the warning in the world. Why didn't she get out of the way? Or hide? She knew that tornado was coming, and she just let it sweep her right up."

"I don't know about that." He looked at me, and I glanced down at the page. "What I mean is, if Dorothy didn't get sucked up in the tornado, there wouldn't *be* a *Wizard of Oz*. She didn't have a choice."

Jake twirled one of his earbuds, thinking. "I guess not."

"Sometimes, you don't have a choice about where you go. Because it's somebody else's story you're living. Plus, she had to get her dog, right?"

"I guess that makes sense." He thumped my shoulder. "Come on, I'll show you the thunder sheet. That way you won't get scared next time."

"I wasn't scared!"

"You could've fooled me."

"Whatever. It takes more than a thunder sheet to scare me," I said, crossing my arms over my packet, even as a smile snuck onto my face.

Jake laughed, an easy, musical sound. "Tell that to my toes."

28

YES AND NO

"IT WAS GOOD, YES?" MRS. RAVELLI ASKED ON OUR WAY HOME after the production meeting. Most of the snow had melted, except for the lumpy hills the plows had left on the street corners. But it still felt like the Arctic outside, or at least what I imagined the Arctic must feel like.

"It was fun," I admitted, "but I have no clue how to do anything." My breath left a trail in the air.

"Yes and no," she said. "This is okay. Sometimes, it is hard to see the way when you are in the middle of things. My uncle, he come to America one year before me. He let me stay with him, and he get me a job at his deli, too. My first day, I broke the cash register! *Ay*, it was hopeless!"

She rested a hand on her forehead, as though the memory alone might make her faint, and I laughed. "It took me many days to learn the new ways," she said, "but I did it. You will learn, too. This I know."

While we walked, I told her about all of the different sounds we had to create, and how they would make the play seem more real to the audience. When we got to the apartment building, she mentioned that she'd seen Mr. Lipinsky that morning, and that he was feeling much better since our visit on Monday, which made me happy. I didn't like seeing him confused.

On our way up the stairs, I whistled a song from *The Wizard of Oz*, and by the time we got to the third floor, I could hear Sylvie whistling back. Sure enough, Mr. Lipinsky's door popped open. "Keep it down out there," he said before he slammed the door, but he didn't really look that angry. In fact, I thought I might have even seen him smile.

Upstairs, Mom and Val were already home. Mom was sitting at the dining table with a bunch of papers. And for the first time that week, Val was on the couch instead of back in her bedroom.

"T!" he said. "I rode the 4 train!" He held up a new model subway car.

"Let's keep it calm," Mom warned, and Val set the train down again, although he was obviously feeling a million times better.

Mrs. Ravelli gave him a little wave and headed into the kitchen.

"How'd it go today?" I asked Mom.

"Pretty well." She glanced up, and I thought she was going to ask me how my theater meeting went, but she just said, "Dr. Everett says we can expect the 3F8 infusions to go better later in the week, but the first few days of treatment will always be hard." I knew I should have been happy that she was sharing something with me, but all I heard was the word *always*.

"Did Dr. Everett say when we can go home yet?" I asked, and Mom's face closed up.

She glanced at Val. "Let's not worry about that right now." She gathered her papers and said, "I'll be in my room." Then she left like she couldn't get away from me fast enough.

I wanted to shout at her the way Cori did, but then I saw Val watching me from the couch. That's when I knew. I didn't want to be there, and he knew it.

Talk about a horrible feeling. I was the worst sister on the planet.

I plastered a smile on my face and plopped down next to him. "Guess what?"

"What?" he said eagerly. Val loved news. And secrets.

I leaned closer. "I learned how to make fake thunder today," I whispered, like I was letting him in on a very, very important piece of information.

His little blue eyes lit up. "Can you show me?" he whispered back.

Mom was still in her room. "Okay, I'll be right back." I snuck into the kitchen and stole a wooden spoon and one of Mom's sheet pans, right behind Mrs. Ravelli's back. In the living room, Val sat up on his knees, grinning with excitement.

"Ready?" I asked.

He squealed.

Then I nailed the sheet pan with the spoon, and a super loud (and pretty terrible) crash exploded in the air. It wasn't exactly right for thunder, but it was startling as heck. Mom and Mrs. Ravelli both came running. When Mom saw me standing there with the spoon and the pan, she looked like she wanted to strangle me. Val grabbed the spoon and started whacking away at the pan.

"Sorry!" I shouted over the racket. "I'm just practicing for my theater group."

But the truth is, I wasn't sorry at all.

◎◎

The next day at lunch, I went straight to the auditorium and got there ahead of everyone else. The door that led backstage swung open silently, and for a split second, I felt like I was sneaking around somewhere I wasn't supposed to be. Then a woman's powerful voice burst into song from beyond the stage curtains, in the direction of the piano. Only there was no music, just the sound of her voice.

I crept past the trunk of sound props and peeked past the stage curtains. Mrs. Smith was there, sitting at the piano while she waited for us to show up, singing "Somewhere Over the Rainbow" a cappella. But not the way I was used to hearing it. This version of the song was slower, more drawn out, and with a different beat. Words melted like whispers into the highest notes. And in between the words, the most beautiful hum filled the silence. I let the words wash over me, even though I felt them stirring something up—some sorrow buried deep down inside.

"*Where troubles melt like lemon drops, away above the chim-iny tops, that's where, you'll fi-ind me.*" As I stood there, listening, tears sprang to my eyes, fast and hot. The kind of tears no

I looked up. I hadn't marked the call on the Calendar of Us like I usually did. "Shoot. I'm sorry. I've just been busy working on stuff for the Spring Fling."

"Well, I can't talk long," Shani said.

"Me neither." I thought of all the things I wanted to tell her. About sound production, and Jake playing his Dad's guitar for me, and Val—

"Well, if you don't have anything to say . . ." Now she sounded mad.

"No, no. I do! Val finished his second round of 3F8. It wasn't as bad for him by the end of the week, either. He actually laughed."

"Does that mean you're coming home soon?"

"Well, Val still has to have his treatment for February. Then he has to have scans, and it takes a while to get the results, so I think it's going to be a little longer—"

"I meant *you*," Shani said, and it finally clicked.

"Oh. No, I haven't asked my parents yet."

"Well, how much time do you have now?"

I looked at the Thyme Jar. I hadn't exactly counted every single slip since Shani and I had talked the weekend before, but with the time I'd earned that week, I had to have over a hundred and thirty hours saved up. Which was so much time.

So. Much. Time.

What was I waiting for?

Shani was quiet for a minute. Then she said, "You're never coming back, are you?"

amount of blinking could hold back. It felt almost like homesickness again.

Then the stage door slammed open behind me, and Mrs. Smith stopped singing.

I hid my face as the other kids filed inside carrying bag lunches from the cafeteria. The air heaved in and out of my lungs in great, rattling bursts. It was like Mrs. Smith's voice had reached right into my chest and squeezed the feelings out of my heart.

Mrs. Smith walked past me. "Thyme!"

I wiped at my eyes. "I, ah, I just got here. I wasn't sure what to do."

"Well, first you eat lunch with everyone else. I don't need anyone running on empty when we have so much to do." Her voice sounded stern, but when I looked up, her smile glowed.

I ate with the rest of the sound crew, including Jake. Then Mrs. Smith gave me a list of sounds to work on with Amelia, while Jake worked with Davis. "Remember, these sounds will be amplified by microphones. But we need them to really *snap*!" She snapped her fingers for emphasis. "Show me what you can do."

Amelia dug in the prop trunk while I read Mrs. Smith's list aloud. Some of the sounds seemed easy, like a cowbell. Others I had no idea how to make, like howling wind.

"How do we make something howl?"

Amelia's head popped up from the trunk. With her

straw-colored hair going this way and that, she was a perfect match for the Scarecrow. "That's a tough one. We'll have to brainstorm some ideas. We might need some new materials for a good howl. Here's something." She twisted a blue plastic place mat into a cone and blew through the smaller end. A sound came from the cone, but it was more like a foghorn than a howl.

She tossed the place mat back on the pile. "Close, but no tamale."

"So . . . where do we get new materials?"

"Look around at home. Or in the art room. Try to find stuff that might work. Mrs. Smith said that's what they did last year. If we can't figure it out, she can buy some stuff. But we have a really small budget, and she needs to save it for CDs if we can't make the sounds ourselves."

My mind raced with possibilities for making sounds, like Mom's old plastic watering can. I wondered what kind of noise would come out of it. Then I remembered I hadn't seen the can since we'd moved. What did we need a watering can for in the city? We didn't even have a yard.

I ran my finger down the list of sounds, noting the ones that seemed toughest. It would be fun to figure these out. Movies were full of cool sounds. Someone, somewhere, had to make every single sound. I could be like the Wizard himself, the one behind the scenes, making the magic. Which sounded just about perfect to me.

29

NO TAKE-BACKS

AT THE END OF THAT WEEK, VAL FINISHED HIS SECOND of 3F8, which meant he was done for January. H tired, but he still helped me work on sound props o weekend. We used things we had around the apar like rubber gloves tied to a ruler to make a flapping for flying monkey wings. Mr. Lipinsky called it a "h contraption" when I ran downstairs to show him on S afternoon, but it got a smile out of Val even though still puffy and itchy. Mom warned me not to wear hi but she smiled when she said it.

Right before bedtime on Sunday night, the phon Dad appeared in our doorway, and Cori pulled her phones off. "Is it Liam?" she asked.

Dad smiled. "No. It's Shani, calling for Thyme handed me the phone. "Just a few minutes, or we'll ha warden in here."

Cori put her headphones back on, and I pressed the to my ear.

"Did you forget?" Shani said. "We were supposed t yesterday."

"No! No, I am. I am no matter what. You should see how cold it is here. It's like living inside a giant walk-in freezer, only there's no free ice cream."

Shani didn't laugh.

I glanced at Cori. Her eyes were shut. "I'm serious. I'm going to ask soon. It's just been hard with everything that's been going on with Val."

"Well, you said he's doing better."

"Yeah, that's right. And you're right. I'm really sorry I forgot about yesterday."

"Look, if you're going back on what you said, you should just tell me now." Shani was practically yelling, and she never yelled.

"I'm not taking it back. I promise."

There was a pause. "You know how you didn't tell me that crimping my hair made me look like a poodle because you didn't want to hurt my feelings? This isn't like that, right? Because you can take it back and I won't blame you," she said, sounding like that's exactly what she was doing—blaming me for not trying hard enough. For not being a good enough friend.

"I'm not going back on what I said. I've been really busy, but I'm earning plenty of time, too. I just need to save a little more. I'm getting close to a week." That was it, right? That's what I was waiting for. To have enough time . . . only a little voice in my head said I could go ahead and ask Mom now, if I really wanted to.

"This isn't easy, you know." Shani sounded sad all of a sudden. "Jenny is nice, but she's not you. I thought it would be okay, but it's not."

"I'm sorry." I didn't know what else to say. It sounded like she was giving up on me.

Shani was quiet for a minute. Then she said, "I have to go."

"I'll call you next Saturday," I promised, but Shani said she would be gone for a soccer tournament, so it would have to wait. She hung up, and I looked at the Calendar of Us. Then I grabbed a marker and circled January 26, which was two weeks away. I put stars all around the date, too, just in case. I wasn't going to forget again.

◎◎

At school the next week, Emily acted like she and Lizzie had never been best friends in the first place. She rolled her eyes whenever Mr. Calhoun had them rehearse together and spent all of her time with Rebeccah. Lizzie pretended like she didn't care, but during rehearsals on Wednesday afternoon, I caught her watching Emily joke with Rebeccah while they waited to be called onstage.

"Rebeccah is such a kiss-up," I said.

Lizzie shrugged and went back to winding a length of yarn from the costume table. I wondered if you could pass some invisible point in a friendship where there was no turning back, where your friend was lost forever. I kept imagining Shani staring at her phone, waiting for me to call. And me not calling.

After a minute, Lizzie said, "I think I'm going to quit."

"Why? You're such a good singer."

She frowned. "It's just so hard. I've been counting like my doctor told me to, but every time I go onstage, all I see is everyone staring at me. And that's just Mr. Calhoun and his helpers. What happens when there's a whole audience out there? What if I freak out?"

"We can practice together if you want."

"Thanks." She didn't look very optimistic.

"There's got to be a way to fix this," I said, more to myself than to her, and someone laughed. Emily and Rebeccah had moved closer to us.

Rebeccah looked at Lizzie. "Some things are unfixable, duh."

Lizzie kind of folded in on herself, and I saw a flicker of sadness on Emily's face.

Just then, Jake walked up to me with a dowel rod for one of the sounds we were working on. "I think I got it," he said. "We can make notches in the wood—"

"That's so cool," Emily said, smiling at him. He stopped talking, mouth hanging open, seeming to only just realize that I was standing there with three other girls.

"Are you playing your guitar in the show?" she asked. Jake shook his head and took a step back. "Ooh, I know! You should play at the Valentine's dance. Mr. C says they have a student band every year. They put a stage and lights in the gym and everything."

Jake took another step back. "I don't know about that—"

"You'd be awesome," Emily said with a smile that turned into a blush, and it occurred to me that maybe she liked him, too.

Jake mumbled that he'd see me later and snuck away.

Then Mr. Calhoun finally called for Lizzie and Emily, and Lizzie hurried away from us.

"She's so lame," Rebeccah said to Emily. "If she keeps messing up, you'll get the part for sure."

Emily smiled, but she didn't look entirely happy even though Rebeccah was kissing up as hard as possible. As she walked away, the smile fell completely off her face. That's when I saw it: that invisible moment when you could lose your friend forever. It was right there in front of me. The same sadness that I'd heard in Shani's voice was on Emily's face.

I ran after her and grabbed her arm.

"What are you doing?" she said.

"Just listen to me for a minute. Remember when you said this was just a misunderstanding between you and Lizzie? Maybe that's all it really is. There's got to be a way to fix things. You guys are *best* friends. Don't listen to Rebeccah about this. She's not your friend. Lizzie is."

"What does it matter to you?" Emily said.

"It doesn't," I said, only I realized that it did. Somewhere along the way, I'd started caring about these girls and their stupid problems. I even missed sitting at the lunch table together, listening to Emily and Lizzie argue about stupid stuff the way best friends do. The way I used to with Shani.

When I looked back at Emily, she had a frown on her face. "I've got to go," she said. Then she marched onstage, leaving me standing in the wings.

30

AN ACCIDENT
WAITING TO HAPPEN

I GUESS EMILY AND LIZZIE'S FIGHT WAS REALLY GETTING TO ME, because I spent most of the following weekend hanging around the apartment in case Shani called, even though I knew she wouldn't. On Sunday afternoon, Dad showed up at my bedroom door. "You all right?" he asked.

I shrugged.

"You know what you need?" he said. "A good old-fashioned butt-kicking." He held up our checkers set. "You up for a Champions Tournament?"

We settled on the living room rug to play. First checkers, which I won. Then Blokus. Mancala would be the tie-breaker if we needed it. Every once in a while, we heard laughter from Val's room. He and Mom were catching up on his schoolwork. Cori was out with her drama friends. They had a new idea, something sure to get the school's attention—*and Mom and Dad's,* I thought.

I set a Blokus piece on the game board, and Dad cleared his throat in warning. His long legs were folded underneath him, his chin propped on one arm. He'd trimmed his beard super short, like a shadow.

"What?" I said.

"Oh, nothing." Then he picked the exact same piece and played it on his side of the board.

"Copycat."

He grinned. "What can I say? You learned from the best."

"You're right. Cori is pretty good at this game."

"Hardy-har," Dad said just as an alarm erupted in the hall.

He frowned. "I better go see what that's all about. No cheating while I'm gone." I rolled my eyes, and he went into the hall. But he came back right away. "Get your boots and coat on," he ordered. Then he ran down the hall to Val's room. The alarm was still blaring in the hall.

I got ready as fast as I could. "What's wrong?" I asked when he came back with Mom and Val.

"Looks like a fire," Dad said. He grabbed Val and stuffed his feet into his boots, while Mom threw on her coat and scarf.

"I don't want to go outside," Val whined, but Dad just zipped his coat up anyway.

Mom ran past me to the shelves by the dining table and came back with a stack of photo albums.

Dad shook his head. "Hon—"

"Don't argue with me," she warned. "I'm not leaving without them."

Something tightened in my chest. "What about my jar?"

"Sorry, honey," Dad said. He scooped Val into his arms and opened our door. There was smoke billowing into the hall.

"But, Dad—"

"Thyme. *Now*," Mom said, and we all ran out of the apartment.

"Keep your head low!" Dad shouted as we rushed down the stairs. The alarms were so loud, I couldn't think, and my eyes burned. But I could see a little, and as we passed by Mr. Lipinsky's door, I saw smoke pouring out from under it.

On our way out of the building, firemen rushed past us, up the stairs toward Mr. Lipinsky's. There were more firemen outside on the sidewalk. And fire trucks. And police. And about a million people who had no business being there, but stared at us anyway, like we were putting on a show.

I looked down. I was still in my pajamas with the bright pink hearts and flying elephants. Of course people were staring.

I pulled my coat closed, and a fireman directed us off the sidewalk into the street, where the fire trucks had blocked off part of the road. There were other people from our building standing there, so we stood next to them and stared at the building, too.

"I'm cold," Val complained, and Dad rubbed his arms.

Mom made an angry noise. "We forgot his hat." Dad took off his own hat and put it on Val. Mom tucked it over Val's hearing aids. "He shouldn't be out here like this," she said.

"What do you want me to do?" Dad said, but Mom just clutched the photo albums to her chest.

"What about all of our stuff?" I asked.

Mom frowned. "I don't know."

Just then, a fireman came through the door, pulling Mr. Lipinsky behind him. Mr. Lipinsky was waving his arms around and yelling, but the fireman forced him over to our area.

"I have to get back in there!" Mr. Lipinsky shouted.

"Sir! You've got to calm down."

"Don't tell me to calm down! Sylvie's still in there!"

"Sir! If you want us to save your bird, I need to get back in there. Stay here and let me do my job. You hear me?"

The fight went out of Mr. Lipinsky's body. "I didn't mean for this to happen. The oven timer didn't go off, I swear."

The fireman let him go. "Can I trust you to stay here?"

Mr. Lipinsky's head dropped, and the fireman took off.

Mom turned to Dad. "I told you. That man is an accident waiting to happen."

"No he's not," I shot back.

Mom shook her head, so I turned my back to her and crossed my arms over my coat, fighting the cold that was creeping through my thin pajamas. Back home, Grandma Kay was all alone in her house. To talk to Mr. Ravelli, Mrs. Ravelli had to go to the cemetery. I thought of Lizzie and Emily tearing each other up, and I thought of Val, and how I at least had him, while Mr. Lipinsky had no one. His wife was dead. His best friend had moved away and was never coming back.

I walked over to Mr. Lipinsky and tapped his arm. He looked at me, but he didn't say anything. It was like he wasn't there, all husk and no cob.

"Mr. Lipinsky?" I said. "It's going to be okay."

"I don't know about that, kiddo." He looked back at the building, his gray eyes shiny with tears.

I hoped maybe he was wrong. That there was a little luck out there for him, and for Sylvie. The firemen knew what they were doing. They had hoses and axes. Surely they could put the fire out.

The thing about fire, though, is it's not the flames that kill you. It's the smoke. That's why they make you crawl on your hands and knees during fire drills. Because high up in the air is the worst place to be during a fire. That's where all the smoke is. But birds don't know any better, even a bird as smart as Sylvie. All they can do is fly higher.

☉☉

That night, long after the firemen had left, I waited until everyone else was sound asleep. Then I crept out to our landing. The hall smelled like an ashtray, and the wall above Mr. Lipinsky's door was streaked with black smears that stood out against the paint in the moonlight. I whistled extra loud, just in case, but there was no answer from apartment 3B.

31

THE SILENT TREATMENT

FOR THREE DAYS AFTER THE FIRE, MOM AND MRS. RAVELLI scrubbed every inch of the apartment to get the smoky smell out. Cori kept asking to sleep over at her friend's house, but Mom said the air was safe thanks to Val's new air purifier. She'd sent Dad to buy it right away. Mrs. Ravelli believed in the power of fresh air, too. She propped the windows open for hours every time Mom and Val were gone, even though it was still completely freezing outside. January was almost over, but winter wasn't.

We washed everything that smelled, too, so I earned plenty of time slips for lugging loads of laundry up and down the stairs. I kept an eye on Mr. Lipinsky's door as I passed by, but it stayed shut no matter how hard I stomped my feet. I even wrote him a note and taped it to his door, the way he used to when he was mad at us. The note stayed there for days, until it finally disappeared.

Mom said it was for the better, and that I should leave him alone. But she was wrong. Being alone never made anything better. I wished he would just open his door and shout at me like usual. I knew what to do with a grumpy Mr. Lipinsky, but the silent treatment was a lot harder to take.

✪

That same week, I'd also started trying to figure out the sound for the tornado at school. We needed something that howled and scratched and whirred—something that *terrified*. I'd dug around in the prop trunk, testing different materials, but nothing had sounded right. I'd stolen the colander from our kitchen, thinking the holes would make a nice whistling sound, but Mrs. Ravelli had flipped, so I had to bring it back. As it turned out, making fake sounds for real-life things was way harder than I'd thought.

We were supposed to share our new sounds with the team at the end of every week. Jake and Davis had been working with Mrs. Smith on the sound sequence for the yellow brick road. They had the Tin Man's feet clinking (teacups) and the corn rustling (a broom), but the sounds couldn't happen at the same time or they blended together into mush.

On Friday at lunch, Mrs. Smith clapped out the beat while Davis clinked the teacups and Jake swooshed the broom in between each clink. Finally, they got the rhythm down, and with Mrs. Smith playing the piano, the whole effect sounded great. They finished and the people around us clapped, and Jake looked right at me and smiled. At the end of the day, he walked out with me, too.

"You're really good at this sound stuff," I said, wishing I'd had more to show for a week's worth of work. The tornado sound still needed to be solved.

"Thanks." He glanced at me from beneath his puff of hair. "I spend a lot of time on it. When my dad was working on a song, he practically lived in his music room. It had foam on the walls, and all of his guitars. He said if you want to figure out a song, you've got to give it everything you've got."

"Well, I'm trying everything I can think of, but the tornado is impossible. And I don't think Mr. Calhoun would like it if I started living in the auditorium to work on it."

"Maybe if you bribed him with a bow tie."

We laughed. "What kind of music did your dad play?" I asked.

"Everything, but mainly blues. And jazz. He loved Stevie Ray Vaughan. You know him?" I shook my head. "You should look him up sometime. He covered the song I was working on. The one I played for you." He smiled, and I could feel a hot red blush coloring my face.

"Did you play it for your mom?"

"Yeah. She loved it."

I thumped his arm. "I told you so."

He laughed. "What's cool is, Stevie didn't even write this song, but he played it so well, it sort of became his, too. The original was by Jimi Hendrix."

"What's it called?"

"'Little Wing.' It's about having something good, but knowing it could take off and fly away, like a bird." He got quiet, and I could tell he was thinking of something else. Maybe his dad. "So I'll see you," he said all of a sudden. Then he took off down the hall.

But when he got to the big red doors, he stopped. "Hey. Maybe I could help you with the tornado next week?" he called, and my heart lifted.

"Sure," I called back. "That would be great."

◎◎

I woke up that Saturday excited to talk to Shani. It had been two weeks since our last call. After lunch, I propped the tablet on my pillow and got the Thyme Jar out so I was ready to talk to her. I even counted the slips early so she'd know I was on top of things again. One hundred and forty hours of time. I could hardly believe it, but other than the Christmas gift from Mom, I'd earned every single slip. Shani had to see that I was serious about coming back.

But when I called at lunchtime, she wasn't home. Her mom said she was gone for a sleepover with Jenny. That she would be gone all weekend.

"Thanks," I said, and hung up.

I looked at the Thyme Jar, sitting at the foot of my bed, and thought of all the things I'd wanted to tell Shani—about sound production, and Jake, and the fire and Sylvie. There was so much she didn't know. I could've just e-mailed her, but it wasn't the same as talking face-to-face. Her mom said she'd have Shani call as soon as possible, but with the way Shani had dodged our call, I was pretty sure Mr. Lipinsky wasn't the only one giving me the silent treatment.

32

A GOOD SIGN

THE FOLLOWING WEEK, VAL'S HAMA TEST FROM HIS SECOND round of treatment came back negative. A good sign, according to Dr. Everett. It meant that Val could go ahead with his third round of 3F8 in a couple of weeks, and that hopefully, the medicine was doing its job. There was no way to know until Val had his scans, but first he had to finish the treatment. "One thing at a time," Mom said, with no mention of what that meant for us.

For once, I let it go. I was happy for Val, and that was enough. Plus, I had plenty to keep me busy now that Jake and I were working together on the tornado at school.

So far, we had a train whistle and some reeds rubbing against a board. But the sound wasn't right yet. We still needed the *whoosh* of the wind. Like the howling for the flying monkeys, but different. Faking a tornado was hard, but it was easy to work with Jake. He never made fun of my ideas, and he laughed when things went wrong. Shani would have been the same way. It was hard not to think about her, and wonder what she was up to . . . or if she was going to call.

Mrs. Smith said it was okay if we didn't figure out the

perfect sound for the tornado. She had an old tape recording we could use as backup, if it came to that.

"I don't want to use a tape," I said to Jake on Friday after we'd shown Mrs. Smith our progress at lunch. "It sounds lame."

"I listened to it in music the other day," he said. "It's pretty scratchy, like an old record."

"Shoot." I didn't want to settle for some scratchy tape that would make it sound like we couldn't figure out how to do our jobs.

"Don't worry," Jake said. "We'll figure it out."

Lizzie waved as she walked by. She and Emily had actually done all right in their rehearsals that week. Emily didn't look happy, but she didn't seem to be going out of her way to be mean, which was something. Rebeccah still hovered around her like a mosquito, though.

Jake bumped my sneaker with his. "Mrs. Smith asked me to play 'Little Wing' at the dance."

I almost said, *What dance?* Then I remembered it was February first, which meant the sixth grade Valentine's Day dance was only a couple of weeks away, and this weird, sick feeling rushed over me. Was Jake about to ask me to go with him? I couldn't tell if that was what I wanted or not.

"The thing is, I don't know if I want to play that song for the whole school," he said, and I almost laughed at myself. I was so dumb, getting all worked up when he just needed a friend.

"You'll do a great job. You played it for me."

"Well, you're not most people," he said, and all those nervous feelings came right back. "You're going, right? It's during the day, so you don't have to get a ride from your parents or anything."

I swallowed. My throat was so dry all of a sudden. "Sure," I said, and he smiled.

I knew I should have been happy that Jake sort-of, kind-of asked me to the dance, but for the rest of the day, I got that same weird feeling every time I looked at him. I liked working with him, and joking with him, and even walking to the auditorium together every day. But the idea of dancing together on Valentine's Day? In front of everyone?

No way.

෧෨

On the way home, Mrs. Ravelli and I stopped by Mr. Lipinsky's apartment. She didn't get out her key, but she did wait while I tried to talk to him through the door. "I'm working on sound production at school, but I'm really terrible at it. Do you know how to make a fake tornado? We've tried everything, but nothing works. I could sure use your help."

I was thinking of how Mrs. Ravelli had tricked him into coming inside that day by asking for his help. I hoped maybe he'd barge into the hall and tell me exactly what I was doing wrong, but there was no reaction from inside. I hadn't seen him since the fire.

I tried a different tactic. "This theater stuff is dumb, anyway. No one cares if I get the sounds right. Everyone I know would rather watch the movie instead."

Mrs. Ravelli shook her head at me, but I heard a shuffling noise coming from inside apartment 3B. Then, "Go away or I'll call the police!" His voice was gravelly and strained, but it still made me grin to hear it again.

"*Ay!* This is enough for today," Mrs. Ravelli said, though she looked pretty pleased, too. She started up the stairs. "I must ask you, *bambina.* Why do you tell Mr. Lipinsky of the play, but not your mama and papa? This makes no sense."

"I don't know. I guess I didn't want them to get the wrong idea, and anyway, they're too busy with Val and work and stuff to listen to me."

Mrs. Ravelli stopped. "This is not true. Your mama, she tell me all the time about you. You like the turkey in three slices, like a fan. You like chocolate milk and pastries. You like to hear stories. All the time, your mama tell me these things."

"She does?"

"Of course! How else would I know? I am not magic, *bambina.*"

I followed Mrs. Ravelli up the stairs, thinking of all the little things I'd appreciated about her, and how many of them had been because of Mom. Mom was the one thinking of me and reading my mind.

Mrs. Ravelli turned her key in our lock and pushed the door open to the sound of a fight.

"What on earth were you *thinking*?" Mom shouted. Not like she was annoyed. Like she was actually going to kill someone.

I pushed past Mrs. Ravelli and saw Cori sitting at the dining table. Dad was home, too, sitting next to Cori while Mom paced the floor, her tiny frame bursting with anger. She waved a crumpled slip of pink paper. "Ten days of detention. Ten *days*? And now three days of suspension!"

Dad lifted his hands. "Now, hon, let's—"

Mom turned on him. "You're the one who always says we need to give her space. That a little independence would go a long way. Well, boy, did it ever. It sent her all the way to a suspension!"

Dad's face turned red above his beard. *This is it,* I thought, only I didn't want Dad to fight back. I didn't want him and Mom to fight at all.

"Just give me the lecture and let me go," Cori said.

Mom stopped in her tracks. I thought she really would kill Cori right then, but she just turned to us and said, "Thank you, Mrs. Ravelli. You can go ahead now. Have a lovely weekend."

Mrs. Ravelli swept through the kitchen to gather her things and leave, but not before tapping my chin and whispering, "*Ti amo,*" which meant "I love you."

As soon as the door shut, Cori rolled her eyes, which were thick with black eyeliner again. "Can I just *go* already?"

Mom pointed at her. "Don't you ever speak to me that way again."

"Right," Cori said. "Wouldn't want to embarrass you in front of the help." Her voice dripped with anger, but she was blinking fast, like she was trying not to cry.

"You will not speak about Mrs. Ravelli that way," Mom said. "She is a wonderful, decent woman whom I can never repay."

"At least Thyme has her! You've never even been to my school!" Tears flooded down Cori's face.

That's when Val padded up to us in his Batman costume.

"Honey, I told you to wait in your room," Mom said, but Val just went straight to Cori and wrapped his arms around her.

"I'm sorry, C," he said as Cori gulped for air. My eyes were aching, too. Mom pressed her hand to her mouth to hold back a sob, while Dad's shoulders slumped. We were a mess.

Cori dropped to one knee and wrapped her long arms around Val. "Don't you ever, *ever* apologize," she said, resting her cheek against his scruffy head. "You. Are. Awesome," she whispered, and my chest caved in. I knew exactly how she felt. She was mad, but that didn't mean that she didn't love Val. She loved him the most.

"Cori." Mom's voice was softer now. "I am sorry." Those were the last words I expected to hear her say, but she was looking straight at Cori like she really meant them.

"Mom—" Cori said, her voice cracking.

Val saw me and came running. "T!" He wrapped his arms around me the same way he had with Cori. That hug felt like a million bucks.

Mom took Cori's face in her hands. "I see you. Do you

hear me, honey? I see you." Cori nodded, her face streaked with tears and black eyeliner. "Good," Mom said. "That's good. But you're still grounded." Then they both laughed, and I wondered how something so terrible could turn so good in a single moment, with a few simple words.

33

YOU SHOULD TRY IT

AFTER THE FIGHT WITH MOM, CORI TURNED INTO A COMPLETELY different person. All weekend, she made jokes that weren't mean. She laughed. Getting grounded seemed like the best thing that had ever happened to her. Technically, her suspension was only for three days, but Mom said Cori had to stay home for a week, just to make sure they had enough time to "reconnect." After that, Cori would go back to school and it would be time for Val's third round of 3F8.

"What did you guys do all day?" I asked Cori after school on Monday. It was weird to think that while I'd been in class, she had just been home with Mom and Val.

"We rode the F train," Val shouted as he lined his model subway cars up on the linoleum tiles in the kitchen. "We're going to ride another train tomorrow, too."

Cori laughed. "You've ridden almost all of them now," she said to Val. Then she leaned close. "A word of advice. If a subway car is empty, skip it. I nearly died from the smell on that F train."

"Good to know, but I'll leave that to you and Mom." I had zero intentions of riding the subway.

Cori was looking funny at me. "What?" I said.

"You should try it," she said, like she was reading my mind.

"The subway? No way."

"No, not that. You should try talking to Mom about everything. It helps."

I shrugged, but part of me wondered if Cori was right. Shani still wasn't talking to me. I'd left her messages over the weekend, but she hadn't called me back. I wondered what Mom would think about that, if I told her. Maybe she would actually listen.

⊗⊘

That Wednesday our production meeting finished early, so I stayed to watch Lizzie rehearse a scene with Mr. Calhoun on-stage. Big pieces of the set were in place. Lizzie wasn't wearing her costume yet, but the play was starting to look real. Then, when Mr. Calhoun signaled Lizzie, she missed her cue. They started over and Lizzie messed up again.

"Let's take a quick break," Mr. Calhoun said, and Lizzie buried her face in her hands.

"I told you she'd fall apart," Rebeccah said to Emily. They were standing just a few feet away from me, watching. "They never should have given her the role."

"You don't have to keep saying that," Emily said. When she caught me looking at them, she actually moved away from Rebeccah a little bit, too. Maybe she was getting tired of all the kissing-up.

Onstage, Lizzie looked like she was about to burst into

tears. Despite Mr. Calhoun's rules about keeping off the stage during rehearsals, I walked over to her. "What's wrong? You know this part."

It was one of the final scenes in the play. The one where Dorothy shuts her eyes and says, "There's no place like home."

Lizzie sighed. "I'm trying to calm down, but I feel so nervous. They're all staring at me."

I took her hand and squeezed it. "Why don't you pretend you're singing in the bathroom again? That was a piece of cake, right?"

"But I'm not."

"That's why it's called pretending, *duh*."

She cracked a smile, and I grabbed both her hands. "Repeat after me. 'There's no place like home,'" I said, thinking of how Dorothy wanted to go home so badly, she left all her new friends from Oz behind.

"There's no place like home," Lizzie said softly.

"Louder."

"There's no place like home!" she said with just the right amount of hope and sadness.

Mr. Calhoun started clapping. He was standing at the front of the stage again, watching us. "Excellent, Lizzie! That's perfect. All right, folks, that's enough for today."

Lizzie grabbed my arm as we walked to the wings. "That was so much easier, pretending I was in the bathroom. I can't believe I did it."

"I wouldn't say you did it," Rebeccah said, and Lizzie stopped in her tracks. "More like the rest of us suffered through it. But I bet if you keep at it, you'll get some of it right in the end."

Lizzie's face fell, and Emily frowned. Then she turned to Rebeccah. "The only people suffering around here are all of us, listening to you run your mouth all the time."

Rebeccah stared at her. "Are you kidding me?"

"No. You're kidding yourself if you think you can say that to my best friend."

"But she stole your part!"

"Well, that's the thing." Emily looked at Lizzie. "She didn't."

Rebeccah stomped off in a huff, and Lizzie and Emily just stood there. For a minute, they didn't say anything at all. Then they both said "I'm sorry" at pretty much the exact same time and hugged each other. Then they hugged me, too, which felt new and weird and good at the same time.

"I'm sorry about Dorothy," Lizzie told Emily, wiping at her eyes. "I just wanted to be in the play, but I won't do it if it hurts your feelings too much."

"No way," Emily said. "I'm not letting you miss out on this. But now that we're working together, let me tell you, you have got a *lot* of practicing to do." Lizzie laughed, and Emily looked at me. "You were right, you know. You said I had a choice. I don't know why I've been such an idiot."

"What made you change your mind?"

She thought for a second. "I guess I just needed time to get over it."

"Well, you didn't have to wait so long," Lizzie said.

I thought of Shani, waiting for me to come home (assuming she still wanted me there). I told myself I just wanted to crack the tornado sound first. After that, I would leave.

☉

Emily needed help making parols for her grandma's birthday, so we made plans to work at Lizzie's apartment on Saturday afternoon. Emily would give me a ride. She was supposed to pick me up at eleven o'clock, but our buzzer rang early.

I grabbed my book bag and threw my coat on, and when Mom tried to say something, I just said, "I know. Be back by dinner, and have a good time, and be safe. I will and I will. And I wrote Lizzie's number by the phone."

Mom handed me a box. "I thought you might like to take some cookies?"

"Oh. Thanks."

I took the box and rushed out, while Val shouted good-byes down the stairwell after me. Mr. Lipinsky's door was shut, so I whistled on my way by, in case he was listening.

Emily's car was standing at the curb. Her driver opened the door for me, and I climbed in.

"Thanks, Jennings," Emily said.

The driver tipped his hat and shut the door. The inside of the car was dark, with black leather everything. Emily pressed a button on the console between our seats, and a glass partition rose between us and the driver.

"I wanted to say thanks for helping Lizzie all this time."

"It was no big deal," I said, but Emily shook her head.

"You don't understand. Lizzie is like . . . she's like my sister or something. I don't know because I've never *had* a sister, but sometimes it feels like we're actually related."

"That's probably why you fight so much. Sisters are like that."

Emily looked at me like she was waiting for me to say more. I didn't, because talking about Cori would lead to Val. What would Emily think when she found out I had a brother and a sister I'd never mentioned once, in all the time that she'd known me?

When we got to Lizzie's building, which was four stories and redbrick just like mine, Jennings carted our supplies upstairs. Unlike us, they had the whole second floor, although with three brothers running around, it still felt cramped. Jamie frowned when he saw me, and I wondered if he remembered running into me at Emily's holiday party. It was crazy to think that was over two months ago.

Lizzie led us past her brothers, who were wrestling over a pile of toys. "Sorry about that," she said. "My brothers are crazy. You know what Eric says when my mom asks him to help fix dinner?"

"What?"

"'Why? Is it broken?'" We laughed, and I thought of how much happier Lizzie was now that she and Emily weren't fighting. "And the best part?" Lizzie said. "I get stuck helping instead, because my mom thinks he's just hi-*lar*-ious."

Lizzie's room was a little smaller than mine and Cori's, but all her own. The walls were a soft shade of yellow, with brightly checked curtains and a bookcase loaded with

Playbills and picture frames. Just like at Emily's, most of Lizzie's pictures were of the two of them.

Emily had ordered rolls of beautiful, sparkly paper in every color. We spread them out on Lizzie's floor and spent the afternoon cutting and stapling, creating beautiful stars in every color of the rainbow.

"You should be in charge of decorations for the Valentine's dance," Lizzie told Emily.

"Like I need another party to plan for." Emily looked at me. "You're going to the dance, right? Don't say no! You're stuck with us now."

"Sure," I said. Going with Emily and Lizzie sounded like it would be all right. Right?

"I know who Thyme's going to dance with," Lizzie said. "He's got crazy hair, and he listens to music all the time—"

I wanted to crawl under her bed and hide. "Cut it out!" I shouted, and Lizzie broke into giggles, while Emily shook her head at us like we were crazy.

"What? You said he was cute," Lizzie said, and Emily blushed. I wondered if this was when she'd say that she liked Jake, too.

But she just shrugged Lizzie off. "Yeah, he's okay. But it's so weird how he wears those headphones all the time."

"I think it's kind of cool," I said. It just slipped out.

Emily tilted her head. "Then you're just as weird as he is. Which means you're a perfect match."

I groaned, and Emily and Lizzie laughed. It was almost like we were friends.

34

LITTLE WING

THE NIGHT BEFORE VAL STARTED HIS THIRD ROUND OF 3F8,
I dreamed that I was back home. Shani and I were sitting
in her room, but we weren't alone. Emily and Lizzie were
there, too. At first, everything was okay. We were working
on parols together. Then Emily and Lizzie started fighting,
and when I tried to stop them, Shani got mad at me. Soon
everyone was yelling, only I didn't even know what we were
doing there together in the first place.

I woke up covered in sweat and extremely glad that I
wasn't in Shani's room.

Then the guilt hit.

Of course I'd rather be in Shani's room. It was way better
than this stupid apartment, even if I was starting to wonder
when she would ever talk to me again.

In the morning, I went into the kitchen expecting to see
Val in a new costume, but he was wearing Iron Man again.
"You doing okay, buddy?"

He smiled. "Sara's bringing her Wii. We're staying this
afternoon to play." It was the happiest I'd seen him on a
treatment morning.

"That's great." I waited to see if he said anything else, in case he was worried or scared.

Sure enough, his brow furrowed. He held up two of his lovies. "Who should I take, Leo or Mikey?"

I tapped the stuffed Ninja Turtle. "Definitely Leo."

Val considered. Then he tossed Leo aside. "Nah, I'm taking Mikey."

Ten minutes later, he and Mom were out the door. Val didn't even give me a hug good-bye. Which hurt more than I would've expected. I guess I was used to those hugs, too.

೧೦

At school, everyone was talking about the Valentine's dance coming up on Thursday. It was going to be held after lunch in the gymnasium. We could wear our fancy outfits to school or bring them with us to change before the dance. I didn't even know what I was going to wear.

When Mrs. Ravelli and I got to the apartment that afternoon, Val was on the couch with the tablet. He looked puffy and tired, but he smiled despite the pink hives on his skin.

"How did it go today?" I asked.

"Good."

"Want to play Math Mysteries?"

He shook his head. "I'm playing Minecraft with Sara. She has it on her iPad, too."

"Looks like you're off the hook," Mom said with a smile, but that just made me feel strange. I was glad Val was doing better, but how could he not need me all of a sudden?

I went to my room to look through my clothes. Of course

I didn't have anything for a Valentine's dance. I thought about asking Mom to take me shopping . . . but would she really have time to do that?

"What should I wear to a dance?" I asked Cori when she got home.

Her owl eyes sprung wide. "Do you mean a *Valentine's* dance?"

When I didn't answer right away, she said, "Thyme! Do you have a boyfriend? Listen, I know I told Mom that Liam's just in charge of the drama club, but the truth is, we're sort of going out." She said the last part in a whisper, but by that time, my guts were swirling so hard, I thought I might be sick. I didn't have butterflies in my stomach, I had a *tsunami*.

I sat on my bed, hard, and Cori said, "Whoa, whoa. Relax. It's just a dance."

"Well, I've never been to one before."

"Well, then this will be the best dance you've been to, guaranteed." She gave me a big smile, and I managed to give her a small one back. "That's more like it. Now, let's find you something to wear."

⊚⊚

On Valentine's Day, I woke up early so that Cori could do my hair. She said I looked awesome, but I wasn't sure about the braids. Well, not braids, but one braid that kind of looped over the top of my head. It kept my bangs out of my eyes, and Cori said it was cool. But I just felt lame, especially when I walked into the kitchen and Mom did a double take.

"Well, look at you," she said. "Why so fancy?"

"There's a dance at school today."

She sighed and ran her hand through her hair. It was long enough to tuck behind her ears now. "That's right. It's Valentine's Day, isn't it? One of these days I'll be back in the real world again, and I'll remember things like that." She smiled. "Do you need something to wear?"

"No. Cori let me borrow a dress."

"Oh." Mom's smile faded. I thought she would ask which one, but she just said, "Well, I guess you're all set, then. Have fun, honey." I could've been wrong, but she seemed a little let down.

At school, I hung Cori's dress in my locker for later. Mrs. Ravelli had wrapped it up in a bag so it would stay clean. The dress was white with giant painted flowers in red and orange. They reminded me of Grandma's poppies in the middle of the summer, when the sun was so bright, the petals glowed. I wondered if Emily and Lizzie would like it. Then I saw Jake in homeroom and wondered if he would like it, too, which made me even more nervous. He'd decided to play a song at the dance, but he hadn't said which one. Would it be 'Little Wing'? And would he want to dance with me? I still wasn't sure how I felt about that. I spent the morning trying not to think about it, but my brain kept bringing it up.

After fourth period ended, the entire sixth grade was dismissed to the gymnasium.

I met up with Emily and Lizzie in the locker room to get changed. Lizzie put on a puffy skirt with a big music note on the front that looked like something our math teacher would have worn—old-fashioned, but cute. Meanwhile, Emily looked as cool as ever in a shiny red dress with a black bow around the waist. The ruffles at the bottom had rhinestones that sparkled when she moved. Next to them, I felt kind of plain, but Emily gave me a thumbs-up when she saw my dress.

"It's so California," she said. "In a good way."

I prayed she was right and followed everyone to the gym, which had been transformed into a dance hall with giant paper hearts and glitter balls. The floor was still as squeaky as usual, but with the lights turned down, the air felt electric. There was music playing, too, but there was also a stage set up in front of the folding bleachers.

"When is Jake going on?" Lizzie asked.

"I don't know. He said they were playing regular music for a while first."

We went to the drink tables to get some punch and met up with the other girls from the lunch table. Celia and Delia were wearing matching dresses, of course, pink ones with puffy sleeves. Rebeccah was there, too. When she saw Lizzie and Emily together, she just turned to talk to one of the other girls.

"Can you believe Mr. C is dancing with Mrs. Harris?" Emily said, pointing across the gym to where the two teachers were swaying back and forth. They were the only ones on the dance floor.

Lizzie smiled. "I think they're cute together. His bow tie matches her vest."

We laughed and stood there talking about who was

standing with who and drinking punch until the music cut off and the lights flashed three times. The crowd started shouting and squealing, because obviously *something* was happening. Then Mrs. Smith went up to the microphone at the front of the stage.

"Happy Valentine's Day, sixth graders!" Everyone cheered until she waved for quiet. "We have a special treat for you. I'm proud to introduce Jake Reese, who is playing 'Little Wing' by Stevie Ray Vaughan for us today."

My heart jumped at Jake's name. He stepped onto the stage, and everyone crowded closer.

Then Mrs. Smith moved over to a standing drum, and Jake stepped in front of the microphone. He was wearing a crisp white shirt over his jeans. "This is for my dad," he said. The crowd got quiet, and Jake started playing his guitar, the one with the swirly red wood. The notes started out slow. Then Mrs. Smith joined in, tapping out a beat on the drum that went along with Jake's playing.

"Wow," Lizzie said. "He's really good."

"That's his dad's guitar," I said, feeling happy for him. Jake's playing picked up speed, and the blues sound turned into something louder and more urgent. Mrs. Smith started humming along as well, adding the same kind of notes I'd heard her sing backstage that day. They traded back and forth, Jake's guitar and Mrs. Smith's voice. When the song slowed down, I felt sad. And when it sped back up, I felt like I was flying. Then, when they were done, I could hardly hear over everyone cheering in the gym.

Jake bowed, and Mrs. Smith wished us a happy Valentine's again. The regular music came back on and some kids finally started dancing. I kept my eyes on Jake, but when he climbed off the stage, I lost him in the crowd. I wanted to tell him how amazing his song was, and what a good job he'd done. I was struck with this weird fear that he could disappear right then, and I'd never see him again.

"Thyme," Emily said. Then she looked past me and blushed.

I felt a tap on my shoulder and turned around. It was Jake.

"Hey." He peeked at me from under his puff of hair.

"That was amazing!" I shouted over the music.

He grinned. Then he held out his hand. "Want to dance?"

I glanced at Emily. "It's fine. I like Davis's moves better, anyway."

"Really?" I looked at Davis, who was jerking his knees toward his elbows like a chicken.

"Yes, really," Emily said. Then she marched off to the dance floor and I turned back to Jake. He took my hand, and I felt like I was flying again.

When we got to the center of the dance floor, Jake stopped and pulled his earbuds out of his pocket. "I have a song for you," he said, leaning close. "I think you'll like it."

We each took one earbud and plugged our open ears so we could hear better.

It was a song I knew from Dad's records, one about a brown-eyed girl, and dancing and laughing in the sun. "It's perfect," I said, and Jake grinned. We listened to the song

together, and after a while, we started moving, too, swing-
ing our arms around and laughing to the sound of our own
music. It was weird at first, dancing with Jake, but we'd been
working side by side for weeks, making sound out of junk.
We were friends. He started doing goofy dance moves, sticking his legs out like Davis. I made up my own moves, too,
and for once I didn't feel stupid or awkward at all. I felt just
right.

35

BUTTERFLIES

THE WEEKEND AFTER VALENTINE'S, MOM SAT NEXT TO ME ON THE couch and said, "You and I should go do something together." She'd been chasing after me since the dance, wanting to spend time together. Now that Val's third round of treatment was over, she was trying even harder.

"There's a new exhibit at the Museum of Natural History. It's about *butterflies*." She whispered the last word, like the idea of a butterfly was so enticing, I couldn't possibly resist her offer.

"I'm calling Shani at noon." We didn't exactly have a call scheduled because Shani still wasn't talking to me, but I was planning to call her anyway.

"I mean after that," Mom said.

"What about Val?" He'd finished his week of 3F8 in the best spirits yet, but he was still pretty wiped out. He'd been on the couch all morning, watching his Transformers.

"Your father can watch him." She wasn't giving up.

The truth was, I did want to go with her, but some part of me didn't want to admit that. Maybe I was still mad about all the times she couldn't do things with me. But this time, Mom looked like she really meant it, so I told her I would think about it.

◎◎

I called Shani at noon, but she wasn't home. Again. According to the Calendar of Us, it had been eighty-five days since I left San Diego, and we hadn't spoken in four weeks. I told myself that it wasn't a big deal, but that hurt. A lot. I wanted to tell her about Jake and the dance. I wanted to tell her about Cori getting suspended but how Mom ended up being nicer because of it. And how Val looked like he was doing well, but we wouldn't know for sure until after his next set of scans, which might not be until after our birthdays. Shani had to understand that.

Frustrated, I put the phone back and got out some of Emily's fancy printed paper—a beautiful white-and-pearl pattern with swirls like clouds. I cut the paper in straight lines and folded the edges the way Emily had shown me. Then I tacked the folded sections together, but they weren't perfectly even, and my star ended up looking more like a squished flower. But that gave me an idea of something I could make for Mr. Lipinsky. He still wasn't talking to me, other than yelling at me to go away. But maybe I could make him something special, to help him feel better.

I took the star apart and cut one of the sections loose. Then I trimmed the others into triangular shapes and tacked the sections back together again. It took three tries to get it right, but when it was finally done, I had a beautiful paper bird that sparkled in the light.

I ran downstairs and knocked on Mr. Lipinsky's door.

He didn't answer, so I said, "I made you something. I'll just leave it out here, okay?"

Then I left the bird on his doormat. Even if he didn't like it, at least he'd know I was thinking of him.

On Sunday morning, I woke up early, but when I ran downstairs to see if he'd taken my gift, I found the bird sitting there, untouched. "Mr. Lipinsky?" I called.

No answer.

I started back up the stairs, and his door creaked open. "You can't leave that there."

A smile pulled at my mouth. I turned around and looked at him. He was wearing the purple robe again. "When someone gives you a gift, you should say thank you," I said.

He looked down at the paper bird, then bent slowly to pick it up. But he didn't smile. Instead, he stared at me, his gray eyes hard and unkind. "Sorry, kiddo," he said. "That's not how this works." Then he crumpled up the bird, right there in front of me. I felt like I'd been slapped.

"I just thought—"

"You weren't thinking at all," he said. "You think a scrap of paper can fix things? I've got news for you. Sylvie's gone. Everyone dies, and there's nothing you can do about it."

Tears sprang to my eyes. I bit my lip to hold them in.

He shook his head. "Sorry, but it's the truth. With that

brother of yours, you should know something about that." His eyes were far away when he said it, like he was thinking of something else, but all I heard was Mr. Lipinsky saying Val was going to die.

"You're wrong!" I shouted. "You're wrong because my brother's going to be fine!"

Mr. Lipinsky started to say something else, but I ran away before he could finish. I was done helping him. Done caring, even the tiniest little bit.

I burst into our apartment, and Mom looked up from the clothes she was folding. "You okay?" she said, but I just ran past her to my room and grabbed Mr. Knuckles.

All I could think was how stupid I was, trying to help someone like Mr. Lipinsky. I'd thought he was my friend. For the first time in a long while, I felt the tug of homesickness again, deep in my belly.

Mom walked into the room and sat on the corner of my bed.

"Thyme."

She put her hand on my leg. It was warm like the sun. Even in the dead of winter, Mom's hands were always warm. "I'm sorry I haven't had more time for you. But I'm here now. And I'd like to do something with you, if you'll let me. But you have to tell me what's going on. I'm not a mind reader."

And I'm lucky you're not, I thought. Otherwise she'd know what a rotten daughter she had. Someone who, at that very moment, would have ditched her little brother if she could to go back home and leave Mr. Lipinsky and paper birds and broken feelings behind.

"Why does he have to be so mean?" I said, swallowing back my tears.

"Oh, honey. Come here." Mom drew me into her lap. Her cheek rested against my head. "He's still upset about Sylvie. It's hard to lose someone you love," she said, but that only made me cry harder.

"I don't want Val to die," I said, hiccupping between each word.

Mom wasn't a whole lot bigger than me, but her arms tightened around me like a shield. "He's not going to die," she whispered. Her voice was all clamped down. She cleared her throat and kept going. "Your brother is going to be just fine. And Mr. Lipinsky will be fine, too. He just needs some time to remember that he's not alone. You're a good friend to him, Thyme, and I'm proud of you."

I pulled away. "I thought you didn't like him."

"Mr. Lipinsky's a mixed bag, but I love *you*, Thyme. And I'd really like it if we could spend some time together. Whatever you want."

I hugged her again, and her arms squeezed my sides. "This is good for now," I said. "But maybe later, can we go see the butterflies?"

"You got it, love."

⚭

The butterflies turned out to be incredible. There weren't just real butterflies in cases, but huge models of caterpillars and cocoons, with parts that lit up and moved, showing how everything worked to change wormy little bugs into a beautiful winged creatures.

And better yet, watching the gigantic wings of a butterfly model gave me a sound idea for the tornado machine. All of a sudden, I couldn't wait to get back to school and work on sound production. We were more than halfway through February, which meant the show's debut was two weeks away, but all of our sounds had to be turned in a week ahead of time, so I had until Friday to get it done. My new idea promised to blow the sound team away. If I could only get it to work.

36

AUDITORY MEMORY

THE THING ABOUT SOUND IS, OUR BRAINS LIKE TO PUT A LABEL on any noise we hear more than once. That's called auditory memory. And according to what I read online, our mental libraries for sound are always growing. Meaning, every new sound we hear gets added to the library and given a name. But when a sound changes, when it doesn't *sound* the way it used to, our brains get all mixed up.

That's why it took Val a while to get used to his hearing aids when he first got them. With a hearing aid, everything sounds different. A cow doesn't sound like a cow anymore, at least not to your brain. The hearing aids change the cow's *moo* just a tiny bit, so that it takes your brain longer to recognize it. You have to learn the new cow sound and retrain your brain.

Auditory memory is also what makes it really hard to fool people into thinking they're hearing a tornado when there is no tornado. If the sound you make is just a little off, people can't recognize the sound at all. They might think they're hearing the ocean, or an airplane, or some other sound in their sound library. But with the new idea from the butterfly wings, I thought I might be able to pull it off.

During lunch on Monday, I went to the auditorium and worked on my design, cutting careful wings from cardboard scraps. It didn't take long to build up a pile.

Jake saw what I was up to and squatted next to me. "Something new for the tornado?"

I covered my work with my arms. "It's a surprise."

"I guess you're a sound nerd after all," he said. Then he bumped my arm with his. Since the dance, it felt like we had a secret language all our own. The arm bump meant "Good job. You can do it."

Every day that week, I made a little progress on the machine, in between practicing with Mrs. Smith and learning my sound cues for all my other sounds. I'd started with a small black fan—the metal kind with two speeds and a wire cage— but the fan wasn't just a fan anymore. Thanks to the butterflies, the cage sported wings around the rim and a cardboard funnel at the center. The end of the funnel was covered in mesh and long strips of ribbon and plastic. When it was off, the fan looked like a winged flower with a colorful ribbon snout.

By lunch on Thursday, I was ready to test the machine for the first time. Jake joined me. While he watched, I crossed my fingers and flipped the fan's switch to low. A sound something like a tornado filled the backstage. After a minute, I turned it off.

"Wow!" Jake said. "It's too slow, but it's really close to a tornado." His face was a mask of disbelief. "How did you do that?"

"These wings, all around here, they flutter so fast, it sounds like wind rushing," I explained, pointing out the different parts of the machine and how all of the little noises added up to the sound of a tornado to our brains. "And when we turn it to high, it should be just right. But I want to make sure it's ready first. I think it needs a couple more wings to be perfect."

"Cool." He bumped his shoulder into my shoulder to emphasize just how cool he thought my invention was. Which sounds awkward, I know. But it was actually really nice.

⊚⊚

That night, I tossed in my bed, too excited about the tornado machine to sleep. I was going to show it to the entire sound team the next day at lunch—our deadline for new sounds. Except for Jake, no one had any idea that I'd cracked the tornado sound. As far as they knew, I'd failed, and we were stuck with the dreaded substitute for real sound effects: a tape recording.

I sat up and rearranged my pillows for the hundredth time, and a noise filtered in from the hall, loud enough to hear over Cori's snoring: Dad's voice, muffled but urgent. I slipped out of my bed and snuck across the floor, taking care to avoid the squeaky spots. When I pressed my ear to the door, Mom's voice came through loud and clear.

"What if it doesn't go down?"

Dad responded, but his voice was too deep to understand through a thick wooden door.

A floorboard creaked. "I don't know," Mom said, her

voice rising. "I just thought this once, things would go our way. And now, with a fever—"

"It's going to be fine." Now Dad's voice was close enough to make me jump. "The cancer isn't back. It's probably just an infection like last time. We'll stay on top of it like we always do, and he'll be all right. I promise."

"You don't know that," Mom said.

More creaks. And then a sound like coughing, only quieter, with gasps in between each cough. "It's okay." Dad's voice was distant again. And that's when I realized the sound I heard was Mom crying. She was outside, crying in the hall, while Val slept in their room.

I crept back to my bed, suddenly anxious for the warmth of my comforter. With the fluffy blanket pulled up to my chin, I thought about what I'd heard. Val had a fever. It seemed like it wasn't high enough to be an emergency, but still, it was bad enough to make Mom cry. And that was more than enough to make me worry.

❀

In the morning, I watched Mom like a hawk, but she didn't give anything away about what had happened during the night, and I was too afraid to ask. I was so distracted I ended up late, and Mrs. Ravelli had to wait while I raced around the apartment, gathering last-minute supplies for the tornado machine. "Thyme!" she called as I rooted around in Dad's desk drawers. His plastic report covers would add the perfect slippery rustle to the tornado's sound.

"I'm coming!"

"We have to go. You make us late, Thyme." She held the door open, waiting.

"I have to say good-bye to Val."

"He's still sleeping, *bambina. Vai!*"

"Okay, okay!" I made a quick wish for Val and hurried out the door.

On the way downstairs, I stayed on my tiptoes past Mr. Lipinsky's door. I didn't want to see him. I wasn't going to give him another chance to say horrible things to me.

By the time I hustled up the steps at MS 221, my nerves were jangling. In a few hours, I would find out what everyone thought of my machine, which made me feel like smiling and barfing at the same time. So I tried not to think about it, especially while I was waiting for Mrs. Harris to dismiss us for lunch. Jake must have noticed how I felt, because he nailed me with a ball of paper and gave me a thumbs-up when I scowled at him.

At lunch, he walked with me to the auditorium. "Ready to blow everybody away?"

I swatted his shoulder and he laughed, and then we were there. I dragged the tornado machine out of hiding, and Jake called for everyone to come over, and my heart started thumping so loud, I could hear it in my ears. Amelia and Davis were there. Lizzie and Emily, too, grinning her megawatt smile.

"What have we got here?" Mrs. Smith asked.

"This is the Tornado Two Thousand."

The other kids giggled at the name, but Mrs. Smith just said, "Well, let's hear it."

A flutter of nerves made me freeze for a second.

Then I flipped the fan's single switch to HIGH, and the blades inside the metal cage whirred to life. A roar built in the air—a fluttering, whipping roar, with the dry rustle of leaves and a deep, howling undertone. To my ears, it sounded just like a tornado should. And judging by the smiling faces around me, my machine sounded just like a tornado to them, too.

But then a flap of cardboard flew off the fan and whipped into the crowd. *Oh no.*

Mrs. Smith spread her arms wide. "Everyone, get back!"

I reached for the switch, but Jake grabbed my arm. "It's not safe," he shouted as another part flew off, and then another. Bits of the Tornado Two Thousand flung in every direction. Kids ran every which way. I rammed straight into another girl and fell. Here I was, thinking that maybe I was figuring things out. I must have been kidding myself. I'd wanted so badly to do this one thing. And I'd failed. Completely, totally failed.

Suddenly, the stuttering sound of the tornado cut off. Mr. Calhoun had pulled the plug. His mouth was pinched, and I hung my head, waiting for him to yell at me for making such a mess of everything.

"Thyme. You need to come with me immediately."

His voice was calm, gentle even.

"What?" I looked up. Mr. Calhoun had that look on his face, the one people got when they were acting like everything was okay but things were really not okay.

Lizzie started walking toward me, but I kept my eyes on Mr. Calhoun.

He pointed to the back of the auditorium, by the doors.

Mrs. Ravelli was standing there with her scarf in her hands. She spotted me looking and waved. A little rush of panic rolled up my spine.

"Who's that?" Lizzie said.

I snatched my book bag off the floor. "I have to go," I said. Then I hopped off the stage.

"Is everything okay?" Jake called after me, and I felt bad for not stopping.

I don't know, I thought. *I don't know.*

I raced up the aisle to Mrs. Ravelli and led her outside the auditorium, where we could talk.

"What are you doing here?" I asked. That's when I noticed the bright spots of color in her cheeks, and the way she twisted her scarf in her hands. "Mrs. Ravelli? What's wrong?"

"It's little Val," she said. "We must hurry, *bambina*. Little Val is in the hospital."

Then I heard it. The panic in her voice. That was a sound I knew by heart.

37

LOST

WHEN A CANCER PATIENT GETS SICK, THEY GET REALLY SICK. Their skin turns kind of yellow. Their cheeks get hollow. They suddenly look as close to death as they really are. The last time Val had been in the hospital for chemotherapy, he hadn't looked as bad as a lot of the other patients there. But he wasn't himself. He was thin. Frail. A ghost.

When Mrs. Ravelli and I arrived at the hospital, Mom and Dad were standing in the hall with a heavyset doctor in a white coat. He had a beard like Dad's and a tablet in his hands.

"We've started the first course of antibiotics," the doctor said, "but given that his chest films aren't completely clear and his temperature is so high, we'd like to observe him overnight."

Mom and Dad nodded. Then they saw me standing there.

"Thank you, Dr. Everett," Mom said, saying good-bye without introducing me.

She and Dad walked over to us. "Your sister's in with Val," Dad said. Then he nodded toward the door, like I should go in, too. It was another room where I didn't know what to expect.

Mrs. Ravelli set her hand on my shoulder and squeezed. "I will see you later, *bambina*."

I nodded and went inside.

The lights were turned low. Val was asleep in the narrow hospital bed on the other side of the room, beneath a giant painted mural of Winnie-the-Pooh. Long, clear tubes trailed from the crook of his arm to a stand beside the bed. Machines crowded close to the stand, their displays full of ominous lights and numbers, none of which meant anything to me beyond the reality that my brother was sick.

Cori was in a chair next to Val's bed. She sat up when I walked over. She didn't say anything. She just gave me a hug. After a long minute, she wiped at her eyes and said, "He'll be okay," like she had the power to decide.

"But the doctor said his films weren't good. And his fever is too high."

She frowned. "Yeah, I know. I'm gonna get a Coke, okay? I'll send Dad in here."

"No, I'm fine by myself."

She touched my shoulder. "You sure?" I nodded, and her eyes met mine. She looked as scared as I felt. The chest films were a bad sign. Maybe the 3F8 wasn't working. Maybe the cancer had come back. Even if it was just a really bad infection, Val's body was so weak from all the treatments he'd been through that he could have trouble fighting it off. He could die.

After she left, I stood right next to Val's bed and looked at his face. His bones seemed to stick out too much all of a sudden. I ran my fingers over his arm, and he stirred in his sleep, furrowing his brow like he was about to open his eyes and ask me a tough question. I would have been happy to answer one right about then, but he didn't wake up.

The sky outside grew dark, while Mom and Dad took turns watching over Val and helping the nurses. After so many trips to the hospital, they knew how everything worked. Val's temperature didn't go back to normal, but it didn't climb any higher.

"It's a holding pattern," Dad said as he rubbed at his eyes late that night. "We won't know more until something changes. Why don't you try to get some rest."

I let him tuck me into one of the two reclining chairs in Val's room. Most hospitals had them—a chair that looked regular but stretched out so that you could stay in the room overnight. I lay there for a long time, watching Val, hearing the nurses come and go, thinking I would never fall asleep.

Then it was morning, and Cori was shaking my shoulder. "Come on, T. Time to get up."

I sat up quickly, wondering what had changed, but Val was still in the bed. His face was so pale, it barely stood out against the sheets, but there was a bright red spot on each of his cheeks, like clown makeup, and an oxygen mask over his mouth and nose.

"What time is it?"

"Close to lunch," Cori said as she stretched her arms over her head.

"Where's Mom?"

"Outside," Cori said. "I crashed in the other chair, but she and Dad were up all night."

We went out into the hall. Mrs. Ravelli was there with my parents.

"It's going to be a while until we know more," Dad said. "It doesn't make sense for you girls to stay here all day. Val's stable, so you're going home with Mrs. Ravelli for now."

Mrs. Ravelli gave me an encouraging nod, but Cori's face darkened. "No way," she said. "You can't make me leave."

"Honey, remember what we talked about," Mom told her, and Cori softened. I couldn't believe it. What could they have possibly talked about that would make Cori give up like that?

Dad had a bag in his hands. I realized it was my book bag.

He handed it to Mrs. Ravelli, and she gave me a little wave. I was supposed to follow her like a good little girl. But I had that feeling again, that there was something Mom and Dad weren't telling me. And if I walked out right then like I was supposed to, I might never know the truth. So I stood my ground.

"Why do I have to leave?" I asked. "What's happening to Val? Is something wrong?"

"It's nothing," Mom said, way too quickly. "We just want you to get some rest."

"I don't need any rest," I said. "I slept in the chair."

Dad smiled. "I know you want to be tough for your brother, but trust us—"

"Trust *you*? You never tell me what's going on!"

Cori's mouth fell open, and Mom and Dad looked at each

other in surprise. They could think what they wanted. I was tired of being lied to.

Just then, Dr. Everett walked up to us. "Good morning, folks," he said. "It looks like we can fit Val in for a set of scans a little earlier than I thought."

"What?" I said. Mom and Dad hadn't said anything about scans to us.

Mom glanced at me. "Maybe we should talk inside," she told the doctor, and he smiled like that sounded just fine to him. Well, I wasn't going to let them leave me out anymore.

"What's wrong with my brother?" I asked, looking right at Dr. Everett. I hoped that maybe he was under some medical obligation to tell me the truth.

"We're not sure yet, but we hope to know more soon," he answered carefully, with a smile that said he didn't expect me to understand how complicated all of this was.

I changed tactics.

"Is he rejecting the 3F8? Or is the cancer back? Is that why he's having scans? You need to tell me what's going on. *Now.*"

The doctor raised his eyebrows, while Mom and Dad stared at me like they were really seeing me for the first time.

"Mr. and Mrs. Owens?" Dr. Everett said.

Mom just stood there, but Dad finally said, "All right. First, we're still waiting on the HAMA results, but we don't think the fever is from Val rejecting the 3F8. So far, his immune system's been too weak to fight the antibodies. And yes, he's having scans to check for any signs that the cancer is back. Hopefully they won't find anything."

"So it might just be an infection?"

"It very well might be," the doctor said. "But we have to rule out a relapse first."

"What happens if the scans are clear?" I had this crazy hope that maybe, if Val's cancer hadn't come back, it would mean that we were done, and the New York experiment would be over.

"If all goes according to plan, your brother can continue receiving 3F8 for up to two years," Dr. Everett said, like it was the best news in the world.

Mom let out a deep breath while the words settled in the air.

Two years.

Two years.

As soon as the words clicked, all of those good feelings I'd been having about my new friends and the play vanished. I couldn't stay in New York for two years. I'd thought a few months wouldn't be that bad, but look at what had happened with the tornado machine. It was a total failure. I didn't belong here. I wasn't ready to say good-bye to my life—Shani, Grandma Kay, the secret garden we'd planted together, my room, our *house*.

Dr. Everett excused himself, and Mom and Dad said good-bye.

Then Dad kneeled in front of me. He was so tall, his head was still level with mine, even down on one knee. "Go home and get some rest. We'll call you if anything changes, I promise."

I looked at Mom. She gave me a small smile and nodded.

Mrs. Ravelli took my arm. Numb, I followed her out of the hospital. At first Cori tried to talk to me, but after three non-responses, she gave up. All I could think was that I'd done everything wrong. I'd let myself get close to people when I should have been focusing on getting home. And now Val was sick, and I couldn't leave, when the last thing I wanted was to stay.

☉☉

On the way home, Mrs. Ravelli stopped to pick up doughnuts, but I wasn't hungry. As soon as we got to the apartment, I called Shani. The phone rang and rang, even though it was Saturday afternoon, which meant it was still Saturday morning in California. Someone should have been home, but no one picked up. So I left her a message.

"It's me," I said. "Things are bad. Things are so, so bad, and I know I really messed up. So please call me as soon as you get this. I need to talk to you."

When I got off the phone, Mrs. Ravelli was waiting. "Maybe you like a hot chocolate?"

I shook my head, went straight to my bed, and fell asleep. When I woke up, the room was dark. Cori was still passed out on her bed. I left her sleeping and walked to the kitchen.

Mrs. Ravelli looked up from the pot she was stirring. "*Ciao, bambina.* Are you hungry? I made sauce." She held up the spoon, and my stomach growled. "Also, your friend called while you were asleep," she said.

I snapped awake. "Shani called?"

"No, the girl Emily."

"Oh." I didn't want to hear from Emily. I wanted Shani to call me back. The idea that she might never talk to me again made tears spring to my eyes. How could I have been so dumb?

"*Bambina*," Mrs. Ravelli said, reaching for me, but I pulled away. I didn't want her comfort. I wanted to leave all of this behind. I wanted things to go back to normal.

I went back to my room. Cori was awake and writing something in her journal. She'd been doing that more lately, just writing quietly instead of blasting music and painting everything in sight. It didn't make sense, how she'd changed so much since her big talk with Mom. She probably even thought it was a good thing that we might stay in New York for two years.

I grabbed the Thyme Jar and dumped the paper slips out on my bed.

"What are you doing?" she asked.

"Can you just leave me alone? I'm trying to count."

She watched as I sorted through the papers, but she didn't say anything else.

Seventy-nine, eighty, eighty-one . . .

The phone rang.

"It's for me!" I shouted, running for the phone. I knew it was Shani. She wouldn't leave me hanging when I needed her. My heart leapt when I picked up the handset. Sure enough, the number on the screen was hers.

I pressed the phone to my ear. "Hello?"

"Thyme? Is that you?" It was Shani's mom.

"It's me," I said as a really bad feeling settled over me. "Where's Shani?"

There was a pause. "Oh, baby girl. She wants to talk to you, she really does, but this is so hard on her. Is everything okay? Your message sounded like it was an emergency."

"Val's in the hospital," I said numbly. Shani wasn't going to call me after all.

"Oh, Thyme," her mom said. "I am so, so sorry to hear that. Look, I will get Shani to call you just as soon as she gets home. She stayed over at Jenny's last night. I think it's just been easier for her to be over there instead of here. Ever since that For Sale sign went up in front of your house, it's been hard for her. I mean, we all knew this might happen, but now that it says 'sold,' well . . . she's not taking it well. Speaking of, how are you holding up, sweetheart?"

"I'm fine," I said, because that's what I always said, but my mind was racing.

There was a For Sale sign . . . in front of *our* house.

The truth hit with a smack. *They sold our house.*

My parents sold our house, and they didn't even tell me. I was stupid to think I could stay and finish that dumb tornado machine. I should have left weeks ago—I had plenty of time saved up. It had to be over a hundred and fifty hours. That was almost a week.

Shani's mom was still talking about Val and staying strong and seeing us soon when I hung up. I didn't even say good-bye. I just went straight back to my room and stuffed the paper slips back in the Thyme Jar. Then I hefted the jar into my arms. It was heavy, but not too heavy.

"Where are you going?" Cori asked. With her eyes clear of makeup for once, she looked just like Mom.

"I'm going home."

She made a face. "Don't be stupid."

"It's not stupid! It's what I want," I said, "so stop telling me what to do!"

"Whoa." She held her hands up. "I'm not telling you what to do, T. I just think you look really upset right now. You should calm down. We can talk if you want to."

"What are we going to talk about? How Mom and Dad sold our house and didn't even tell us?"

She winced like she hadn't known either.

Before she could manage a comeback, I hurried to the front door and set the Thyme Jar on the floor. Mrs. Ravelli came out of the kitchen as I stuffed my arms into my winter coat. I heaved the jar back into my arms. "Can you take me to the hospital?"

"Thyme, *bambina*. What is it? You can tell me."

But I couldn't tell Mrs. Ravelli. I couldn't tell her how I'd hidden Val from everyone so I could avoid being cancer boy's sister. That, more than anything, I just wanted to go home.

I snatched a MetroCard from the bowl on the counter and jammed it into my pocket. "I'll get there myself." I brushed past her, out the front door, and down the stairs, gripping the Thyme Jar like my life depended on it. But before I even reached the third-floor landing, Mr. Lipinsky's door flew open.

"You there." He wagged his finger at me. "I need to have a word with you, young lady."

I ignored him and hefted the Thyme Jar in my hands.

"Thyme! I'm talking to you," he shouted, and I spun to face him.

"You've always wanted us gone, right? Well, I'm leaving!" Then I rushed down the stairs as quickly as I could. By the time I reached the bottom, the jar was growing heavy in my arms. Two blocks later, I had to stop and rest on a stoop. After fifteen grueling minutes of trudging down the streets with my arms on fire, the smell of roasted nuts greeted me.

The 86th Street entrance to the subway loomed ahead— the green line, the one that would take me to the hospital. Mrs. Ravelli and I had made the same trip after she picked me up from school the day before, but I'd never ridden the subway by myself.

I shifted the Thyme Jar in my arms for the hundredth time and hurried down the steps, careful not to drop it. Then I heard the screech of a train arriving below. Other people rushed past me, so I swiped my MetroCard until it worked, forced my way through the turnstile, and took the steps two at a time, the jar lurching in my arms with each hop.

When I got to the platform, the train was still there.

I checked the sign. It was a downtown train.

"*Stand clear of the closing doors,*" the speakers warned.

I slipped on board just before the doors slid shut. The train lurched forward, and I collapsed into a seat, my arms screaming for relief. The windows went black as the train picked up speed.

The hospital is on the green line, two stops away: 77th Street, then 68th Street.

Then I could get off, and I only had to walk a couple more blocks to the hospital. Light flashed in the train car's windows. The green and white tiles of a station blinked by, but the train didn't stop, and the chill of panic crawled up my neck.

I strained to read the subway map on the other side of the car, but there were too many heads in front of it. The train stopped, and the conductor's voice crackled over the speaker. It sounded like he said *59th Street*, which made no sense. I was supposed to take the train for two stops, and get off at *68th Street*, like I had with Mrs. Ravelli.

Panicked, I climbed to my feet, swaying as the train took off again. The floor rocked beneath me, but I wove closer to the doors, the Thyme Jar slipping in my sweaty hands. The train started to slow down again, and my eyes caught a word on the lighted sign above my head.

EXPRESS.

I was on an express train! The number 5 train, when I should have been on the number 6. The 4, 5, and 6 were all green lines, but the express trains skipped lots of stops.

The doors slid open, and I dashed for the platform, desperate to get off the train before I ended up on the other side of the city. The sign up above said Grand Central. I stumbled into a crush of people and followed them up a steep set of stairs. I didn't know how I would find my way. I only knew that I needed light. And air. I needed to get out of the subway *immediately*.

A ratty old man was perched at the top of the stairs. "Whatcha got there, missy?" he said. His fingers swiped the jar's glass. "Come back," he called, cackling as I stumbled forward.

Suddenly, a hand landed on my shoulder.

I jumped, but thankfully, the hand belonged to a policeman.

"I'm lost," I sobbed as I slid to the floor. The Thyme Jar clinked against the concrete.

"It's okay," the officer said. His eyes were warm, his voice a relief. "You're going to be all right. Just try to breathe. Is there someone I can call?"

I nodded, wiping the tears from my eyes. "Mrs. Ravelli. You can call Mrs. Ravelli."

38

THE TRUTH

AFTER MRS. RAVELLI AND CORI PICKED ME UP AT GRAND CENTRAL station, we went back to the hospital. When we got to Val's room, the blinds on his windows were drawn.

I looked at Mrs. Ravelli. "Is it okay if I go in by myself?"

"Yes, you go. We wait here." She took a seat on the bench. Cori sat next to her. Shockingly, Cori hadn't said much about me running off. She just gave me a little nod as I turned to Val's door.

This was it. The moment of truth.

I pushed the door handle with my elbow and carried the Thyme Jar inside. Dad was asleep in the reclining chair by the windows. Val was lying on his bed with his face turned away. Mom was sitting on the edge of the bed, holding his hand. She looked up when I walked in.

"Thyme! What happened? Mrs. Ravelli said you were hysterical."

"You sold our house," I blurted out. My eyes were hot with tears, but I had to know the truth. "I talked to Shani's mom. She said there's a sign in the yard and everything. How could you do that?"

Mom tucked Val's hand under the blanket and stood up. Then she approached me very carefully, like she was the one walking on eggshells this time. "I'm so sorry that you had to find out this way. I just—" Her voice caught. "I guess I didn't really believe it was happening, myself. Push came to shove, and we thought maybe we could just rent it, but then . . ."

She shook her head, blinking back tears. Then she wiped at her eyes, and I saw that selling our house hurt her, too. That she didn't have a choice, either.

None of us did.

We'd all come to New York for Val, because that's what he had needed to keep the cancer from coming back—and that getting cancer in the first place hadn't been his choice, either.

She reached for me, but I stepped back. I wasn't ready to let go yet. It was too hard, the idea of leaving it all behind.

"You should have told me," I said.

Mom nodded, her lips pinched like she was trying to hold herself together. I knew that feeling. It was filling up my chest, too, making it hurt.

Behind her, Dad stirred and sat up.

"I'm so sorry, honey," Mom said. "I thought I was protecting you girls by keeping all of this as far away from you as I could. I didn't want you worrying about your brother. I wanted you to have your own lives. I see now that I was wrong. I should have trusted you."

Dad rested his hands on her shoulders, and she took a deep breath. "Your mom is right," he said. "We should have told you what was going on. We're all a part of this family."

"But Val is the broken part," I said, thinking back to what Dad had said about our family being like a printing press. How Val was the broken part, the one that counted.

"Gosh, I can't believe you remember that," Dad said. "That's the thing, though. You need all the parts to make the press work. All of them together. That means you, too."

I looked at their faces. Exhausted. Worried. I wanted to take all of those worries away for them. I knew then that I would still trade every good grade, every good thing, anything for Val to get better. Even Shani. Even home.

"I couldn't have done this without you," Mom said, resting her palm against my cheek. "Thyme, you're the glue. You're the one Val talks to when he's sad. You're so strong and so brave, taking on this whole new place the way you have. You make me so proud."

Hearing those words, something clicked into place. I thought that maybe the missing piece wasn't San Diego after all. It was knowing that I counted. Seeing that I belonged.

I looked down at the Thyme Jar in my hands. There I was, thinking I could bribe my parents to move back to California with a few measly days of time, when what my little brother needed most was to stay in New York. That's when I realized that I wasn't going anywhere. And neither was my family. I glanced at Val, and the truth settled over my heart.

We weren't leaving.

We were staying.

"I just . . . I want to give my time to Val," I said, my voice wavering.

"Oh, honey," Mom said. "What a sweet thing to do."

She reached for the jar, and I let it go.

☺☺

Mom and Dad said that with how things were going, it was best if Cori and I stayed. So we said good-bye to Mrs. Ravelli and waited into the night. Val's fever dipped and wavered, but kept coming back. He woke up for a few minutes at a time, but he was confused about where he was and he kept pulling his oxygen mask off even though the nurse said he needed it to breathe.

When it was my turn to sit by his bed, I ran my fingers over his arm, up and down, just the way he liked. I watched him sleep and worried that he wouldn't wake up. Was that how it would happen? Would he just shut his eyes and never open them again? The idea seemed impossible, so I shoved it down, far, far away from my heart. And from Val.

There was only one thing that I knew for sure: I didn't want to leave him. And I didn't want him to leave me, either.

Early the next morning, Dr. Everett came by with an update. This time, Mom and Dad called us into the hall with them. "He's negative for HAMA, so that's good. We know the fever isn't his body rejecting the antibodies," the doctor said. But I barely had time to feel happy about that, because he kept talking. "I must caution you, however, that we're still waiting for the results from his scans to see if there's any evidence of a relapse. For now, we're proceeding as if these symptoms are from an infection. However, this particular infection seems resistant to the current medication, so we're switching to a different course of antibiotics. We hope to see improvements within twenty-four hours."

"Do you think the cancer's back?" Cori asked, and I swear we all stopped breathing.

"There's no way to know yet," Dr. Everett said. "Not until we read the scans." The way he said it, it sounded like he wasn't making any promises.

Dr. Everett excused himself, and we just stood there. A man rolled past us in a wheelchair, his head dangling to the side. The nurse pushing the chair smiled, but it looked like she was rolling a dead man around. I crowded closer to Mom.

Suddenly, Cori threw her hands into the air. "This is bull," she said. "There's got to be something else they can do. *Something.*"

Mom squeezed her shoulder. "They're doing everything they can. We just have to ride this out."

"I wish—" Dad said, his voice breaking. He pressed his fingers over his eyes. "I wish I had something better to tell you girls. If I could trade places with your brother—"

Dad's knees gave out, and Mom dropped to the floor to wrap her arms around him.

Cori and I both burst into tears and joined them, arms pressed around each other as we cried. We stayed like that for a while, in a family huddle on the linoleum floor.

I was the one who broke the spell. "I'm sorry," I whispered. Because I was the one who'd wanted to go home so badly. I was the one who'd considered what might happen if Val's treatment failed, when I should have put every ounce of my energy into believing in it.

Mom squeezed me harder. "It's not your fault, honey. This is no one's fault."

I wanted to believe her, but that's not how I felt.

∽∽

The light changed from dark to light and back again. It was Monday, three days since Val had arrived at the hospital. That night, I looked at the Thyme Jar sitting on the counter next to Val's bed, and the idea of counting hours or days seemed impossible. All that mattered was keeping Val alive.

I worried that I was too late figuring out what mattered. Too late choosing my brother. It was funny how I'd thought my worries would go away if I could just make it home. But I would have the same problems no matter where I went, because I would still be me, and worries attach to people, not places.

Mom caught me staring at the jar, running my fingers over the glass again and again.

"I'm scared," I said.

"Me too, honey." She looked at the jar. "I'm sorry I let you get away from me for so long. Tell me everything." So I told her, and she listened. It felt good to let it all out. I told her about the secret garden Grandma and I had planted for her, and about the play, and sound production, and how Emily and Lizzie had fallen apart but pieced themselves back together again. Then I told her about Shani, and how I didn't think we would be the same anymore. That I didn't know how to be friends from so far away.

"Maybe you can visit her for spring break," Mom said, surprising me. "I know it's not much, but we all deserve a little normal once this is over . . ." Her eyes lingered on Val. I knew she was thinking the same thing I was: that I only wanted this to end one way, with Val safe and healthy again.

"I'm sorry this has been so hard on you," she said. "I wish I could kiss it and make it better, but it hasn't been that kind of year, has it?" She looked so sad, sitting there waiting for Val to get better. But she always stuck it out, no matter what. She was the toughest person I'd ever known, and I regretted every horrible thought I'd had about her. I'd missed her so much since Val got sick, and shutting her out had only made me miss her even more.

I leaned over to give her a kiss on the cheek. "Better?" I asked, and she smiled through her tears.

"My little girl," she said. "When did you get so grown up?"

I made a face. "Oh, I'm still a goofball," I said, though I knew better. Inside, I felt different. The homesickness was gone. No matter what happened or where I lived, I would never be the same again. I wasn't so sure that was a bad thing, either.

Mom smiled, teary-eyed. "You know what? You should call Shani."

"Isn't it too late?" There was no clock in Val's room, but it had been dark for hours.

"Not in California." She handed me her phone. According to the screen, it was almost eleven, which meant it was only eight in San Diego.

I looked at Val. "Are you sure?"

"Yes. She'll be happy to hear from you."

I nodded and went into the hall. Then I just stared at the phone for at least a full minute. What would I say? What would *she* say?

When I finally dialed, Shani answered on the first ring. "Thyme, is that you?"

"Hey." I wasn't sure where to begin.

"I'm so, so sorry I wasn't here," she said. "I didn't know about Val. Is he okay?"

"We don't know yet."

"This is the worst! I'm sorry I gave you such a hard time. It was just the For Sale sign, and—"

"I didn't know," I said. "But I do now, and I'm sorry, too. And there's something else. I . . . I might not be coming back for a long time. We have to stay here as long as Val can be in the trial."

"Oh." She was quiet for a few seconds. "I think I already guessed that."

"But Mom said I can come visit for spring break."

Shani said, "Yes!" I could hear her smiling over the phone. We were okay. And that was enough.

☙☙

Dr. Everett came back first thing on Tuesday morning with an update. Mom and Dad and Cori and I gathered in the hall again, only this time, we already had our arms around each other. We were a wall against bad news. As long as we stuck together, nothing terrible could happen to Val.

Dr. Everett's expression was grim. He glanced at his tablet, and a sick, tumbling feeling filled my stomach. The cancer might really be back. And it could be worse than before. Val might die, not at some distant point in the future, but then. *Now.*

"According to Val's scans, there is no evidence of a relapse," he said.

For a second, no one moved. Then Cori shouted, and Mom and Dad hugged each other, pulling me tight up against them. Strangely, we were all crying again—only this time, happy tears.

Dr. Everett smiled. "While I don't want to put a damper on this very good news, there does seem to be a significant infection in Val's lungs, most likely a secondary infection due to a virus. As you know, this is common in patients with weakened immune systems." He went on about the medicines they were giving Val to fight the infection for him, because his body wasn't doing a good job on its own.

Dad wiped at his eyes. "What's next?" he asked.

"If he can't get his oxygen levels up, we'll have to drain the fluid from his lungs," the doctor said. "I wish I had better news about that. But the truth is, the rest is up to him."

I didn't want to hear any more, so I went back to Val's room and listened to him breathe instead. I knew he had it in him to fight. I leaned close to his ear and told him that I was waiting to ride the subway with him. That I needed him to try harder to get better, and that I loved him.

At some point, I fell asleep with my head on the edge of his bed. I woke up when a nurse bumped my arm. She was taking Val's temperature again. She checked the line next to his bed and tapped a number on her tablet. The sun was brighter in the room. It had to be hours since the doctor's update.

When she walked away, a beam of sunlight caught Val's cheek. His eyelashes twitched. And then his eyes opened. His face was still puffy from all the medicines, and his skin was waxy with exhaustion, but his eyes were as blue as ever.

"T. You're here," he said like he was seeing the best thing on earth.

"Of course," I answered. "Where else would I be?"

39

BREAK A LEG

AT THE END OF THE WEEK, FEBRUARY TURNED TO MARCH, AND WE got to take Val home. He was still weak, but strong enough to shout, "Cake!" when we walked into the apartment on Friday afternoon and found one of Mrs. Ravelli's Italian cream cakes waiting on the dining table.

"Oh, how I owe you," Mom said, embracing her.

When they parted, Mrs. Ravelli blinked hard and clapped her hands. "*Ay!* There is no crying on this happy day." Then she walked over to me. "There is something for you, too. Your friend with the hair stopped by while you were gone." She winked and pointed at a box sitting by the door.

Inside the box were the parts for the Tornado Two Thousand.

Plus a note for me: *I hope you're okay,* it said. *Mrs. Smith wants to use the tornado tape, but this way you'll have all the parts. Just in case. Your friend, Jake.*

Dad looked over my shoulder. "What's this?"

"It's for the sound machine I've been working on. For the play at school."

"Shoot," he said. "Did we miss it?"

293

"No, it's this weekend. It opens tomorrow."

His face brightened. "What do you want to do? I'm up for an eleventh-hour save if you are." I thought about how I felt when the machine fell apart at school. How I figured I would never go back there again. I'd told myself that I didn't care, only that wasn't true anymore. I cared about the machine, and the play. I didn't want to let anyone down—including myself.

I looked at Dad. "Let's fix it," I said, and hoped for the best.

◎◎

Early on Saturday morning, while everyone else slept in, Dad and I worked on the Tornado Two Thousand. The parts were littered across the carpet when there was a knock at the door.

"I'll get it," Dad said, climbing to his feet. "You keep working."

We had the fan and most of the machine reassembled, but I was still trying to figure out how to keep everything intact. The packing tape stuck to the fan's metal, but wouldn't stay stuck to the paper I'd used for the wings and streamers. Cutting holes in the parts hadn't worked, either. They just tore apart at the hole when we switched the fan on high.

"Oh, hello there," Dad said.

I looked up to see Mr. Lipinsky standing in our doorway. But he looked totally different—his hair was neatly combed, his trousers pressed. No purple robe in sight.

"Good morning," he said, extending his hand to Dad.

They shook, and Dad raised his eyebrows at me, like he was counting on some really interesting theatrics to follow.

"I believe I owe your daughter an apology," Mr. Lipinsky said, keeping his eyes on Dad.

"Sure, of course. Thyme, can you come here?"

I walked over to them, but I kept my arms crossed so that Mr. Lipinsky would know not to mess with me. But then he smiled, for the first time ever. A big, full, wrinkly smile. "I'm sorry for all the trouble I've caused you folks. And I'm especially sorry to you, Thyme. What I said before was out of line. I really do hope your brother gets better soon."

The way he said it, I knew he really meant it. He knew what it was to lose someone you love. He'd lost his wife and Sylvie—but we still had Val.

I gave him a smile, and he looked relieved. "Thank you," I said, and Dad added, "We appreciate that. It looks like he's out of the woods for now, but there's still a long road to go."

Mr. Lipinsky nodded and looked down at his hands for a moment. Then he glanced at the gobs of parts spread out across our floor. "Is this the machine you were going on about outside my door?"

"Yeah, if we can get it to work."

"We're close." Dad was trying to be encouraging, but at the rate we were going, I didn't know if we'd make it in time for the show.

"Everything keeps flying apart when we turn the fan on," I explained.

"So I heard," Mr. Lipinsky said. "How about I grab my toolbox, and we'll get this sorted out?"

Dad looked at me. "I sure think we could use the help."

I nodded, and Mr. Lipinsky went to get his toolbox. When he came back, he said, "Back in my day, we rigged everything by hand—lights, props, you name it. We didn't have all the fancy machines they have now. I'll never forget this one night I spent crouched in the eaves, clapping coconuts together for a director who thought it sounded just like horse hooves."

At that moment, Mr. Lipinsky's eyes twinkled the way Mrs. Ravelli's always did, and I was glad he was there with us. "Let me see here," he said, digging in the toolbox. "I think I have just the thing to fix this contraption of yours." And as soon as he said the words, I knew he was right.

☙❧

Along the way to MS 221, crocuses were just beginning to appear around the base of the sidewalk trees. Soon, it would get warmer, and the spring flowers would take over. It was March second, four days before Shani's birthday. It was still weird to think I wouldn't be there, but we'd promised to talk. And this time, I knew we would.

When we got to school, the sidewalk was full of parents and students on their way to the show.

"Are you coming in with us?" Mom asked as she helped Val up the marble steps. Cori and Dad were just behind her.

"No. I need to take this backstage first," I said, lifting the Tornado Two Thousand. The Spring Fling production of *The Wizard of Oz* started in fifteen minutes.

"If you want to stay back there with your friends, you should do it," Mom said. I still felt a little embarrassed about spilling my guts to her at the hospital, but she'd made me promise not to hide what I was feeling anymore.

I gave Val a kiss on the cheek and said I'd see them all after the show.

"Break a leg!" Cori said with a grin.

"Not if I can help it," I shot back, though I felt so jittery as I walked to the stage doors that I almost turned around. Costumed kids and teachers lined the hall, but everyone was so busy with last-minute fussing, no one noticed when I pushed the doors open and slipped backstage. Off to the right, a bunch of kids stood in costume, waiting. Including Emily and Lizzie. But Mrs. Smith spotted me first.

"Thyme!" she exclaimed. "Just the girl I was looking for. How are you doing, honey?"

"I'm good," I said, because I really was fine. For the first time in a long time.

Mrs. Smith smiled like she understood all of that and more. "Is that machine of yours ready?" she asked. I nodded and she said, "Let's hear it."

I set the machine on the floor and grabbed the nearest extension cord to plug it in.

Mrs. Smith raised her hands. "Everybody stand back. Just in case."

I flipped the switch, and the sound of the tornado filled the backstage. Thanks to Mr. Lipinsky's stagehand magic—otherwise known as gaffer's tape, the stickiest tape in the universe—every bit of the machine stayed in place. I switched it off, and Mrs. Smith started clapping. Everyone around us did, too. Including Lizzie and Emily.

"Well done," Mrs. Smith said. "Now get that where it's supposed to be. Curtain in *ten*, people! Ten minutes!" She rushed away, and I walked straight over to Lizzie and Emily.

"Where have you been?" Emily said. "I called you but you never called me back." Only she didn't sound angry. She sounded worried.

"Is everything okay?" Lizzie asked.

"I'm sorry I didn't call you back," I said. "I've had a lot going on, and I should have told you guys a long time ago. The truth is, we didn't come here because of my dad's job. My little brother is in a drug trial for cancer patients."

Lizzie gasped and gave me a big hug, but Emily hung back. When Lizzie stepped away, Emily said, "So this has been going on this whole time?"

"Yeah. And I'm sorry. Val got really sick last Friday and ended up in the hospital. That's where I was all week. I'm sorry I didn't tell you before. I understand if you're mad."

"Well, I've got every right to be," Emily said. Then she surprised me by hugging me, too. "I'm sorry about your brother," she whispered.

"No. *I'm* sorry," I said, and she smirked.

"The only thing sorrier will be us if Mrs. Smith catches us ruining Lizzie's makeup with a sobfest," Emily said. "Now get out of here! And break a leg!"

"You too," I said. Then I left to put the tornado machine where it belonged.

◎◎

When I found him, Jake was hunched over a big blanket with a bunch of sound props in front of him, lined up in the order we would need them for the show. Amelia and Davis were set up at another sound station on stage left with the rest of the props.

"Hey," I said, and he looked up.

He smiled when he saw the tornado machine. "I knew you'd figure it out!"

For some reason that made me blush. "Thanks. You want to hear it?"

He shook his head. "Nope. I trust you."

I set the tornado machine in its spot next to the other sound props, and I told Jake I had something else to show him. I led him to the front of the stage and pulled the curtains back a little.

"There he is." I pointed at the crowd. "The kid with the sort of bald head. That's my brother, Val. He's sitting with my parents and my sister. He's been sick . . . with a kind of cancer. But he's getting better." Val's face was beaming at the stage, bright with anticipation. I felt like he was looking right at me, like I could reach out and touch him.

"He looks nice."

"You should try sharing a bathroom with him."

Jake cracked up, and then he leaned over and kissed me on

299

the cheek. My face burned, but I couldn't hide my smile as we walked back to the sound production area.

"I get it, you know," Jake said. "When my dad died, I didn't want to talk about it, either."

"Thanks." I wished there was a better word in the English language than *thanks*. A word that said, "I'm so glad I know you, and you are the best."

Mr. Calhoun swept past us, clipboard in hand, positioning people on their marks for the start of the show. Mrs. Smith was right on his heels.

"What do you say, people? Are we ready to rock this?" she called out.

"What do you say?" Jake asked. "Are you ready?"

I nodded, and he squeezed my hand. The lights went dark, and we all held our breath, waiting for the show to start. For another new beginning. It wasn't perfect. And it wasn't home.

But I was right where I belonged.

ACKNOWLEDGMENTS

THE FIRST TIME I HEARD ABOUT THE CHILDHOOD CANCER CALLED neuroblastoma, I was a new mother living in Park Slope, Brooklyn. A neighbor's son was battling the disease. That morning, I read her blog and cried like I'd never cried before. I couldn't believe the struggle these families faced. I wanted desperately to DO something to help.

Soon enough, my opportunity arose. Another local mom launched a challenge to bake 100,000 cookies to raise funds for childhood cancer research. Her son Liam also suffered from neuroblastoma. I joined the baking effort, meeting in a half-broken rental kitchen on Stuyvesant Avenue and then at the French Culinary Institute. I loved to bake, and supporting Cookies for Kids' Cancer was something I could DO.

Thank you to Cookies for Kids' Cancer for continuing to lead the fight against childhood cancer (readers can support Cookies at www.cookiesforkidscancer.org). It is my great hope that one day the groundbreaking treatments depicted in this book will be outdated, because childhood cancers will be curable. While Memorial Sloan Kettering and 3F8 are real, Val's story is fiction, and any errors in the depiction of his treatment are my own. To Toby, Angelina, Max, Will, and Erin: I tried my best to show your truth.

To my fearless champion and brainstorming partner, Peter Knapp: your faith in me is a gift. From the moment you wrote during the Super Bowl to say you'd just finished reading my pages, I knew we were a match. It's not often that you find someone who shares your exact sensibility in books, and I'm grateful that I have that in you.

To Stacey Barney, whose keen editorial eye shone a light on every opportunity for improvement, thank you for helping me write the best book I could write. I remember our first call, when you asked me what I wanted—not for the book, not in a publisher, but for myself, as an author. I said I wanted to write a damn good book. You held me to it. Thank you also to my publisher, Jennifer Besser, and the entire Penguin team, including Bridget Hartzler, Marikka Tamura, Theresa Evangelista, Kate Meltzer, and Cindy Howle. Special thanks to artist Pascal Campion for the incredible cover art!

To Rebecca Sutton, for your many reads, texts, commiserations, and hugs—thank you so much. I've got your back. For early reads and words of encouragement, thank you to Jen Malone, Dee Romito, Stefanie Wass, April Wall, Hay Farris, and Heidi Schulz. To Tracy Holczer, thank you for your patience with my countless Facebook messages. Thank you to the #MGbetareaders for being the best group of writers on the planet, and to the Sweet Sixteens for giving me a place to vent.

To the Novel Bites, for sharing every step of this process

with so much genuine enthusiasm and celebration (re: wine): Christine Houseworth, Bridget Lai, Léana Lu, Barbara Quinn, Melissa Biren, Michelle Scotti, and Romaine Williamson. I am so lucky to know all of you incredible women!

Thank you to my friends: Jessamyn, Katie, Natasha, Jeff (for the acronyms), Louisa (for loaning me Tate), Colten (for sharing that heart of yours!), Words Bookstore (for being the best indie bookstore ever!), and the librarians at the South Orange library: Ms. Beth, Ms. Keisha, and Ms. Cynthia. You run the best children's library!

There are people in life who help you grow from a messy lump of feelings into someone with purpose. For me, that person is Vince Foote. For every tough critique in studio, every callout, every smile, and every wink of encouragement, THANK YOU FOR BEING MY MENTOR (you'll get the use of CAPS).

There are also people who are a part of your life from the beginning. Marisa, you've been there all the way. You even stuck with me through a hurricane in twenty-degree weather (plus four bottles of wine). Thank you for being my counselor, cheerleader, stylist, reader, sistah, and friend. Yes, I'm writing more books as fast as I can!

Growing up, I was fortunate to have parents who believed in me. To my parents, Tom and Cheryl Andres, thank you for supporting every single move I've ever made. You taught me what it is to work hard, and how to love. You have always made me feel like I counted. I love you.

To my boys, who are the most energetic human beings I

know: You are amazing people. You are so curious, so brave and determined. I admire you. Thank you, Perry, for helping your brother with his homework while Mommy was working. Thank you, Alec, for all of the hugs and high fives. Yes, Mommy's book is finally real!

Sometimes when I tell people that I married my high school sweetheart, I get a few eye rolls. I always say we tried our best to get away from each other, but that's a lie. The truth is, I never wanted to be with anyone else. Thank you for loving me, Andrew.

Finally, to New York City: The first time I met you, I didn't know what to think. I was just a girl from North Carolina. You were larger than life and so much fun, but loud and strange. That first time, I was happy to leave. It took me a few years to realize how much I missed you. I'm so glad I got to come back. New York, you are magic.

In memory of Jenny Chang. I think of you often.

Photo credit: Lee Seidenberg

MELANIE CONKLIN is a writer, reader, and all-around lover of books and those who create them. She lives in South Orange, New Jersey, with her husband and two small maniacs. Melanie spent a decade as a product designer and approaches her writing with the same three-dimensional thinking and fastidious attention to detail. *Counting Thyme* is her debut novel.